Bitter Sweet

A novel by Francheska Santiago

BITTERSWEET

Published by lulu.com

Cover design brush sets by: TC MAGIC SPELLS ~ MOON: http://treehousecharms.deviantart.com/art/TC-MAGIC-SPELLS-M-O-O-N-371114755 . http://discopada.deviantart.com/art/Feathers-and-birds-Brushes-369492948

ISBN 978-1-304-60590-0

Printed in the United States of America

Dedicated to my daughter Chesilynn, who gives me a purpose to live and follow my dreams, *and* who is also not allowed to read nor touch this book until she is of age. Rated *M* for mature, please ask parent's permission before reading any further, that would mean *me*, Thank You.

One

As the taxi made its way up the gravel driveway Rose couldn't help but gasp. Her green eyes widened and lit up with joy, the mansion in front of her was indeed beautiful. She had done some research on the home her grandfather had left in his will, but she had no idea how big it would be in person. The cab halted to a stop in front of the house. Excited, she swung the door open and took in the scent of sweet England, the smell of pine trees and rain filled the air and she loved it. The man had taken her bags from the trunk and with a smile on his face left them beside Rose who was so lost in her own happiness to even notice. Startled by her rudeness she blushed and handed him a tip. "Have a nice day!" The driver said as he got back in and drove away.

Clutching the hand rails of her suitcases she hauled them up the stone steps and gleamed as the door swung open. Hired movers were already inside connecting the cable, phone lines and televisions. She greeted the men and watched as they aligned her furniture in the living room, everything was ready for her. Rose admired the old English feel of the home and the way the eight foot ceilings arched under the walk ways. She hoped that her decision to move from America would be a good one. Rose had been offered a job here in a high-end business office, thinking it would be a perfect opportunity to get away and start something new she had considered it. After her grandfather's death a few weeks after, and upon reading the will, her decision was evident.

Her eyes watered. She had known her grandfather wanted her to take the job. Grateful for his generosity she vowed to do her best and succeed. She was a single twenty-four year old woman, with a PhD in Science, majored in business and psychology. She had the world ahead of her and endless possibilities that would start in this new country. She wanted to make her family proud, from all the way up in heaven.

Rose turned the knob leading into her room. The scent of fresh and clean linen rose in the air and she smiled as she made her way towards the balcony. Sunshine brightened the room as she pulled aside the curtains. A warm breeze blew by her as she stepped out to enjoy its warmth.

"Oh my god..." She whispered as she gazed down at the miles of acres that was now her yard. A large fountain centered the garden of bushes and flowers directly below and across from that were fields of hills. She didn't have a neighbor that was for sure. Squealing, she ran over to her bed and dropped down on her back. Rose took a moment to think about all the things she had to get done before her first day of work on Monday. What would a woman from England do on a Saturday? She had no friends or family here and that somewhat worried her. She didn't want to be one of those women who lived alone with twenty cats, well, not like that was possible, she was allergic to the beasts. Rose propped herself up from the bed and made her way towards the mirror.

"I look horrible!" She cried and tugged off her messy ponytail, letting her long dark hair flow down her back and around her shoulders.

"There we go...I can't believe I looked like this all day." Rose sighed, she totally let herself go.

The trip was exhausting and all she craved was a warm shower and a nice cozy robe. She waited until the men finished downstairs, yet by the time they left night had already fallen.

After saying good bye she made her way into the kitchen in search of a pot to cook with, it took a while as it was hidden in one of the dozen of boxes that were spread out across the room. All she planned to have for dinner was soup, fresh out of the can.

Back in Florida, she had lived in a dorm room with her room-mate Jen. They would take turns cooking each day, and Rose realized how difficult it would be living alone. She missed her, that was for sure and the crazy parties they would escape to on the weekends. But after their graduation Jen had left to California for a job offer as well, even if she had decided to stay in Florida, Jen would not be by her side.

Running up the stairwell to her room, she grabbed her white robe, shampoo and soap and made her way to the bathroom. She flicked on the light switch and winced as the brightness of the lights blinded her. The marble room was big, and to her right was a long mirror that ran from the start of the room till the finish. It was perfect.

The shower seemed to wash away all the anxiety and purified her mind and soul. It was probably one of the greatest showers she had ever had. Stepping out, she dried herself and slipped on her robe and slippers. She toweled her hair until it was barely damp and combed it, deciding that she'd let it dry on its own, she was too tired to sit for an hour and use the blow-dryer.

Rose was about to step out when she noticed that the bathroom door was opened. She had sworn she closed it shut. Feeling uneasy she stepped away, she had seen too many horror movies to think nothing of it.

After a few seconds of holding her breath and listening intently for any unusual sounds she found herself feeling incredibly stupid. Her scientific expertise shot up, telling her that there must have been something wrong with the door knob, it was an old house.

Feeling like that was enough of an answer for her she brushed away the thoughts and crossed over to her room, which was just opposite of the bathroom. She shut the door this time and locked it, not wanting to take any chances. Her bed whispered to her, taunting her with the pleasure of a warm, comfortable embrace and she found no need to fight against it. She tossed aside her robe and in her underwear, slipped under the covers.

That night was pretty uncomfortable for Rose. She kept waking up from wild vivid dreams. She had dreamt she was running through a town, beads of sweat sliding down her face and tears in her eyes; she was calling out to someone. A figure of a man came into view, and finally she stopped. She couldn't see his face, but it didn't seem to matter. Her heart was pounding and she had a strong urge to hug him and kiss him madly. But the moment she wrapped her arms around him she fell right through him, the instant she hit the dirt road was when Rose's eyes sprung open and she sat up from her bed gasping. She placed her hand over her heart in an attempt to calm it down.

"Why do I feel so hurt...?" She thought. It felt so real, the heartbreak of not being able to feel him.

"I must have drunk too much coffee." She thought back on the three cups she had devoured at the airport and finalized that excessive caffeine was not good for the mind, especially when trying to get some rest. She huffed and fell back down on the pillows, hoping to dream of something more peaceful, like lying under the sun on a beach, listening to the intakes of the waves washing up on the shore and soon enough she was fast asleep, and this time remained that way throughout the night.

Rose awoke to the sounds of birds chirping. It was a beautiful morning. Pulling on her robe she headed to the bathroom to apply some makeup and look somewhat decent. Her plan for the day was to get rid of the boxes that made it almost impossible to walk through the kitchen. After a quick breakfast she began the long process of unpacking. It was almost noon when she finished. Exhausted and ready to give up she decides to store the remaining boxes in the attic. It takes her a while until she finds the door leading upstairs. Stacking two boxes over each other she proceeds to climbed up the steps, knowing that there was a good chance of falling backwards. The attic seemed eerie and she could feel the tiny hairs on her arms stand on end. There was an incredible amount of darkness and her mind flashed back to the times she'd watch horror movies with her best friend. Something creepy was always lurking in the dark and even though she told herself not to think about it she couldn't help but imagine different scenarios in her mind. Her heart begins to beat faster and suddenly, Rose misses a step and screams as she feels the weight of the boxes growing heavier, her body starts to fall back but within an instant she is hauled forward to the top step and onto her knees. The boxes slide off each other and land perfectly in front of her. Rose closes her eyes as she regains her self-control. She couldn't deny the feeling that crept up her spine, that weird warmth on her back that seemed like a palm. It felt as if she had been lunged forward by someone, or something.

She was shaking her head now, laughing at the thought. Although it seemed like she was going to fall backwards, the top box must have slipped forward alleviating the weight on her arms and dragging her forward as well, now that was a more logical explanation, so she thought. She made her way through the dark room, reaching her hands forward and trying to find the light switch, finally she felt the string against her fingers and flicked it on. The room was wide and empty, nothing in it but an old looking closet dresser. Could it have been her grandfathers? Intrigued she walked over to it and pulled the doors open. A cloud of dust immediately sent her into a coughing fit and she looked away for a moment. Letting the dust settle she waited, then looked inside.

"Holy, how old is this?" Rose gasped as she stared at the old vintage looking dress that hung in the dresser. It was an odd faded red color, and by the corset style of it she figured it must have been hundreds of years old.

"But…why would grandpa have this?" It seemed strange to her. Gazing to the corner of the dresser, she notices a small black box. Blowing away the inch of dust on top, she grabs it and slams the doors shut. Rose suddenly felt uneasy and forced herself to ignore the creepy feeling the old attic gave her, the feeling of being watched. She bolted down the steps and shut the attic door.

Once in her room she places the box on her dresser and opens it. Inside she finds a gold rimmed hand mirror.

"Wow, now this looks like something straight out of the Titanic." She said half smiling. Rose stared at her reflection for a second then gently placed the mirror inside. It looked special and she didn't want to be the one responsible for breaking the thing. The ringing of her cell surprised her. She had forgotten she even owned a phone, that's how long it's been since she had gotten a call. She jumped on her bed and answered it.

"Hello?" A wide smile spreads across her lips. "Oh, yes, I'll be there tomorrow for sure. Thank you so much!"

It was her work place calling to confirm her position and letting her know her scheduled time of orientation. Rose couldn't wait and was beyond excited. A new chapter in her life had just begun.

The rest of her day was spent buying groceries and exploring the town boutiques. She bought a couple of new office outfits and spoiled herself a little at the hair salon, figuring that she'd get her hair professionally washed and dried for the big day tomorrow. It was passed eight when she pulled up to her house. Once in her room she hung up the clothes she bought and changed into her nightgown. She stood in front of the mirror and pulled her hair up into a bun. Rose turned towards the bed and froze. "Whoa…" She whispered. Goosebumps ran up her arms. There was a sudden cold chill around her, but within a couple of seconds it suddenly disappeared. Was the window open? She turned to it and her heart stopped as she realized it was closed. She stretched her hand out into the air, trying to find from where the draft of cold air was coming from, but after looking like a fool she stopped and decided to ignore it. *I have to get good sleep tonight for sure; I can't go to work looking like a zombie.* She switched the lamp beside her bed on and shut off the lights. She felt more comfortable with a light on at night, as childish as that sounded. Forcing her eyes shut and clearing her mind of anxieties, she let herself go into the realm of sleep, dwelling into a mist of dreams that would keep her entertained through the night.

Two

Orientation that day was quieter than she expected. Rose, along with a couple of new interns sat around a projection screen, listening and reading about the rules and regulations of the company and what their jobs consisted of. She tried not to yawn, but Rose caught herself covering her mouth a thousand times to hide away the fatigue. She could see others around her yawning as well and they'd shoot her a look as if telling her to cut it out. Rose squinted and apologized, last night had been horrid again. She had dreamt a similar dream and it freaked her out. She was locked inside a dungeon in the castle, no one could hear her cries, and she was alone. The dream brought chills to her body.

"Now, if you all follow me I'll show you to your offices." The hiring manager said, Rose awakened from her thoughts. She scrambled up and followed behind as they walked into the office. Dozens of cubicles lined the room and heads appeared over the walls as they walked by, women whispered and men awed at her. She tried not to roll her eyes, and mentally wished that men wouldn't flaunt to her like they did in college. Mr. Dean, the manager, turned to Rose with a smile. "I trust that you'd be comfortable over here." He said holding the glass door open which led to a private office. She gasped at the view and turned to him delighted, "It's perfect, thank you so much!" She beamed.

"Of course, you were highly requested here, we'd be fools if we didn't offer an office with your position." They were right, she thought. Never would she accept a job half way across the world if they were to throw her in some little corner of the room. He left her with a folder of articles to edit and left the room waving goodbye as he walked out. The other employees peeked above their cubicles once more to stare at her, and she found the glass wall highly unnerving. She didn't have *any* privacy. Sighing, Rose turned her computer on and began to work on her papers, vowing that they would be the best articles she'd ever edit. The ticking of the clock seemed to be the only sound resonating through her head, she hadn't even stopped to look at the time and her fingers were beginning to ache. It was the moment when someone cleared their throat that Rose turned her attention away from the screen, startled.

Gleaming back at her were a pair of sparkling blue eyes. "I'm terribly sorry I didn't mean to startle you." The man half smiled and blinded her with a set of pearly white teeth. He was about six feet, with tussled blonde hair, and in each hand he held what appeared to be coffee cups. Quickly regaining her consciousness she smiled and said hello. "I'm sorry, I was so focused I didn't notice you there..." Rose half whispered. The man laughed. "It's always good to see someone working hard here, I never get to see that." He winked and she fought hard to control her cheeks from flushing. "I'm Andrew. I just wanted to introduce myself. You must be the new intern?"

"Y-yeah, today's my first day, I'm Rose nice to meet you." He took a seat in front of her and got comfortable. "I always treat the new employees for some lunch, but I bought coffee just in case you reject me." Rose couldn't help but laugh. What a ridiculous person, she thought. Trying to keep her wits, she smiled politely and apologized, letting him know that she still had a lot to edit. "A beautiful woman like you must eat lunch, well at least drink something." He handed her the coffee before she could reject. "If you need any help, just let me know I'm right next door." He gave her a smile as warm as the sun and left the room. Trying to hold back the grin beginning to form on her face she shook her head and laughed. *"Well, he was really freakishly handsome, holy…"* Clutching the coffee, she held it as if it were a prized possession. Maybe she'd keep the cup and take it home? She laughed at the thought.

Before the end of the day, two other co-workers had introduced themselves to her. Kate and Jennifer, both had spent a good while warning her of who to talk to, which printer was the best and which one always seemed to jam up the printer paper, gossip that had been going around, and finally about Andrew.

They looked at each other when they said his name and giggled. "He is *totally* hot! "Kate said. "I couldn't agree anymore." Jen pitched. "Rumor has it that he came to see you, is it true? "They said with their British accents, which Rose was beginning to wish she had. She nodded, unaware if it would make them angry or not.

They clapped their hands and smiled, "Andrew never goes out of his way to meet someone; he's usually the quiet one." Her eyes widened. "Wow! That's hard to believe…he's so perfect looking." Rose admitted.

"Well I think it's about time he met someone new, he went through an awful breakup last year." Rose blushed. "He wouldn't want me." They rolled their eyes. "Not to sound weird, but you're like gorgeous, total American girl straight out of a magazine." Kate said. Rose laughed hard. "You girls are too much."

They spent the rest of the work day conversing while Rose tried desperately to multitask on writing and listening, occasionally nodding her head or replying to questions. They had managed to make Rose agree to going to the bar with them, Andrew and a couple of other co-workers on Friday. Not wanting to be the lame one in the office she agreed, all the while feeling less excited about it. She just hoped they wouldn't try to play cupid, they were too old for that game.

The week had gone by in a flash. Rose had finally gotten comfortable at her job, and the house was beginning to feel more like home, besides the occasional cold chills that would scare the hell out of her, she was beginning to get used to it. Five o'clock struck the old clock on the wall and she gasped, she had promised to meet up with Kate and Jen at five thirty. She pulled down her wine colored maxi dress towards her knees. It hugged the curves of her body a little too tightly and she wondered if it was a little too much. Combing her hair to the side she ran to the mirror and checked her makeup. Perfect. *"I can be a bit fashionably late"* Rose smiled, for some reason she couldn't wait to see Andrew. He was such a sweet guy, bringing her coffee every morning and checking in to see how she was doing. After the first couple of days she had felt embarrassed, finding the attention a bit awkward, but Rose knew he meant well, bringing her to the conclusion that if he were to ask her out, she would totally say yes.

Her stomach had butterflies, god, she was excited. Turning into her room she searched for her purse. "That's weird…I swear I left it here." She said facing the bed. "I don't have time for hide and seek. "Rose rolled her eyes and looked at the time; she was going to be mega late. Going down on her knees she pulled the covers up and checked under the bed, on the floor, on top of the dresser, the bathroom, but her purse was nowhere. "Am I going crazy…?" Rose whispered. The half opened closet caught her attention. Rose was sure had closed it. She pursed her lips, breathing deeply she made her way towards it and without hesitating swung it open. Dozens of clothes stared back at her. She felt like a fool, what in the world was she thinking? But it was when she spotted her purse on top of the black chest that her heart dropped to her feet. There was no way in hell it could have gotten into the closet? Her heartbeat raced. Slowly she reached for it and snatched it back, wincing as if an explosive would go off, but there was nothing. She stood for a moment and stared at the chest that contained the strange mirror. Rose had an odd feeling about it, and she didn't understand why it made her feel so uncomfortable. "I need a beer!" She said out loud, the long shifts at the office must be getting to her head. Goosebumps crept up her ivory skin as a strange cold breeze blew.

"What the..." Startled, she turned her heel towards the door and began to walk towards it quickly when out of nowhere her body collided with something. She shut her eyes, heart pounding in her chest, knowing all too well that there was nothing blocking her path towards the exit. Her face was planted against, what seemed to be a broad chest. She could feel a heartbeat beneath her cheek and the curves of a man against her body. It took her a long second to realize what was going on. Mind racing and heart thrashing wildly she stepped back and tripped, letting out a loud wail. Rose's hair fell over her face, obstructing her view of the intruder in front of her. "What the hell do you want!?" She stuttered, her voice was shaking. "I have a gun!" Rose waited a moment for a reply. But there was silence. Her heart was pounding, and her knees were trembling. She hadn't heard anyone come into the room, not even the creak of the floor board just outside her door that always annoyed her. Lips trembling she peeked through the strands of hair and gasped. There was no one. Absolutely, no one.

She scrambled up and fell back against the wall, using the support to hyperventilate. *"Did the thief run out the room?"* That had to be the explanation. No way in hell did she imagine that?

Rose could still feel his heartbeat against her. She held her flushed cheeks and stared at the empty spot before her. She tried to reject the thought of *ghosts* from her head. It was impossible, ghost didn't exist. Things like that were fake, lies made up by people to scare one another. Everything in this world has a logical explanation, and she was not going to let herself be bothered by nonsense. Yet, what she felt was real, he was real. But was *that* real? The way her heart skipped the moment she felt that body against hers, even for a split second a nostalgic feeling engulfed her senses.

Rose quickly slapped herself. "Am I crazy?!" She scurried into her purse and pulled out her phone. "911, There's an emergency." Rose quickly explained what happened, and after, was told to stay in the room with the door locked. "Boy, Jen and Kate aren't going to believe this." She sat on her bed, hugging her chest until she could hear the police sirens outside her window. They arrived within minutes and she was thankful for that.

She opened her window and looked down. "Mam, I'm going to need you to throw down your house keys."
Shaking, she fished for them, and with a steady hand let them drop down below. Within seconds she could hear the footsteps of the officers invading her home, looking for the intruder. *"They aren't going to find him…"* A voice inside of her kept saying, she was so sure they weren't going to. She listened as the footsteps came nearer.

One person knocked, startling Rose from her dream like state. "It's safe to come out." Running to the door she heaved it open with a sigh of relief. "You didn't find anyone?" The officer shrugged. "No mam. No sign of forced entry or anything." The cop raised his brow, as if questioning her sanity.

"I swear, I'm not making this up. There *was* someone in here. He had a hard chest and a built body...I felt it through my-"She stopped, half gasping. Rose realized how crazy she sounded. The cop frowned. "Do you have a boyfriend, or ex who has a spare key to your home?" "No, I don't have anyone..." Rose replied defeated. "Well, if anything strange happens again just give us a call back but I suggest staying over a friend's house tonight." Rose nodded because that's all she could do. She walked the cops out the door and said goodbye. The door shut with a loud bang, but she stood frozen. *"Maybe it was just my imagination, it had to be."* She told herself. Rose laughed out loud. Like her father had once told her when she was younger, the mind can play terrible tricks on you. If you believe in something so deeply, you may be crazy enough to see it.

Grabbing her purse by the table, she swung it over her shoulder and ran to the car. She wasn't going to stay here thinking of rubbish things, she wanted to see Andrew and the others, especially Andrew. Maybe he could take her mind off things. Turning the key into the ignition, the car started up in a roar. She took one last look at the house, which gleamed brighter in the moonlight, and shock her head. She reared down the driveway and watched the tall mansion disappear through her rearview mirror.

Three

"**A**re you serious?!" Kate cried. "—what kind of crazy shit is that..." Rose nodded, but their eyes held a deep confusion. "Hmm, maybe he was a ghost, and by the way you describe his body, a pretty damn *sexy* ghost." Jen said. They burst out in laughter, louder than the music that was blasting against their ears. "There's no way that's possible Jen!" She rolled her eyes. The margarita was starting to get to her, because she was beginning to laugh uncontrollably at everything. "Well think about it Rose, your own personal ghost, you can have him like, steal things for you and stuff." Kate's voice slurred. She was tipsier than all of them. Kate had already stacked nine bottles of Heineken behind her. "Or, imagine having sex with him, I wonder how that would feel." Jen shouted through the noise. Rose laughed so hard she had to hold her stomach.

"Sex with who?" A sultry voice interrupted their ridiculous conversation. Rose turned around and locked into Andrews eyes. "Well there you are it's about time!" Kate cried. Andrew smiled and combed back his hair with his fingers. "Sorry for the wait ladies, I was held back in traffic." His buddies stepped up behind him. "—so is anyone going to answer my question?" Rose blushed and shot Jen a look, but it was too late. "Rose's ghost boyfriend" Andrew raised his brow, paused, and then laughed. "How many shots of tequila did you ladies have?" His eyes sparkled against the neon lights and Rose couldn't help but fall deep into them. He turned to her with a warm smile. "I didn't know you had a boyfriend."

"N-no I don't!" Rose retorted a bit too harshly. "*Ghost do not exist.*" She whispered, trying to make up for her awkward outburst. "I'm glad."

He took her hand and brought it up to his face. All three ladies watched in awe as he slowly leaned forward and placed his lips against it. "You look gorgeous tonight Rose." She laughed, her buzz rising back up. "Thank you, kind gentleman." Andrew smirked, highly amused at her awkwardness. "Can I buy you a drink, my lady?" "*God, he's so hot...*" Jen and Kate elbowed her and smiled sheepishly. "Y-yes." He took her hand into his and winked. Rose followed behind him through the crowd of people towards the bar. The music was loud and the people around them were wild, grinding against each other and downing their drinks like no tomorrow. For a moment it was a bit uncomfortable.

"Whoa!" Andrew cried, he suddenly stopped and dragged Rose into his arms. Rose gasped as her body hit against his and her cheek fell onto his chest. His arm swooped around her back and held her close. She could hear the smashing of beer bottles and a table fall from behind them but she didn't dare look, she stood still listening to his heartbeat. Then she remembered *him.* She swore to herself that she wouldn't think of *him*, or what happened earlier this afternoon, but she couldn't help but compare the way her heart skipped to now. In Andrews arms, she felt as if she were hugging a person, but in *his* arms, the moment she fell against him, her heart did something she'd never felt before. Why was it so different to now?

Rose blinked rapidly, taking in the scent of his perfume and reminding herself that she was crazy. She was in a gorgeous guy arms, she should be thrilled. She leaned her head up the moment Andrew looked down and held her breath. Their lips just inches from each other's. "Thanks..." She whispered. He smiled and pulled her away slowly.

"There are too many idiots in this bar; I can't let you get hurt madam." Rose smiled. God, she wanted him to kiss her. She sat up on the stool and watched as he ordered two mojitos, and wondered if he was trying to get her drunk on purpose. Andrews's phone began to ring and he reached into his pocket to pull it out. Checking the number he answered the call and turned to Rose. "I'll be right back sweetheart, I just have to answer this call." She nodded, inside wishing he'd just ignore it. "Okay, take your time." Rose was alone now, in a bar full of drunken haggard looking men shouting for shots and tripping over their own two feet. She looked back for Jen, anyone she knew, so they could keep her company for a few minutes but her view was obstructed by strangers dancing. She sighed, wondering who was so important enough for him to have left her alone.

Taking the straw, Rose swirled it around her drink, trying to wait patiently as the seconds felt like minutes. She felt a hand on her back and sighed, thanking god he had made it back before she lost her mind. "Finally, what took you so l-"Rose stopped short as she realized it wasn't Andrew. "Get your hands off me." The man ignored her, his eyes glossy and red from the alcohol. "What's a good looking girl like you doing all by yourself?" His hand moved downwards toward her bottom. Rose pushed forward and swung her hand towards his face, the slap was loud enough to capture some attention. His eyes flashed and he took ahold of her hand. Her heart began to race as his smile turned into a frown. "Let go of me, right now!" Rose cried, shaking her arm back and trying to free her hand. He laughed at her struggle. "You crazy son of a bitch!" A couple of heads turned their way and Rose could see a couple of men turn to each other, debating whether to get involved or not.

The stranger grasped the back of her head before she even had a chance to react and pulled her closer to his face. Rose pulled her head back quick. "Get your fucking hands off my woman."

"*Andrew!*" Her heart raced. Rose screamed as Andrew pummeled the strangers face into the counter. "Oh my god!" She cried, stepping back as he turned him around, grabbed him by the collar and shoved his knee into his groin. "Fucking pervert, get the hell out of here before I rip your face off." The man rose to his feet, wiped his bloody lip and disappeared through the cheering crowd. "Andrew, thank god you came." He pulled her into a tight hug and Rose felt safe again. "I'm so sorry I took so long, god I'm an idiot." He squinted, trying to contain his anger. "—I should have known better than to leave a beautiful woman like you at a bar by yourself." Rose flushed crimson against his leather jacket. For a moment she was thankful towards the idiot who made a move on her, because she had a chance to hear his words.

The crowd around them began to applaud and it was then that Rose realized they weren't alone. "These beers are on me!" The bartender shouted at us. We looked at each other and laughed. Jen and Kate came running towards us, their jaws dropped to the ground. "Wow Andrew, who would have thought Mr. Nice guy was such a badass." Jen cried slapping him a high five. "That was kind of hot." Rose blurted without thinking. His eyes gleamed as he looked down at her. "You think so?" His arm swooped around her neck and they all headed towards the bar again. "*Get your hands off my woman.*" His words resonated through her head and she tried hard to hide the grin. "So I never asked where you live." She looked up surprised, feeling like she was caught thinking about him.

"I live here in Birmingham, by the border of Edgbaston Pool apparently. I haven't had a chance to check it out." His eyes gleamed. "Oh nice, we thought you lived outside the city, it's good that our work place isn't too far huh?" Rose nodded. "Yeah, I'm glad my grandfather left me a house in such a good city, everything's here." She laughed. "He left you a house?" Kate asked. "Yeah, he passed away and left his mansion on the will for me." Her eyes widened and for a moment she looked as if she were thinking deeply about something. "Whoa, are you talking about the mansion a couple miles away from the castle?" Their lips parted as they waited for her response and Rose was almost afraid to answer. "Yes…why are your eyes popping out of your heads?" Jen and Kate look at each other and scream. "The haunted mansion!"

"What are you guys talking about?" Andrew pitches in. "Stop joking guys, after today that's the last thing I want to hear." Rose said. "Were not joking, Google it, the mansion with the three acre yard? Boy, that house has some history." Rose stopped her eyes from popping out of her own sockets. "All I remember is that as a kid, we'd go there and peek at the house, even threw rocks at it to see if anything creepy would happen." Rose frowned. "So you mean to tell me my poor grandpa was tortured by kids who believed in obnoxious stories?" She rolled her eyes and felt an ache of sympathy for her grandfather. Jen laughed. "Well, if anything, don't you find it strange what happened to you today? Bumping into a man that wasn't actually there?" Andrew looked down at her with startled eyes.
"Is this true, Rose?" She nodded, embarrassed that she didn't have a rational explanation to give, but told him about it anyways.

"Well, if you allow me, I'd like to follow you home tonight, and make sure you get inside safely, if it's alright with you?" Rose could feel the grins on Kate and Jens faces, she didn't have to ask to know what they were thinking. "Y-yeah sure, if you want..." He took her hands. "Of course I want to. "Andrew reassured her. "Well, enough about this haunted house crap, lets drink!" Rose said as she tossed up her glass. Glasses clicked together and separated. "Welcome to England Rose" Kate said and took a shot of vodka. "Don't welcome me too much or you won't be able to wake up tomorrow!" They all laughed.

The night descended into deeper hours and Rose couldn't help but feel amazing. Andrews arm was around her, twirling her in the dance floor and pulling her close. Everything was going perfect, and Rose couldn't be happier. *"If time could only freeze for a moment..."*

Four

Rose's heart was beating and her mind was flooding with thoughts as Andrews car pulled up behind her. She was not going to be one of those easy women, nor was she going to have a one night stand so why did she feel so nervous? Her hand gripped the steering wheel tightly before she stepped out and turned towards him. "Hey, I want to scope out the place first." Andrew said as he crossed the distance to her. Rose tried to keep her hands from shaking, god, she was such a loser. She climbed the steps to the door quickly and turned the key in. The door creaked open into darkness. "Whoa, looks really eerie." Andrew laughed and turned to her. "—I'll go in first, just stay close behind me." Rose knew there was nothing inside her home, or that's what she kept telling herself that way she'd believe it. Her hands felt against the wall for the light switch. They moved through the kitchen together, then the living room, dining room and finally upstairs. They neared her bedroom and her heart began to thrash wildly. "This is where I felt him…" She whispered into his ear. "I'll kick his ass if he's in there, don't stop me." Andrew whispered back. The way he said those words was so attractive, her body warmed to her core and she couldn't help but grip his arm tighter.

Her bedroom was empty, just like she imagined. There was no one. She turned to him with a sigh. "I think Jennifer's ghost tales are starting to get to me." He turned to her suddenly. "Don't let them, there's no such thing." Andrew smiled and caressed her cheek. "I think it's so cute how you blush when I look at you." Startled by his comment Rose covered her cheeks. "I was hoping you didn't notice!" He laughed.

His phone buzzed and he took it out, turning away he checked his text. "Sorry about that." The alcohol was making Rose's head heavy and she wished Andrew would leave now. Well apart of her did. She stood smiling into his eyes and then suddenly the moment came. The moment when he looked at her lips then back into her eyes. Rose held her breath as his hands slid down her waist and pulled her closer. "Slap me now if this isn't what you want..." He whispered, inches from her lips. Rose stared wide eyed, there was no debate. She wanted him to kiss her. A thud startled them from behind, Rose gasped as she looked at the remote that had fallen from her dresser.

"That was nothing babe, just the wind." He said, but she knew that it wasn't. The window was closed, it was always closed. His eyes were sultry, a deep want behind them, did he like her? Or was it the alcohol in his system making them that way. She didn't know how she felt about that. She was so against the thought that he wanted her only because he was so drunk of beer. It was a sudden anger that surprised her, Rose had never felt that way till now. It was sort of nostalgic in a way but she couldn't remember a time she felt that way. Rose ignored the remote and turned her attention back at him. He leaned back down and with one hand pushed her into him. Her chest collided with his and almost instantly his lips were on hers. Rose grunted from the impact, and kissed him back. His lips were hot and each kiss grew deeper until his hands were caressing her back and groping her bottom.

She could feel his *want* for her getting stronger and her heart beat a little bit quicker. He moved forward, ravishing her, until Rose could feel the bed behind her knees. She groaned as she fell backwards onto it. He was wild on top of her, feeling her legs, arms, and chest.

Rose was getting a bit uncomfortable. This was not what she had imagined. He broke free from her lips and began to kiss her cheeks, then down to her neck. Rose looked up towards the ceiling with wide eyes. Her jaw slightly dropped, she thought on how to stop this. Before she could protest he caught her lips again and silenced her moan. Rose squeezed her eyes shut. Her mind yelled for her to put an end to this, but her lips refused to speak.

It was when his hands ran up her dress that her eyes sprung open. "Andrew..." She meant to say but instead it came out as a moan. She tried to squeeze her legs close but he was a barrier in her way. He didn't stop. "Stop..." Andrew continued, ignoring her silent pleas.

Suddenly there was darkness. Rose screamed and Andrew jumped off of her. "Whose here!" He shouted. Rose backed into the bed and hugged her knees, secretly thanking whatever made the lights go off, but terrified of what did.

Breathing heavily she stared through the darkness. A hand touched her shoulder and the moment it did, goose bumps ran down her arms, a shiver shot through her spine, she froze, like a block of solid ice. The hand squeezed reassuringly and she figured Andrew was by her side. But, when the lights flickered back on and she saw him across the room near the light switch, her heart stopped. She turned her face to the side slowly, prepared to scream in horror, but there was no one. "Are you alright?" Andrew ran to her, noticing her pale complexion. "It must be a power outage, there *is* a storm coming tonight..." He said, but behind his words there was a sense of doubt. Rose cleared her throat and shook her head. " —I think you should go, I'd like to get some rest. I'm already freaked out as it is." Her eyes were apologetic. She hoped he understood and didn't take it the wrong way. "I understand, I'll walk myself out." He leaned down and kissed her cheek. "I'll see you at work Monday, if anything call or text me babe." Rose nodded, but she wasn't focused on him, her mind and body was paralyzed. Someone had touched her, someone had helped her. *"Someone knew I was in trouble..."* She wasn't crazy. *"Maybe what Jen had said was right, maybe this house is haunted".*

A couple weeks had passed since *that* night, and after searching online through dozens of so called, "Haunted houses of England" and finding nothing related to hers, she concluded that she *was* crazy. Nothing out of the ordinary had happened after that and day after day she felt bit better. She didn't need to buy a plane ticket and run away to Florida. "Hey beautiful." Rose quickly grabbed the mouse and closed the browser. She didn't want Andrew to know she'd been looking up haunted houses again. Now that they were dating, she didn't want anything to scare him off. He was beyond romantic, and had taken her to see the Eiffel tower, lakes, the old castle, and so much more. Rose didn't know if she was in love, but she sure had fallen quite deeply. Andrew leaned down and kissed her on the lips. "What are you doing?" Her eyes gazed into his. "I just finished editing, almost ready to go home. Were you waiting for me?" Rose said flirtatiously. Andrew smiled. "Of course I was baby. I can't leave without saying goodbye." She laughed and caressed his hand against hers. "You are so hooked on me, aren't you?" The phrase was bold and Rose wondered if it was a bit too much. "Of course babe. I'll see you this weekend right, maybe tomorrow?" "I'll call you." Rose said with a wink.

She watched his back turn to her and walk out of her office. Closing her laptop, Rose turned to her purse and hauled it over her shoulder. Suddenly Andrews's phone buzzed with a text. Startled, Rose jumped, not expecting Andrew to forget his phone, the man always had it with him. She didn't mean to intrude on his privacy, but when she looked down at it and saw the name *Vanessa* her heart sank. *"Who is Vanessa?"* Her face flushed. Andrew was such a good guy, there was no way he could be unfaithful.

The running footsteps she heard made it evident that they were Andrews. Trying to avoid an awkward situation she leaned down to the ground began to fix her heels. Andrew barged through the door and snatched his phone. Cautiously, he looked at her, his eyes wide, holding back much more than she wanted to know.

"I-I forgot my phone." He said. "O-oh I didn't even notice!" Rose laughed awkwardly. He gave her a tight hug and kissed her again before leaving the room. There was something about the way he looked at her that made her heart heavy. God, she wished the feeling in her chest was wrong. She left her workplace in a hurry. Right now, her priority wasn't to imagine what that text could have said, but instead to research some more on her house. Rose drove to the library just a couple of miles away and parked her car. Walking through the aisles of books, Rose felt utterly lost. Were in the world could she start? There were thousands of books and she was embarrassed to ask. The librarian noticed her confusion and walked up to her, startling Rose with her presence.

"Can I help you find what you're looking for?" Rose bit her lip and looked around, making sure no one was near enough to hear. "Can you point me in the direction of haunted houses?" The librarian's eyes widened. "Are you researching a certain house?" The librarian knew she could help her better if she knew which home. Defeated and tired of searching Rose decided to confide in her. "I heard stories about my late grandfather's mansion being haunted so I just wanted to research what they say about it." Surprisingly the librarian didn't laugh. "I'm a master at these, what's his address?" Rose followed behind her quickly. "110 Boldmere Road" Her eyes lit up. "Oh, that house, there definitely is something special about it." "What? What is it?" Rose blurted. "Come, I'll show you." She led Rose towards the back of the library, into an isolated aisle. Watching eagerly, the Librarian scanned her eyes through the tittles of books.

Growing desperate Rose crossed her arms, tapping her heel on the ground. Was she even prepared to see what was being said? She didn't know if she could handle it and for a moment she thought about leaving. It was better not to find out, she wouldn't live a day in peace again if there was something horrible. The librarian smiled as she found the book. "Come, there's more." Confused, she followed her towards the front desk where she pulled out a magazine article and handed it to her. "First, you must read the story on your grandfathers' home, afterwards read this magazine. You will find the answer you are looking for." Rose couldn't be any more desperate to rip the book open and read. She thanked the librarian and scattered out to find an empty table away from world. "Here we go..." She whispered. Her hands trembled as she felt the leather cover beneath her fingertips. Without another second to lose, she flipped the page open and scanned the words with her eyes.

"Upon the great valley stands a mansion belonging to the famous Lord Leon Evenwood in the fifteenth Century. The man, who was one of the kings most trusted and favorable guards, was killed in his home for the Rape of the Kings young daughter, Margaret. Furious of this finding, the King

ordered his guards to exile him immediately, without questioning or without a trial.

It is said that the body of Leon Evenwood still haunts the mansion, seeking justice for being wrongfully committed. But the world may never know if this famous commanding officer was indeed innocent, or guilty as charged. Overall Lord Leon Evenwood was a great man who led many battles into victory with his smart tactics and free spirited attitude. Leon never married and spent many days at the pubs, he was said to be a bit of a womanizer."

Roses' jaw was dropped the entire time reading. The man was rapist. The *ghost* in her house was a damn rapist. Her mind flashed back to his touch and the way he had made her feel. *"Was he trying to make a move on me? Is that even possible!"* She didn't feel safe anymore, going back into that house was the last thing she wanted to do now. It was a bad idea to come here. Her eyes scrolled down to a photograph. "Is this him...?" Wow, she couldn't help but awe at him, he was extremely handsome.

He had a strong, defined chiseled face, with deep set grey eyes. His dark black hair was combed back, a popular style back in his time. Dark tights wrapped his lower body and a white collared shirt under a coat dressed his upper body. It didn't make sense, Rose thought. *"How could a man so handsome, successful and rich, rape the Kings daughter?"* And if it was true, why was his *ghost* haunting the mansion, for being wrongfully killed? Rose felt crazy. A call from her cell interrupted her fluttering thoughts. It was Andrew. "Hey, so I couldn't wait for you to call me, how about dinner tonight?" Rose laughed. "Don't you have patience?" She thought fast. "What about my place? I'll cook for you." The words rolled off her tongue.

If there was ever a more perfect time to have a guest over it was now, especially when she was terrified to go back home. "Cool, I'll meet you in about an hour." He says. Hanging up she looks down at the open article and decides to finish reading it tomorrow. The chills resonating through her body warned her not to read anymore, if she did Rose wasn't sure she could keep her sanity.

Five

"**S**weetheart, your stew is amazing, I don't think I've ever tasted one this good." Rose smiled. "Oh please, you're lying." She could see he really did enjoy it, and it surprised herself how good it tasted. It wasn't often that Rose cooked meals, and she was proud of herself for not messing up this time. He laughed that dashing laugh of his, which made his blue eyes sparkle even more than they already did. "Your amazing Rose, I can be myself around you and not feel embarrassed." She blushed. If only she could feel the same way. Rose couldn't feel like herself around him, she was so afraid he'd judge her. "I'm serious I've never felt that way around a woman before." Rose stood crimson in her little black dress, soft curls, and red lips.

She didn't know what to say. She's been so wrapped up with this Leon guy that she hadn't been as focused on Andrew like she should have been. She wanted to make it up to him. He was her boyfriend after all. Rose grabbed his hand and his eyes lit up in surprise. Rose led him to her bed room and shut the door behind her.

"Why not have some teenage fun?" He laughed and lunged at her, kissing her wildly. "Shhh, we have to be quiet or the ghost will hear us." Andrew whispered. The joke didn't amuse Rose at all but she laughed anyways. Andrew dug into his pocket and threw his phone and wallet on the bed. He pulled his t-shirt over his head and flung it on the ground. Rose froze, realizing he had gotten the wrong idea. "Andrew...I'm not ready for *that*." She said. Her eyes were wide, hoping he'd understand. Rose had been saving herself till marriage, or till she met someone she knew she was in love with, someone who'd make her heart skip. The

way her heart skipped that night. *"Whoa, clear your head Rose, you're thinking about a man who doesn't even exist!"*

"We won't if you don't want to" He said between breaths. Andrew kissed her neck repeatedly, inching closer towards the bed. Intent on making her take back her words. Rose gasped as she fell backwards, not expecting to cross the distance from so fast. He met her lips and this time she kissed him back, playing a game of tag between his lips and hers.

"You're so beautiful." He whispered in her ear. Rose curled her toes and smiled. She enjoyed his presence and kissing him, but what she wanted was to cuddle with him in bed and watch the sunset through her window together. His hands roamed up and down her thighs, spreading them slowly. She clasped his hand with hers and brought it onto her stomach and away from *that* area. But instead Andrew grabbed her breast. She let out a small groan as he stroked it harder. Rose felt wrong, bothered, and hot. It didn't feel right, she didn't feel right and she didn't understand why. Andrew was her boyfriend, yet why was her body so against his?

"Andrew..." He lifted his head above hers and stopped. His face suddenly angry. "Aren't I your boyfriend?" He was frowning now. Rose flushed, embarrassed at how childish she must seem. "Yeah...it's just..." She didn't have an explanation. "You can't just look the way you do, and expect a man not to *want* you." He shakes his head. " — and then reject them once you've turned them on."

Rose couldn't possibly figure out how she turned him on. He was doing all the touching and kissing, she just wanted to lie in bed together. His weight was starting to crush her and without thinking she shifted and let out a moan. He rammed his mouth into hers and began to kiss her fiercely. Rose's eyes flung open and her pulse began to quicken. He grabbed her bottom and forced it upwards against his lower body. Andrew really wanted her and tonight would be the night that he'd finally have her. He waited too long, and his patience had run out. Rose groaned from beneath his lips and squirmed under him, trying to get away.

"Andrew I'm serious, I don't want to do this." She said out of breath. The room was getting hotter and her mind cloudier. He wasn't the type to force her. Andrew was too nice of a guy to do something so horrible. But who was she bullshitting, the guy was on her like a dog. With her hands, she grabbed a hold of his shoulders, but it wasn't enough to stop his hands from feeling her body. It was when she felt her underwear being pulled down that she snapped. "Get off of me!" She cried, hitting against his back with her hands. But he was a boulder; there was no way her small body could go up against his. He continued, and with one hand caught both of hers and held them above her head. "Shhh." He whispered.

Rose watched in horror as he unbuckled his belt and sprung it free. "Are you serious right now Andrew, this isn't funny!" She cried through the tears that now streamed down her cheeks. "Shut up." She screamed and kicked knowing there was no point in crying out for help. He stared her down. His eyes were different. This wasn't the same guy she grew to like. Andrew was in a daze, his gaze staring right through her as if she weren't even there. Rose brought her knee up swiftly and kicked him in the groin. Quickly, she broke free, reached for his phone and crawled up to it. She caught it just as a text from Vanessa came through. Andrew caught her by the waist and brought her back down against him, not realizing at first that she held his phone in her hands, ready to call the police and have him arrested.

"Hey baby, when are you coming over again? My body misses you so much." Anger, hurt, and pain rushed into Rose all at once as she read the text message on the screen. "You've been cheating on me?" She cried, holding up the phone for him to see and totally forgetting the point of grabbing it. She was so angry and heartbroken. All this time Andrew had been lying to her and seeing someone else, no wonder he would hide his phone from Rose, never did it leave his side. Rose bit her lip. *"This piece of shit!"*

"Go screw your whore and get off me, were done!" "No baby, trust me, she's just someone who wants me, an old ex-girlfriend" Andrew pleaded. "I don't care who or what she is, I want you out of my house!" Rose saw the sudden anger in his eyes. He snatched the phone away from her hand and threw it over his shoulder. The pieces of it were now scattered around the room, leaving no way to call for help. "You don't tell me what to do." He threw himself on her again and pulled her dress up. She screamed but he covered her cry quickly. Rose could feel a cold breeze run up her legs. She screamed again, yet her voice was muffled by his strong grasp. She didn't want to give up, she couldn't give up so easily. He'd have to break her arms first before she did.

She clenched her thighs closed and with every inch of her soul cried for help. But Andrew was too strong for her and with one final heave he spread her legs apart. Exhausted from struggling Rose let her arms drop in defeat. She turned her head to face away from the monster on top of her, ready to ruin her and all that stood for. He grabbed her breast again and she shut her eyes. Praying god would kill her so she wouldn't have to go through this.

Suddenly Andrew screamed, Rose looked up just as his body flew into the opposite wall. The impact caused the room to shake and picture frames to come crashing down. *"What?!"*Rose pulled her dress down and sat up quickly. Horrified she looked down at Andrew. Blood was oozing from the side of his head and he was cursing, unable to get up and move. She looked up at the dent on the wall then back at him.

Rose stared down in disbelief. She didn't do that. She had not pushed him that hard. Her eyes scanned around the room for the person that had thrown him off of her but they were alone and creepily, Rose already knew that. Panting, she grabbed the standing lamp shade and pointed it at Andrew. "G-get out right now or ill call the police and have you arrested!" She screamed. "What the fuck was that..." Andrew stood up, groaning from the excruciating pain that penetrated his body, it was apparent how much the blow had impacted him as he staggered upwards and balanced himself against the wall.

"Damn sure I'm leaving, you and this haunted house, you freak." Rose's heart seemed to break as she watched the man she thought she could trust walk out the door. "Fuck this shit!" She could hear the smashing of plates and cups they had left on the dining room table, and then finally the front door slam shut. The house shook, then stood still. Rose dropped to her knees and sobbed. *"How in the world did things turn out this way?"* She cried hard, ignoring the fact that whoever this Leon was had saved her from something she'd regret for the rest of her life. Rose felt miserable, dozens of thoughts were rushing to her head, some that didn't even make sense.

A cold breeze chilled her body and for a second she stopped crying and held her breath. She looked up at the empty space beside her. She could feel someone, or something. Ice cold fingertips touched her face and she froze. Petrified, her body locked down and refused to move. *"The rapist is touching me..."* was all she could think of. *"Did he save me so he could have his turn?"* Lips trembling she tried to speak but couldn't. Gaining an ounce of courage her lips quivered as she thought of what to say. She stuttered something inaudible, clearing her throat she forced the words out again. "W-what do you want from me?" Suddenly the magazine the librarian had given her flew and landed right in front of her. She wiped her eyes, was this really happening?

Horrified, she looked down at the flying sheets of paper as they began to turn violently and gasped when it stopped. It was on the article she had read this morning, the one about Lord Leon being framed. She didn't have the mentality to read right now, her mind was trying to make sense of something so unreal. Rose didn't understand, was this person Leon? Or was he someone else? "Who are you?" She asked. "You know who I am..." A whisper as soft as a feather replied. Within an instant Rose flew to the ground and knocked herself unconscious.

Six

"**A**h, my head..." Rose rubbed her side and winced, remembering the events of last night like a plagued nightmare. The bruises on her body reassured her that it was not just a dream. She sat up, letting the covers fall down to her legs. Rose did not remember climbing into bed, nor did she want to remember what happened afterwards. From her peripheral she could see the magazine. She gasped. Leon, he had spoken to her last night. He was the one who put the magazine in front of her, why? She didn't know, but wasn't sticking around to find out. Scrambling up, she put on her shoes, snatched the magazine, car keys, and shot out of the house like a lightning. Halfway to the car she stopped out of breath and looked back at the house. Boy was no one ever going to believe this.

With coffee in one hand and the magazine in the other she was ready to see what Leon had wanted her to read. The library was empty this morning, mostly because it was just barely seven, but Rose didn't mind. She had run out of the house like a fool, without even fixing her tussled hair and smeared makeup. She looked wasted. How freaking embarrassing. Rose took a deep breath before flipping the page.

"*Lord Leon Evenwood, who was a rich and famous man, favored by King Henry himself, was charged with Rape, without trail or hearing and exiled immediately. It is said the Rape happened during the time of King Henry's expedition, in which the King and his men were ambushed and attacked by the French. The King had been betrayed and led into a trap. Angry of this outcome, Henry held no remorse for any of his men, especially Leon; he could no longer trust anyone.*

Rose scanned through the passage quickly, trying to read something she didn't already know. *"Two weeks ago, archeologist Ben Deward, discovered the diary of Princess Margaret. In it she states how she covered her affair with a fellow guard, by claiming Leon had raped her. In her diary she claims to have lied about it all, not wanting to take a chance for Leon to tell her father and have her lover killed."*

Rose couldn't help but gape. "Wow, what a selfish person!" She cried. "How can she have an innocent man killed...?" Rose suddenly felt a pang of guilt for Leon. She closed the magazine and gathered up her things. *"Was this what he wanted me to read...?"* With a car full of grocery bags, she pulled into her driveway and heaved the trunk open. Hanging them all on her frail thin arms she ran up to the door, opened it and collapsed them on the kitchen counter. "My god! I'm not man enough to do this." She sighed. Rose looked down at the scattered glass still left untouched on the ground. Grabbing a broom she pushed it into a pile in the corner and cleaned it up.

Jen and Kate had been calling her like crazy today and she imagined they already knew what had gone on with Andrew and her. She was not in the mood to chit chat, she just wanted to fill the tub with lavender oil, rose peddles and soak her body for hours. After putting the groceries away Rose ran up to her bedroom and pulled out a towel. She paused and looked around, pushing back the thought that Leon was in this house somewhere. *"Is he looking at me, right now?"* She couldn't help but think and it made her skin crawl. Rose backed away slowly and crept into the bathroom, where she undressed and slipped into the tub. The warmth of the water was exhilarating and she felt like a solid block of ice melting under the scorching heat of the sun. Her head was clearing and the aroma of pedals filled her senses with sweet memories of home. Her parents are who she really missed. Rose had spent the day debating whether to move back home or not. She didn't want to live in this *freaky* house anymore, nor did she want to go back to work and face Andrew. Moving to England was a bad idea and she just wished god had given her a sign before.

The minutes went by quickly. Rose was alarmed when she glanced up at the time, she didn't mean to lie in the tub for a whole hour. She got out and wrapped a towel around herself. Freeing her hair from her crocked bun she turned and stared at her reflection. God, her dark circles were evident today. She added concealer on the area below her eyes just for the hell of it. It depressed her to see herself so sickly. Her long wavy hair curled down to her waist and stopped just below her belly button. She had promised herself she wouldn't cut her hair again, but she didn't know if she could keep that promise anymore. It was proving to be a pain to maintain such long hair.

Rose finished up in the bathroom and headed back into her room. The sight of the chest stopped her dead in her tracks. She screamed and dropped back, landing hard on her bottom. Rose clutched her towel tightly from falling and stared wide eyed at the box. "What is this?" She cried. She got up on her feet quickly, beginning to get angry. Maybe it was Andrew that sneaked into her home? But that was unlikely. Rose was tired of this. She didn't want to deal with anything. She was on the verge of just hopping in the car and driving to the airport, not caring if her valuables would be left behind.

"O-okay." She stuttered. "I-I know you've been wrongfully committed, I get that, it's pretty messed up and now the world knows that. You don't have to worry anymore and you can clear your conscious now and go up to heaven, please I just want to be left alone."

Rose couldn't believe she was talking to herself. She grabbed the chest and opened it again, the mirror was inside. What did he want her to do with this now? Rose didn't have time or the energy for mind games. She frowned and slammed it shut. "The hell with this chest!" She cried as she swung it up above her head and prepared to toss it across the room but as she swung her arms forward two hands suddenly gripped her wrists. She screamed and tripped forward, landing onto Leon chest.

His hand swiftly nudged her back into his body, keeping her steady and balanced. Rose couldn't even think over the sound of her beating heart echoing through every inch of her body. Her face flushed crimson and she sprung her eyes open. She was staring at her dresser. But her body was against a tall, built man who she couldn't even see. Her heart stopped when she felt her towel slipping from under his grasp, she screamed and grabbed the edge of it before it could expose her anymore. His touch was cold as ice, and she could feel it as he removed his hand from her back.

"I can't help you, please find someone else!" Rose cried. Her hands were trembling. Would he hurt her? Strike her against the face because she refused to help him? She stepped away slowly. "Please, just listen to me." A deep, masculine voice said.

Rose shrieked and fell back onto the bed. The chest fell from her hand and back onto the mattress, where it sat just seconds before. She grabbed a pillow and held it above her head. "I don't hear you right now, it's not possible. I'm dreaming!" Rose cried. She was panting now, staring at empty space, somehow convincing herself that she was crazy. But suddenly, he appeared. Rose had to force herself from fainting. He stood tall, about six feet. Midnight black hair combed sleekly, hard chiseled face, just like the picture she had seen of him.

She had to blink several times to prove her sanity, but his image didn't fade. His lips were set in a straight firm line and his dark grey eyes were staring at her deeply. She swallowed as her eyes roamed down his face and down to his body. My god, why wasn't he wearing a shirt?

Rose couldn't breathe. He was truly what she imagined him to look like. He was perfection in tights, like a Greek god. She blushed hard, realizing seconds had passed since he appeared and she had just been staring, jaw dropped, and gaping at him. He stepped forward, closing the large gap between them to just a couple of feet. Rose stared wide eyed back at him in mortal silence. "You're not dreaming." He said. Leon could tell she was horrified and he didn't mean to startle her that badly. Her face was a mix of pale and pink. He was hoping she didn't faint again like last night. Tears began to fall from her eyes and Leon flinched. Inside him a strong urge to hold her flared, and it surprised him, he had never felt it before. He had to look away from her to keep his actions at bay.

"Why are you doing this to me...?" Rose wailed. Embarrassed and flustered she wiped the tears from her face and inched backwards away from him some more. "I'm not going to hurt you, please trust me." Leon said. His chest was heavy from the sight of her crying. Rose studied him through blurry eyes. "I need your help." "There's no way I can help you...you're a ghost." Rose said. Leon frowned. "I need you to go back in time with me." Rose squinted, looked around the room then gave a pathetic attempt of a laugh. "Alright, am I in a reality show? Scare tactics maybe? You can quit filming now you've freaked me out enough." "This is not a laughing matter mam. I do sincerely wish this of you. The mirror incased in that chest is the gate that leads you towards my time. I want you to help prove my innocence, with those articles, you call *magazines*."

Rose didn't want to laugh, but she couldn't comprehend what he was saying. He had just convinced her that ghost exist, but he couldn't possibly think he could make her believe that she could go back in time through a six inch hand mirror.

"That's crazy..." She muttered. "I'm not a time traveler; sorry you have the wrong girl." Rose stood up from her bed and looked at the door. She was going to make a run for it, run straight out of this house and to the nearest hotel in her towel. He blocked her path as if reading her mind. She jumped, startled by the sudden close proximity between them. "Step out of my way." She said calmly. "Please, I cannot, you are my only hope." Rose ignored him and rolled her eyes. "You're a ghost; I can just walk right through you." She stepped forward and smacked right into him. Startled, Rose gasped and placed her hand against his chest. "How is this possible...?" She looked up at him, eyes wide with horror.

Leon looked down as her eyes met his and froze. He had never seen such a beauty before. He had to fight against the urge to rake his hand down her hair and pull her closer to him. "You are the woman meant to help me. I've waited an eternity for you." Leon took a step back and Rose was glad she could finally breathe again. He had convinced her, she knew he couldn't be lying. But Rose chose to believe that it wasn't possible, she didn't know how to help the poor guy. "I don't know how to help you...I'm sorry, I would if I could." She said. Her voice was as soft as the wind and Leon found it intoxicating, he had dreamed of being this close to hear it. Leon himself didn't know how to get the gate open himself. The Grim Reaper had only told him of her arrival, and about the mirror to which both of them would be able to travel back in time with.

"I just need you to want to try," Leon said.

Rose's heart fluttered. His pleading eyes were digging a hole in her heart. It was not like Rose to deny someone who truly needed help; she was always the one volunteering at special needs groups in college. She loved helping people. But this was different. This type of *help* scared her. "I'll give you some time to think about it." He gave her a soft smile and inside she melted. "L-Leon?" The sound of his name on her lips was intoxicating, he could almost grab her face and kiss it. "Yes?"

"How do I know where you'll be?" Rose was suddenly shy, blurting out what had bothered her since she found out about him. Inside, she knew she owed him a favor. He had saved her from Andrew, she couldn't forget that. "Just call my name and I'll be by your side."

Seven

That morning Rose woke with wide eyes. She looked up at the ceiling and slowly scanned her eyes around the room. How could she tell where Leon was? What if he was watching her, right now? Her hands were still trembling. She was plunging into something new and unknown. She wondered if it was all just a dream, but the way her heart beat against her chest, and the way she envisioned him perfectly in her mind proved her sanity. Rose was not crazy. Yet she couldn't help but feel paranoid. Now that she knew, he *really* was in her home she didn't think she could ever shower in peace again. Or change her clothes for that matter. She had to speak to him again and set some rules and boundaries.

If they were going to live together, things had to change. Rose kicked the covers off of her and ran to the mirror. With both her hands she fixed her tussled hair, she couldn't let Leon see her like this. Rose shook her head. Why was she suddenly caring how she looked like in front of him, she wasn't trying to impress him. *"You totally are Rose, you're trying to impress a hot ghost, someone who's not even alive."* She mocked herself, knowing all too well that her mind was right. Like a child not wanting to get caught by their parents, she tippy toed into the bathroom and shut the door softly. She should freshen up before seeing him again, she thought. The shower was fast, lasting a couple of minutes. She swung the towel around her body inside the tub, not waiting till she stepped out like she usually did. Rose felt like a fool and she didn't like it.

She slipped on a pair of jeans and her blue blouse, finally settling her feet into her flip flops. Her hair laid around her shoulders and down her chest in soft waves.

She double checked her makeup, making sure there was no obnoxious line or smudge caused by her nervous shaking while she applied it. She was going to speak to him again.

It excited her and she couldn't deny that feeling. Rose knew she should be afraid of him and be cautious, she didn't know what kind of person he was after all. Making her way to the kitchen she started the coffee machine. It was foolish of her to drink this poison, knowing all too well it was only going to make her heart palpitate even faster, but the taste of it would wake her up and maybe put some sense into her.

With the cup in her hand she sat down on the living room couch and took a long sip, ignoring the fact that it was scalding hot. Her intestines burned as the liquid made its way down to her stomach. "Ouch! Jesus Christ!" She cursed under her breath.

"Are you alright?" A voice spoke out suddenly. Rose jumped and the coffee mug went flying from her hand. She screamed and edged back, luckily avoiding the third degree burn that would have been on her feet. "My god Leon!" She sat panting, angry as hell. "I apologize I didn't mean to startle you." She could see Leon now standing a couple feet away. The sunlight beamed against him, in a way he looked so magical, sparkling from the rays that seemed to reflect off the lake outside her home. "We need to talk." Rose said, keeping her eyes to her hands and away from his bare chest. "Yes, mam, have you decided to help me." Rose sighed. This wasn't going to be easy.

"Leon...I don't know how to help you, I honestly would if I could. But I'm willing to try if it's any consolation." Leon looked into her eyes, which seemed to be avoiding his and it bothered him. There was something about this woman that made him feel as if he's known her for all eternity. "That I do appreciate,

Ms. Beaumont." Rose looked up at him, and their eyes locked together. "How do you know my last name?" A smile spread across his lips. "Well, your grandfather lived before you here, Mr. Beaumont. As his granddaughter I figured you shared the same name."

"You knew my grandfather?" Rose was intrigued now, wanting to know as much about him as she could. "Yes, he and I spoke for many nights. I told him about my fate and about my deal with the Reaper. He knew much about me." Leon said. His brow rose. "He told me a lot about you too."

"Did he…" Rose whispered. "I was excited to meet you, but I surely didn't know you'd be the one who would be able to see me." Rose blinked a couple of times, everything was so surreal. She kept reminding herself that it was not a dream by secretly pinching her hand. "What was your deal with the Reaper?" Leon looked down to his knuckles. God, he was handsome. "I was told I would meet a person, not like any other, who would be able to see me. That person would be the one to help me find my way back and bring justice to my name." Wow, Rose couldn't believe her ears. It was like a damn movie, this whole thing. It took her a lot from saying something stupid. "I would have never thought I'd be going through this…" Rose said brushing the pieces of fallen hair from her face. Leon eyed her, studying her distant expression.

"Um so there are things I'd like to talk about." Rose blushed and interrupted Leon's' attention from her beauty. "About?" She pointed at him with her finger. "You." Leon smiled, and it took all her willpower from blushing again. Fight the feeling, she kept telling herself. "I want to see you, all the time." Rose realized that came out wrong. She panicked, shaking her hands in the air. "Not in that way, I mean like when you happen to be around me, I don't want you to be invisible." He couldn't help but laugh. "Are you afraid of me, Ms. Beaumont?"

"N-no..." She looked down at her feet. "I-it's just that I don't trust you." He arched his brow, a look of surprise yet again on his dazzling face.

"Like when I shower and stuff..." Rose felt like an idiot as the words left her mouth. If he weren't in front of her she swore she'd hit herself a thousand times against the wall. Rose practically sounded like a child and she was embarrassed. "Ms. Beaumont, trust me, I would never invade your privacy." Leon was being honest, but he did not want to apologize, nor mention the times he had accidentally walked in on her changing or in the nude. Besides, he couldn't see through walls. He'd keep that secret to himself, and the images of her, which invaded his memory many times a day.

"Okay, I'm going to trust you then." Rose felt a bit perplexed about his situation, but she was willing to give it a try if they worked together. "As you should, my lady." Leon nodded to her and there was a moment of silence between them.

"Are you always..." Rose knew she shouldn't have started but the words flew from her lips. " — without a shirt?" Leon looked down at his bare chest and Rose suddenly noticed the scar on his stomach. "I am to roam on this earth wearing the clothes I was killed in, I apologize if my nudity disturbs you." He tried yet again not to laugh, he could tell Rose did not feel too comfortable around him and he wanted to tell her he wished she would but her face had fallen and now an expression of guilt framed her face. Rose felt horrible.

"I'm sorry...It doesn't." She was lying through her teeth and she wished he didn't notice.

The day dragged on at work and the whispering continued. Rose had not seen Andrew yet but she was now sure the news of their breakup had spread. She noticed how some of her coworkers would sneer and roll their eyes her way while others gave a sympathetic smile. Rose had been squeezing her fist the entire day swearing she would try not to cause a scene if he were to show up in front of her. Jen and Kate had waited for her in the office that morning, like two dogs wagging their tail, waiting for the treat. In this case waiting for the gossip of what had happened between them.

Rose thought long and hard about it before heading to work. She had two options, either tell them the truth, or tell them he had cheated, which in fact was also the truth. Like a humble person that Rose was, she decided to go with the second option. She knew Karma would one day punish Andrew, hell, the best payback was to see her happy and smiling. Make him feel like the biggest loser on the planet and see her with someone else. God, how she wished Leon could help her out with that one. To pose as her boyfriend for only a night would be the greatest revenge she could think of.

Jen and Kate sat gasping at each other. Their bulging eyes turned towards her with utter distraught. "It can't be! Good Ole Andrew?!"

"Good ole my ass..."

Rose nodded awkwardly, not expecting such shocked reactions. "Oh hell no girl, did you slap him? I would have kicked him in the..." Kate stopped short and lowered her voice. "I did a little more than that..." Rose admitted.

"That explains why he looked so beat up this morning!" Jen pitched in. She described how he had walked through the office with his head down, staring at his phone without looking up, not even for a second. He had even ignored her usual *good morning* and slammed his office door shut.

Rose shuttered knowing that the creep was just next door. Kate put her hand on her shoulder. "You can do so much better anyways, you're hot." Rose smiled, appreciating her friends honest suggestion of going out and meeting someone new.

"Thanks, but I'm not stressing it. I feel like an idiot that's for sure, because I should have known earlier. The way he always had his phone on him was sort of suspicious but I just never cared enough to look...I thought he wasn't that type of guy." Rose said. "We didn't know he was that type either..."Their faces fell and Rose could tell they felt a bit guilty for hooking her up with him in the first place.

"Hey what can I say, the good guys nowadays are all gay, and if one's not, their like a rare clover, hard to find."

" —and hard to lose." Jen said with a smile. They all laughed knowing damn well how life was like now a days, faithfulness was so hard to come by. "Hey, how about we show that dickhead a little revenge? I talked to Tommy last night and their going out to the bar tonight to drink. Let's dress you up in the sexiest thing you can find and let him see what he really lost."

Rose automatically hated the idea but deep in her gut she wanted Andrew to suffer. "Okay, screw it, what time should we meet up?"

"Eight o'clock should be good." Her mind was not in the right place but a little revenge felt nice, and with Jen and Kate, there was no way she could reject the offer.

They slapped hands and silently cheered like young high school girls.

As time progressed Rose liked the idea more and more. The machine by her desk beeped, silencing the women from their gossiping. "Oh, I ran out of printer paper." Rose said under her breath. "I'll be right back, please ladies, and at least look like you're doing something productive." She laughed, surprised they weren't all fired by now. Jen and Kate shooed her off, they knew they lived a life of procrastination at work.

Rose felt a bit awkward as she slid open her office door. The noise of the keyboards typing away filled the room and she found comfort in the fact that no one was watching her anymore.

She crossed the room in a hurry and swerved into the supply room.

"Whoa! Sorry!" She cried as she collided into someone. She caught her balance quickly and looked up at Andrews wide eyes. Rose's face was pale. She stepped back, closer to the wall, eyeing him, ready to defend herself with a stack of rulers she now gripped in her palm.

"I..." He started. Andrews face was hot with embarrassment. He had reflected all weekend on what he had done, and god, did he feel like the biggest dick ever. He shat bricks all day expecting the cops to show up at his door and arrest him for what he did. He regretted it. But he didn't want her to know, no, he wasn't going to look like a pussy.

"About that night, I apologize. I crossed the line."

Rose's eyes were electrifying, she couldn't believe what she was hearing. "I don't believe you." She shot back.

"—you're a rapist, I can't believe you tried to force me..." Rose's chest began to ache. She had grown enough feelings for this guy to feel pain and she couldn't deny the fact that the thought of him hurt her. "I am not a rapist."

" —I admit, I was a bit out of line...it was the alcohol."

Rose sighed. "Andrew you had *one* cup of wine." His brows burrowed. "Listen. I'm not here to argue, just to say that I shouldn't have done that."

"Are you apologizing for cheating on me too?" Rose stared up at him and crossed her arms. She had to keep herself from shaking somehow.

"That..." Andrew smirked.

"I can't really apologize for."

Rose gasped. "How can you say that?" Her breathing was heavy now with the thought of clawing his eyes out. Andrew rolled his eyes, finding her presence now an annoyance.

"You, you're hot and everything, but your worse than a Nun. A guy can't live without sex, and I was not about to wait till marriage, or whatever loser fantasy you had in your mind. I'm a man, I *need* satisfaction. I don't appreciate teasers. I tried to be with you, but after a couple of dates I wasn't getting any. So I spent my nights with someone else, someone who could pleasure me."

Rose didn't think before she raised her hand and slammed it against his cheek. The sound echoed through the tiny room and his eyes shot up, a scowl twisting in his usual warm face.

"You're the loser here."

Rose stormed out of the room with a fiery temper that could explode on anyone who crossed her path. She was capable of murder right now. As she sat down on her desk she wiped her lips with a napkin, angrily regretting ever kissing the fool. Sure, she admitted she was a bit different, she was a bit reserved and respectful of her body, but wouldn't guys want that? A woman they knew they could trust?

She thought wrong all along. Rose was never going to try to like a guy again. Her conscious was right, all men were the same, and all men wanted the same thing. The one thing she hated most in the world was a Casanova womanizer, she damned him and the very path he walked on.

Eight

Leon tried hard to keep his composure. He tried hard not to show how much it bothered him. He watched as Rose retreated to the couch and threw herself back. Her face was crimson. Narrowed eyes shot fire towards the empty air, her gaze was deep, and he watched as her lips moved angrily while at the same time trying to concentrate on what she was saying.

"I can't believe he said that!" She cried.

Leon stared at her, not knowing whether he should comfort her or just stand like a fool. He crossed the living room swiftly and sat down in front of her. Her eyes followed him and she blushed, embarrassed.

"I'm sorry, I'm venting on you and I don't even know why."

"It is fine. I feel not bothered by your words, but bothered by the filth of a man you were with."

Rose was positive Leon didn't know she knew about his past as well as his womanizing days. "I just feel so...stupid. I want to get back at him, and I will. He's going to see the type of girl he likes in me tonight, but the satisfaction would be seeing him look at me, with someone else while he's in front of his friends." Rose smiled a mischievous grin. "I can't wait for tonight."

Leon's heart felt a sting. This beautiful woman should not lower her standards for any man, even if it was a lie. For some odd reason Leon felt angry. Angry that he was not alive, so he could take this woman into his arms and ravish her right in front of the pig.

"I think it's dangerous."

Her eyes shot up. "How so?"

"A lady such as yourself should not be going to a bar full of men...and dare I say testosterone, looking as beautiful as you do. It is not a good idea."

He held back a smile as her cheeks turned crimson again. "I will be with my friends you don't have to worry..." Her voice was low as she studied him.

He could tell her heart was beating as fast as his. Leon could only nod and look past her towards the open window. There was no way to stop her and change her mind. Rose was a persistent woman, going after whatever she wanted to do. An attractive quality, one which was not permitted in his time. Maybe that's why he felt so attracted to her. Her voice, her smile, her spunk and personality baffled him. The way she was, was so different from women in his age. They were secondhand to men, dared not to speak out, and stood by them silently. Cleaned their boots and tailored their clothing, cooked and cleaned and raised the children. They were not allowed to work and to go out. They did everything a man would ask. Even in the bedroom.

But no, he had seen the way Rose spoke as she watched movies on television, yelling vulgar things at the men who in some way, shape, or form had disrespected a female. At first he was a bit repulsed by her use of language, but after some time Leon had found the humor in it and found himself laughing time and time again.

"Well...I'm going to get ready for tonight, it's almost time anyways."

"Please don't go, forget the fool and stay here with me. Keep me company, find ways to go back in time with me, anything."

The words hung on his lips but he didn't dare speak. In that moment he made his decision and he knew what he was going to do.

Rose spent a while in the bathroom holding her chest. Leon had called her beautiful, and she replied his voice over and over in her head. Yet, she was not aware of the sorrow behind his eyes when he tried to convince her not to go.

"Get it together..." She told herself.

Her makeup and hair was done, all that was left to wear was her slutty looking dress. Rose stared at her reflection from the mirror before stepping out in her towel. Her hair was voluminous, with curls that framed her face and swiveled outwards towards the back of her head. Her smoky eye makeup made her eyes pop and her red lips made her look seductive. She liked it.

Rose cracked open the door and looked around before heading out, making sure Leon was nowhere around. Getting in her room she quickly pulled up the bodycon dress that hugged her curves and stop dangerously short.

"It's time."

Leon was about to climb the steps when he looked up and froze. His breathing quickened as he watched Rose make her way down the steps. What a gorgeous body in such an obscene dress, he thought.

His eyes raked upwards, from her heels, up her long legs, over her breast and finally at her face, although her cellphone was used as a barrier between their eyes. Leon wanted her, and god did he wish that he was alive just to feel the warmth of her skin against his. She wasn't looking as she walked down the steps, putting one shaky heel in front of the other. Leon backed away as not to startle her but as she put down her phone and met his eyes, she screamed and stumbled forward. Quickly, Leon stepped forward and scoped her into his arms. Her arms wrapped around his neck as her body collided into his, falling into place perfectly. A moan escaped her lips and in that moment Leon felt hot as he felt the curves of her body through his clothing. His mind teetered and he fought hard to control his thoughts and imagine her naked body against his. His hand held her tightly, just inches above her bottom. Leon cleared his throat and carefully pulled her back before she could *feel* the thoughts running through his head.

"Oh my god...Leon I'm so sorry!" Rose held her heart and shut her eyes, trying to calm the sound of her beating heart. Her back was burning, not from the fall but from the place his hand had held her. She didn't understand why her heart beat like that around him. Childish thoughts rammed through her brain, wanting to fall again and again into his arms just to feel that muscular god-like body beneath hers.

"I suggest you don't stare at that thing while walking Rose." Leon was worried now. This woman was prone to accidents. He had remembered what the Reaper had once said. *"Only by appearing to others, shall be the day in which your time on earth will be settled."* Leon knew that meant he would be cast to the underworld, or heaven, whichever his life before lead him to. He thought about it hard while Rose was preparing herself.

He could accompany her, cheat death for a day, but after the sunset tomorrow, he'd be gone forever. Leon couldn't stand the thought of not seeing her again. Evidently his fate was exactly that. He was only an apparition. There would be a day when he would no longer see her again nor would she see him. He knew the future, for it was told before him.

There would be a day you meet a woman, in which she would be able to help you, but only she can open the portal.

Even with if he were to be gone, fate had made it so only Rose was the key of time. It didn't matter if Leon was no longer on this earth. But would he really risk it all just to be with her? His heart said he would even though his mind rejected the decision.

After watching her silently for so many months, Leon had felt as if he knew everything about her. He'd give up a thousand years just for a day by her side, *alive* and together.

"Okay, well I have to go now before I'm late...I'll see you later." Rose said, she scurried to her clutch and shoved her phone inside. Walking towards the door she turned back and gave a faint smile, a part of her wanted to stay there with Leon but she knew Jen and Kate were anxiously waiting.   "Be careful." Was all Leon could say.

"How about that hot guy over there!" Kate yelled through the music. Her hand stuck out in front of Rose's face. Rose looked up towards her direction and instantly noticed the guy she was talking about. She felt a nervous wave in the pit of her stomach. The alcohol was mixing with her nerves and it made her heart beat much more than usual.

"I don't think so..." She said awkwardly. "C'mon Rose, you have to choose a hot guy already, Andrews over there and he hasn't even noticed you yet." Jen pitched.

She was jumping up and down to the rock song playing, spilling her drink down the side of her hand. Rose looked around while taking in another shot of Tequila.

The liquid burned down her throat and she gasped. "God that's awful!" Rose cried. They all laughed, finding amusement in everything and everyone. A couple of minutes gasped before Kate gasped and grabbed onto Rose's startled shoulders.

"Oh my god...look at that hunk!" Jen saw him before Rose and took a step back. "He's coming our way...he looks like he stepped right out of a movie." Rose was too focused on her drink to see who they were talking about. Her mind was high and she felt like running around the room chugging everyone's drink into her mouth. She was pretty sure she had downed more than ten drinks already, but she wanted more. It was the only way to drown out her nervousness.

She was drunk and ready to hook onto some random guys' waist and show Andrew what he's missing out on. She could be crazy too. Rose wasn't a Nun living in a convent.

Kate nudged her shoulder and Rose looked at her wide eyes and blushing cheeks then turned to meet where her eyes had frozen to.

"*Leon...*" Rose exploded into a laughing fit. There was no way in hell Leon could be standing right in front of them. "Guys, guys, I don't know what you're staring at but he's just a ghost, see?"

Rose took a drunken step forward and swung her hand to his broad muscular shoulder. She felt the muscle beneath her palm and laughed again.

"There is no way this is possible."

Leon stood there with a worried expression on his face. His eyes were set straight in disappointment, staring down her. He was angry she had gotten so wasted, knowing how dangerous it was.

"Rose...that's so rude." Jen whispered and pulled her away. Rose didn't understand, she blinked several times but Leon still stood before them. *Is this for real?*

Rose began to panic, her head was spinning now. "I'm sorry to interrupt, but I just happen to come into the room and was spellbound when I saw your lovely face."

Leon looked at Rose, his face warming up with a smile. Rose nearly choked on her drink. Her eyes were wide and some sense was coming back into her system. "That's so sweet, did you hear that Rose." Kate said.

She gave her a small push forward into Leon. She held her breath, as the proximity between them sent a wave of warm desire down her core. This sexy ancient guy was really here, and everyone could see him. How was that possible?

Before Rose could open her mouth to speak, Jen quickly launched forward and grabbed his arm.

"So what's your name?"

"Leon."

Rose felt a slight tear in her chest when she looked down to Jens arm wrapped around his. She was angry, maybe it was the alcohol but damn did that image bother her.

"So my friend here, Rose, needs a little help. You see, she had an asshole boyfriend who's right over there..." She paused to point at Andrew on the bar wrapped around one of his lady whores.

"If you could help her out, you know, making him jealous, that would be lovely." Jen winked and Leon knew what she meant by that. He was glad he had made it here before she asked some other man to do his job. On contrary, He wouldn't allow that, Rose was his, whether she knew it or not.

His for the time being..." A thought crept back at him.

"I would be honored to."

Leon slid his arm around her waist and pulled her to him, claiming her for himself. Rose gasped a short muffled one. She looked over at her giggling friends and glared. This was awkward and confusing, why would Leon agree to this?

But in her heart she knew this was what she dreamed about, she couldn't believe it was coming true. "Will be right back" Rose shot them a smile and they waved them away. Rose pulled Leon into a corner, away from their sight.

"How is this possible, why can they see you?!" Rose was baffled. Leon caressed the side of her cheek with his fingers. Goosebumps quickly emerged from her body.

"I came to help you, do not worry, today I am alive, just like you." He took her hands into his. "See..."
Rose's eyes widened. "You're warm."

Leon laughed and Rose was mesmerized by the way his eyes lit up. His hair fell forward as he bent his head to whisper in her ear.

"I do apologize for what I am about to do tonight." Rose felt a dull ache in her lower belly as his breath hit against her ear. *Whoa whoa...calm down hormones, he didn't mean it like that.* Rose could only nod. She didn't know what he meant by that and frankly she didn't care. He took her hand and led her through the crowd towards the bar. Rose could see other woman eyeing him as they made their way towards Andrew. She stuck her chest out and gripped a bit tighter, feeling proud that this sexy medieval man was hers, for the night of course.

"And now the acting begins."
"Baby, can you get me a drink, I'm *so* thirsty."

Rose put her back against the granite counter, knowing all too well Andrew was right next to them, on the other side of his whore. Leon was a bit surprised, but quickly fell into play. Rose leaned back so Leon, and everyone else, had a full view of her curvy body. She smiled, enjoying Leon's hot gaze on her.

"Anything for you baby."

Rose had been too classy the night she spent with Andrew at the bar, only sipping a few cups of wine, too afraid he'd judge her if she ordered anything else. The bartender slid a couple shots of Tequila their way. Rose grabbed Leon by the shoulder and pulled him closer so he was against her. She watched as he downed two shots, hissing from the taste, and then looking down at her hungrily.

He wanted her.

Right there on the bar. He imagined pushing away the drinks, pulling her up on the counter and spreading her legs open. Leon shook his head and calmed his thoughts. Rose caressed his chest with her hands, feeling the soft cotton fabric of his tight black shirt. She wondered how he had gotten it, then concluded that he must have snuck it or stole it out of a store. She missed seeing his bare muscular stomach.

"Feed it to me..." Rose whispered giving him a wink that could have shattered him right then and there. Leon took the small cup and hovered it above her big red lips. He teased her, dropping a few drops down her mouth, then he poured it. He watched as she swallowed it and licked her lips slowly. Her pink tongue teasing him. He couldn't take it anymore.

Leon took her waist and grabbed her hair, he pinned her against him and swallowed her mouth with his. The scent of alcohol traveled up his nasal cavities and he knew his self-control was becoming weaker with every second. She followed his lips as they moved in unison together. Rose bit him and when she did he growled hungrily, kissing her deeper. For a second she had forgotten what they were there for.

Rose pulled away and with wide, nervous eyes looked into his. Leon had to regain his self-control.

"Rose...?"

She froze and looked to her left. Andrew stood with his hands on his hips, a smirk of disbelief on his face. "Oh."

Rose rolled her eyes. "What do you want?" Andrew squinted. What a tease, he thought. He'd been with her for so many months and not once had she acted like that with him. He grew angry. Rose looked so hot and sexy, downing shots, with some random guy. She had never done that with *him*. Was she drunk? Was this dick trying to get with her?

"I think you should come with me." Andrew said, he reached out and grabbed her hand.

"What the hell are you doing!" Rose cried as she stumbled forward into his arms. His grip was hard. She knew her tactic had worked and from a distance she could see Jen and Kate running over.

"Get your filthy hands off of her." Leon growled.

His eyes were dark, murderous. Rose could see the tense look on his face and the way his veins seemed to protrude more profoundly. "Mind your business. This is between *my* girlfriend and I." Andrew smirked.

"Girlfriend?"

Rose met Leon's eyes the moment he said those words and that was enough to lose his composure. He reached out and wrapped his hand around Andrews's throat. Rose gasped, he released her arm and she ran behind him.

"I'm not afraid to kick your ass *again*." Leon threatened. Andrews face was turning red. Before Leon could kill him, he released his grip. Andrew breathed in and out profoundly, letting the oxygen re-enter his lungs.

"What do you mean again, I've never seen you before!" Leon smiled, remembering the satisfaction he felt when he threw him against the wall. "And you, you became a whore now?" He began shouting at Rose.

Leon turned to see her eyes widen, her lip quivered, obviously embarrassed at such a statement. Rose pulled her dress down and held back the tears. All she wanted was to get him jealous, not be embarrassed in front of everyone. His blood was boiling; he wanted to rip him in half for hurting her.

"You're calling me a whore? Look at these stanks you're with, who are you to call me a whore! I'm nothing like them." Rose shot back. She grabbed the nearest drink and splashed it on his face.

"What the fuck, you bitch!" Andrew shot his arm up to hit her and that was his breaking point. Leon swung his fist in the blink of an eye. Andrew flew to the ground, stumbling against the onlookers who were gathered around to see the fight. Leon had enough of this sorry excuse for a man. He pummeled him over and over. He didn't stop until he saw blood, until he knew Andrew was hurting more than Rose. His mind was so focused on murdering him that he didn't feel nor hear Rose's cries beside him. He stopped slowly, noticing Andrew had been knocked out for a while.

"Leon please stop! "Rose sobbed. His heart wrenched. Leon had lost his mind for that second, if he hadn't heard Rose, he was sure the man wouldn't live to see another day.

He got back up slowly as the crowd cheered and raised their beer glasses. "I'm sorry Rose..." Leon felt horrible.

Rose was so beyond embarrassed. She didn't want things to turn out this way, she never imagined Leon beating him up. But deep down in the core of her mind she was satisfied. This was exactly what she wanted. "Someone call the police!"

"That's our cue to go!" Rose said as she snatched Leon's hand and ran through the crowd. They were nearly to her car when they stopped out of breath and burst into laughter.

"I can't believe you punched him, I don't know why I was crying!" Rose cried. "Trust me; I wanted to do more than that." Leon smirked, relieved to see her smiling.

"Thank you." She put her hand against his heart, feeling the beat of it on her palm. The world around her was beginning to spin as the alcohol started to take effect.

"I guess we should head home and celebrate!"

The car ride home was amazing. Rose never imagined how charming and entertaining Leon was. He made her laugh hard, in a way that she hadn't in a long time. Her mind kept roaming to his past, wondering if his charm was what made him a womanizer.

"So I read a lot about you." Rose said.

Leon frowned, not wanting to hear what was going to be said next. "You were a bit of a womanizer?"

Rose shut the front door behind them as they strolled inside together.

"I...admit, indeed I was, but I know now of my mistakes."

Rose watched his expression sadden and immediately felt stupid for even bringing it up. She ran over and poured two glasses of wine, filling each to the rim.

"I don't know how you're alive right now, or if I'm even dreaming, but let's have some fun tonight!" Leon looked at her then at the glass.

"I think you've had a bit too much to drink tonight already." Rose stuck out her lower lip. "Awh, c'mon you're no fun." Suddenly she remembers the way he kissed her at the bar and her insides warm.

Leon noticed how wasted Rose was and he knew not to take advantage of a woman in this state, but if she kept looking at him so seductively with that glass in her hand, he couldn't promise that he wouldn't rip that tiny dress off her body. Rose took careful steps towards him with the glasses in her hand and shoved one to Leon. "Drink with me please?"

Her eyes twinkled and Leon was defeated. Whatever happened tonight couldn't be avoided. Leon gave in and took the glass, taking in her scent as she walked by him and collapsed on the couch. "Whoa!" Rose laughed. Leon was cautious, eyeing the giggling beauty carefully, watching her so she wouldn't hurt herself.

Rose chugged the wine and cheered as she placed the cup down. She was amazed to have drunk such a dry wine in less than thirty seconds.

"Now it's your turn!" She cried out to Leon.

Her face was like a gravitational pull, he couldn't resist. He swallowed the wine and hissed from the burning flavor it left in his throat. He had never tasted anything like it, all he drank back then was good ole Ale, something he noticed didn't exist in this time period.

Rose sat up and clapped and Leon couldn't help but notice the way her dress was riding up her thighs, it was nearly exposing her bottom. She ran to the counter then back at him with the dreaded wine.

"One more c'mon baby!"

She laughed as she poured the foul substance into his glass, filling it yet again to the rim. "Chug, Chug, Chug." She sat on the coffee table in front of him, her eyes eager, waiting for him to put the glass to his lips. Leon had to force himself but managed to gulp it down again. He coughed, realizing the room was getting a bit warmer. He looked up and stared in awe at the lag between the floor and ceiling. Before he could realize what was happening, his cup was filled again.

"Rose, I can't..."

His lips were silenced with her finger. His eyes widened. Threatening her in his mind that if she didn't move her skin from his lips, he would devour her completely. Rose smiled sweetly and caressed his hair with her fingertips.

Leon held his breath, fighting the urge to lift her off of her seat and onto his lap. Hell, if she kept the wine glasses coming he didn't have the confidence to stop himself.

Rose had downed the bottle of wine and was laying on the coffee table telling Leon stories of her childhood, of the boyfriends she had, and of all the heartbreaks. Leon just sat there, head dizzy, admiring her beauty and the way her lips moved when she spoke. "I'm sick of men calling me a Nun, a loser just because I don't have sex with them!"

Leon winced. Women in his time were not allowed to speak about such intimate topics. "I'm not a Debby downer I just, you know, never really had the urge to." Her eyes were watery, hurt clearly apparent behind them.

"You're beautiful Rose. You deserve a love much more than simple pleasure. One day you'll meet your husband, the man you love, and you will find the urge to. There is no rush..."

The words hurt to say. Mostly because he knew he could never be *that* man. Rose leaned up on her elbows and stared at him. "Why are you so nice to me?" Her voice was hoarse and throaty.

"I feel like I've known you for so long Rose, I don't know, there's just something about you..."
"You're magnificent."

Rose smiled, hearing that from him made her believe it. She leaned back down and closed her eyes, humming a lullaby that she learned from god knows where. It was time for Rose to rest. Leon had been staring up at the clock countless times, watching the hour hand move while she spoke. He listened to her quietly, until there was a moment when she spoke no more.

Leon bent down and picked her up. Her head landed on his chest and she snuggled against his heart. He carried her through the kitchen and up the stairs to her room. Gently, he placed her body on the mattress and turned on the bedside lamp. He worked his way down to her feet and stared down at the viciously tall shoes, in his time these could be used as weapons. Struggling to unfasten them, he finally found the release and slid them off of.

Through the dim light he gazed down at her long eyelashes down to her perfectly shaped lips. Leon didn't know when exactly he would disappear, and he had not told her yet, but he wished he could stay for one more day. He leaned down and kissed her lips gently. "Goodnight...and farewell."

He turned to go when suddenly her hand gripped his arm.

"Don't go..."

Before Leon could say anything, Rose had sat up and captured his lips. Rose was acting on impulses, she wouldn't be a loser tonight, no, it was the last time a man would call her that. She pulled his body closer, until one knee was on the bed between hers.

"Rose...I am finding it difficult to resist you, and I apologize for what I am about to do."

"You don't need to apologize." Rose said through their kisses. She slid her hand up his stomach and chest, sliding his shirt above his head. Leon took no time to toss it to the ground. It was his turn now. He turned her to the side and unzipped her dress, quickly pulling it down to her knees and off her feet. She was perfection, a sweet pale body and he wanted to explore every crevice with his mouth. She stared up at him, teasing him again with those green eyes.

He unlatched her bra and threw it to the side, her lace underwear quickly followed. "My god, you are a goddess Rose." Leon whispered.

His mouth sucked her tongue into his hungrily. She moaned and arched forward, making Leon feel her breasts against his chest. He kissed her until she was shaky, breathless, and aching with pleasure.

He pulled away and Rose gasped, beads of sweat beginning to form on her angelic face. Leon trailed kisses down her neck and breast until he reached her nipple. Rose clutched the bed sheets as his cold, wet tongue swirled around it. She clenched her thighs, feeling the ecstasy down to her groin. His strong hands roamed her body, trailing his fingers down every curve. His hand reached her bottom. Leon squeezed gently, the bulging erection in his jeans getting stronger.

Rose gripped her hand into his hair as the ache grew stronger and stronger. She wanted him, God, so badly she'd cry if he teased her anymore. Leon ran his lips down her navel, kissing lightly and slowly, taking in the sweet scent of her pleasure. She shuttered beneath him as he kissed her thighs. He wanted to explore every part of her, feel every nerve. Make her remember him forever.

"Please Leon…" She moaned.

He pulled away and unfastened his belt. He kicked aside his jeans and faced her. Rose's eyes grew wide at his manhood. Boy, did he want her and god, did *she* want him. Leon was breathing unevenly. All he could think about was how lucky he was to be with her tonight. He crawled up to her and took her mouth again, sliding his tongue inside and sweeping the insides of her mouth.

"You taste delicious." He said breathlessly.

Rose spread her legs, inviting him in openly. Her arousal swept through her like a tidal wave, she needed to *feel* him, connect to him in the most natural way ever. She ran her hands down his abs while they kissed. His skin was hot, blood boiling with intensity and she loved it, he was alive with her. Her hand reached above his groin and Leon heaved a sharp breath.

Rose took his length in her hand and squeezed gently. Leon moaned. It's been centuries since he's made love and every touch seemed like the first with Rose. Her hand roamed upwards, gliding up and down the impressive length, enjoying the way Leon tensed above her. With her thumb she circled his head, Leon groaned, feeling like shattering beneath her touch.

"Dear god…" He muttered hoarsely.

His hands reached down to caress her thighs and to feel the wetness of her pleasure. They were like ticking time bombs. "Wider" Leon murmured into her ear as he pushed her thighs farther apart. Rose arched forward, feeling his erection slide down her belly.

This was her first time and she didn't know what to expect or how much it would hurt, but she didn't care. Leon moved swiftly and entered her. She cried out as the sharp sting hurt her and clutched her fingers onto his back. The pain quickly subsided as the fullness of him surrounded her, scraping against nerves she never knew existed.

His blood roared through his veins like wildfire as he plunged deeper and deeper. Rose was hanging on tight, moaning to every thrust, wanting him to go harder. Every movement was pulling her; the ecstasy seemed to grow stronger each passing second. She rocked her hips against his in a rhythmic motion. "Rose" He groaned over and over as the ache of release grew closer.

Her breath was hitting against his neck, her breasts were bouncing up and down beneath him, he shut his eyes as he released. With that last deep trust Rose lost herself completely, a sensation so intense she couldn't contain it. She let out a cry of pure pleasure and wrapped her arms around his neck. Her legs shook from the intensity and she lay there still, smiling in satisfaction beneath him. Leon panted, slowly pulled his way out and laid back, pulling Rose against his chest.

Neither knew how long they laid there in silence, listening to the sounds of their heartbeats in their heads. Leon took her hand in his and squeezed gently. Rose was still spellbound to notice. Her heart was fluttering a million beats per second. She was exhausted but she didn't want to fall asleep, for fear of waking up to this being just a dream.

Nine

Rose groaned from the headache beginning to resonate through her head. She leaned to the side and froze as she fell against Leon's chest. So it wasn't a dream. Rose didn't know what to say to him or how to feel. Were they both just drunk? Or did they make love out of passion? Real feelings? She knew *she* did.

"Hello Darling."

His voice startled her out of her thoughts. She stumbled with her words, heat quickly rising to her cheeks. He noticed and smiled. "No need to be embarrassed." Leon said as he watched Rose pull up the sheets to her face.

"I'm sorry, I'm just..." Rose couldn't find the words to say. All kinds of emotions were fluttering in her chest, happiness, love, and terror. What would there future be like? She knew she wanted to be with him, it was apparent to her how his presence affected her. She didn't mind living a ghostly life with him, if only he'd forget the past and just live with her everyday together. Rose didn't care. She knew it was love when she prayed that she could relive yesterday again and again. *"But what is in his heart?"* She thought. Was he only using her to help him?

He reached over and grabbed her hand and it was then that Rose realized she was over thinking. "What time is it?" Leon asked as he searched around for the time. Rose looked out the window, seeing darkness but a hint of light beginning to emerge from the horizon.

"It's almost sunrise, six thirty."

A look of horror fell upon Leon's face. He forgot, god, he forgot to tell her last night, now he was terrified of her reaction. Would she be angry? Would she think they only made love because of it?

Leon grabbed her shoulders and it startled Rose and made her gasp.

"What's wrong?"

"Listen Rose, I don't have much time."

Her eyes widened, what could he be talking about? "I made a deal with the reaper, long ago. And in this deal I was not to show my true self to the living, for if I did I would be forced into the underworld by the following sunrise. Please forgive me. I have failed to tell you this yesterday..."

Leon brows burrowed. He knew he'd give up a thousand years for one day with Rose, but he didn't expect to feel this terrible. "W-what...no...you can't!" Rose cried. "Not now, not after this, please..." Her heart shattered, breaking into a million pieces. Tears streamed down her face like the endless flow of a river, she couldn't hold them back nor control them. Her soul was crying.

Leon forced back the tears and embraced her with a grip so tight he feared he might hurt her. "I'm so sorry, please forgive me, I realize now I don't want to be apart from you. Even if my existence on earth means nothing, I'd still want to be by your side, forever." Rose looked up to him with blurry eyes. "Why, why did you come to me yesterday? You idiot, you stupid idiot! We could have been together...we could have li-" She couldn't finish her sentence, it hurt too much to say.

"Because I love you Rose, and I'd die a thousand deaths than to see you hurt or in danger...and dare I say alongside another man." She tightened her grip around him, thinking if she didn't let go maybe he could stay.

"I love you too…" The words came out as a sob. It was the first time she had ever said those words to anyone. Leon pulled her back and cupped her face in his hands.

"Please don't cry anymore. I'll love you for all eternity, beyond death and where ever I shall go. You are mine, my heart, always remember that. There is still hope, I don't know what the future has in store for us but I know I will see you again. You are meant to go back into my time and help me, I know it."

Rose couldn't believe this was really happening, now more than ever she wished everything was just a dream. She could only nod, swearing she'd do whatever it takes to see him again. Rose leaned forward and kissed him, inviting him to her lips and enjoying the sensation of his warmth around her. Leon stopped and held her hands. His body was getting colder. Something was happening.

His lips shivered and it was hard to speak.

"I must go now it seems."

"Wait no Leon you can't…" Rose stood up pathetically as Leon backed away from her. Her eyes sorrowful and swollen with tears.

"Farewell…"

Within an instant he was gone and Rose was on her knees sobbing, cursing at the world, at the Reaper, at everything for taking him away from her.

Hours passed and it was almost noon. Rose had been lying in bed like a zombie, whose heart had been eaten out of her chest. The sheet beneath her head was drenched with tears. She could feel the swollen bags forming under her eyes, but she didn't care. At one point the doorbell and her phone had rung, but she ignored it. She thought about Leon, every second, for hours on end until finally she looked towards the window and night had fallen again. Cringing, she sat up and let the dull back ache fade from her body.

"Where did I put them?"

Rose could have sworn she had put Leon's magazine article on her desk.

"Damn it, where are you!"

Rose swerved her hand across the desk, tossing pencils and paper onto the floor without an ounce of care. She pulled open the drawer and gleamed when she found it amongst the mess. "Wait for me Leon!" She said as she ran into her closet and pulled out the chest. Heaving it open she grabbed the hand mirror and gasped. Her reflection was appalling.

"Now what do I do?"

There was no way her body could fit into a tiny mirror. Rose felt so foolish. She inspected the mirror, around the gold rimmed frame, the handle, but there was nothing to be found. There was no magical button to press, nothing to give her a clue. Rose sat down exhausted.

"Please, pleaseeee help me." She said through the mirror.

"I want to help him, I need to. I feel like the purpose of my existence is to help this man...sure he's more than a hundred years old and nonexistent in this time period, but for me, he's everything. I love him...and I'm not afraid to help him. I need to see him again." She whispered as tears began to form again. Rose looked up and fanned herself, enough of the crying she had said. Crying was not going to get Leon back nor was mopping in bed all day.

"Get yourself together Rose." She told herself. But Rose couldn't help the overbearing feeling of helplessness as it invaded her whole body. To feel so useless, without having any idea of what to do consumed her. All she wanted to do was have Leon by her side again. Her eyes crept back into the reflection from the mirror and she cringed, noticing how her mascara now reached the bottom of her chin. Her eyes looked as though she'd been up all night partying, and her hair, god, words couldn't explain the horror. Would she really be okay with letting Leon see her like this?

"I have to pick myself up...this is not me...crying for a man." Rose whispered. Hope was beginning to creep back into her now dark hollow heart. It took a nice cold shower and four glasses of wine to make Rose feel human again. She was calmer now, kneeling on the ground with Leon's magazine on one hand and the mirror in the other.

"Maybe if I say some sort of spell, things can get going?" Rose paused for a moment before speaking into the mirror. "Abracadabra, portal open up and take me to my love?" Rose squinted. Nothing. She let out a sigh. "This is so stupid."

Rose sat on the ground for a long time staring back at herself. Her grip on the handle tightened dangerously. Anger was rising through every pore of her body threatening to unleash at any moment. She spun her arm forward and screamed. The mirror flew from her hand, twirling in the air several times before it finally crashed against the wall and shattered. Rose shielded her eyes from the flying pieces of glass and gasped. She looked at her hand then back at the broken mirror.

"The hell with it!"

Her hands were on the carpet now as she breathed viciously. The alcohol was flowing through her system. She didn't quite realize what she had done at the moment. "Why the hell did I even get so involved with him, he's just a ghost! It's not like we'd ever be together anyways!" She was spouting nonsense but her heart was aching.

Rose crawled towards the broken pieces and glanced down. "I just want to see you again…"With tears in her eyes, her finger caressed a broken shard. Rose didn't notice the pain until she saw her blood oozing down her nail. Rose didn't care. The pain in her chest was much greater than a small paper like cut. Rose went as far as to even think about death, wondering if she could meet him again in the afterworld.

Tears flowed down her face again, and all the while she prayed to god that she could see him again one day. It took a second for Rose to notice her hands had gone numb.

"What…?"

Her gaze shot down to her legs. Had she sat for so long that her feet had fallen asleep? Rose began to panic as the numb sensation spread throughout her body like a tidal wave. "I can't move…" She whispered. Was it the wine? Rose watched as her hands began to fade, horrified she watched her arms disappear as well and suddenly, there was only darkness.

A chill ran down her spine. Her fingertips were ice cold. Rose groaned, her head was aching and she couldn't remember where she was or what she was doing. There was a tightness around her body and she found it hard to breathe. The smell of the room was unfamiliar. Rose forced her eyes open and when she did she froze. She was facing a dark grey brick wall, in front of it stood a small table, on it a candle burning low but bright. The room was small and empty besides a dresser on the far right corner.

"That dresser…" She whispered.

It was the same dresser that was in her grandfather's attic. Rose sat up quickly and screamed. She was wearing a red and black corset dress, and not just any modern kind, one that appeared to be from the fifteenth century.

"What is going on here, how did I end up in this?!" Rose was wearing the same dress that hung up in her attic. Her hands were shaking now, terrified and confused. She placed her feet on the ground and found it hard to keep her balance, as her body swayed and crashed onto the bed again. There was an ice bag beside her pillow, which explained why her forehead was damp. It took Rose a while to realize that just maybe she wasn't in the year twenty thirteen anymore.

"Leon…did I go back in time?" She asked herself.

The walls spun around her like a carousel. She tried to reach for the horse that Leon rode on, but she couldn't reach him. He disappeared from her sight, but as quickly as he left he appeared in front of her again. He was facing her, but his eyes looked right through her, as if she wasn't really there.   Rose felt a cold sensation on her face and her eyes shot open.

"Whoa dear!"

A middle aged woman, wearing the same dress, looked into Rose's startled eyes. Her grey hair was tucked flawlessly in a bun and her face held the lines of old age. Her lips spread in a smile, horrified, Rose's lip quivered.

"What year is this…?" Her voice was shaky, she could not control it or her harsh tone.

"Dearly, did you hit your head that hard? It is the year 1583." The old woman frowned, realizing her condition was much worse than she thought.

Rose's eyes widened. She breathed heavily, clutching the sheets into her hands, finding it to be the only way to hold herself together. She didn't know how she did it, but she managed to go back in time, yet some part of her didn't believe it. She needed confirmation, proof, she needed to see Leon.

"Oh my god, are you serious?"

"Yes, dearie. " The woman arched her brows, never before had she heard Rose speak so foreign. Rose looked down at her hands and smiled.

"It worked…I don't know how but it worked! I have to find Leon." She was about to jump out of the bed when her arm was grabbed.

"No dearie, you're not ready to go out just yet. You hit your head pretty hard protecting the Queen from that vase. You've been asleep for nearly a month and now you're talking gibberish! Please, lass, you must rest. I have been instructed to take care of you, Queen's order."

"Queen? What are talking about? How did I protect her, how have I been sleeping for a month?" The dull ache in her head rose yet again. The information was too much to handle. Rose was beginning to feel nauseous again.

"You don't remember? Lass, you nearly lost your head! As you were escorting your Highness to her chambers, a worker on the upper level knocked against a structure, causing the vase to fall down towards the Queen. Luckily you spotted it quickly and pulled her out of harm's way. She is very, very thankful towards you and has instructed us to take care of you and allow you to work more freely. Isn't that great lassie? You don't have to follow around the Queen all day anymore."

"So the vase hit me and I've been in a coma?"

"Yes, Lass. I've been taking care of you."

Rose put her hand up against her head. That explained the pain. When she thought about going back in time she had no idea she would actually be someone else. Rose thought she'd be herself, find Leon, give him the magazine and that was it.

"The magazine!"

"The what...?"

The woman's dumbfounded expression was enough to startle anyone in her path. She knew Rose took quite a fall but she didn't expect her to be this way. Did she remember anything at all? About her duties as the Queens maid? It was hard to tell when she was talking about none sense and saying things she's never heard of.

"Rose, dear, relax." Rose looked up in surprise.

"You know my name? I mean, is that my name?" Her eyes were wide. "Of course, you know mines as well, Agnes."

Agnes was more worried now than ever. The young woman must have really suffered a memory loss. It pained her to see such a bright woman so lost and confused and she wished she could help her.

"I'm sorry Agnes, I know this all sounds strange to you, but I have to find Leon. Do you know if I had a magazine with me?"

"I do not know of what you speak of my dear, what is a *magazine*?"

Rose realized it too quickly. She must have gone back in time and anything from the future stayed there. That explains why she wasn't wearing her normal clothes. How the hell would she help Leon now? She was beginning to panic.

"Please, tell me where to find Leon!"'

Her eyes widened.

"I don't know a Leon I'm sorry Rose."

Rose hadn't realized that she was speaking in an old English accent, and this time she didn't have to force it, it was natural. "I-is there a mirror I can see my reflection with?" Agnes stiffened, but stood up and walked over to the dresser. Rose's eyes widened as she watched her pull open the doors, Agnes opened the chest and pull out the gold rimmed mirror.

"This was you're mother's, don't you remember Rose?" Agnes noticed her startled expression. *"Why was that there? I broke it...I clearly remember breaking it."* Rose stood silent this time, not wanting to freak out Agnes any more than she already had. She took the mirror and held her breath. Slowly she looked down at her reflection and sighed. She was the same. Rose expected to see someone she didn't recognize staring back at her but she was still herself, with her long dark hair and pale white skin.

"Lass, I'm going to get you a cup of tea and let the other's know you've finally awakened. Please wait here."

It was not long before Agnes was back from reporting to the Queen and other castle maids about Rose's condition. The Queen was disappointed, but felt sorry for Rose. She agreed to let Agnes re-teach Rose and Agnes was happy about that. Woman who are let go from their positions were always sent to spinning shops across the village in order to prevent them from spreading castle secrets to the enemies.

"Here drink up."

Rose took the tiny cup from her hands and took a long gulp. She was glad to have something moisten her dry throat.

"We are going to have a walk around the castle, the Queen has agreed to let me teach you how to be the perfect maid, as you once were." Rose could hear her talking but she wasn't really listening. Her mind was trying to process what was going on. She could only nod in response. Rose stood up and this time found it easier to stand.

"Oh no, wait!" Agnes cried as Rose reached for the door.

"You can't go out with your hair down."

"Why not?" Rose spun back in surprised

"You know better than to let a man see you with your hair down. Only a husband can see a woman like that, unless you're a whore in the pub bars, it's very important."

Rose was shocked. To think that in the twentieth century woman exposed much more than their hair. She sat back down as Agnes twirled her long hair into a bun. Rose winced, she hated her hair up but right now all she cared about was finding Leon and feeling his arms around her. The truth was she was terrified, and just being by his side would make everything feel better and make sense.

"Okay. Let's get going."

Rose followed behind in awe. The castle looked just as Rose would imagine a castle to look like. With the long red carpeted hallways, gleaming candle sticks on the walls that bounced eerie shadows along the corners, and paintings of what she presumed to be ancestors on every wall. She peeked through every room as they walked by.

She saw other maids cleaning, making tea, and even polishing men boots. They had passed by a library, multiple bedrooms, living rooms, and even a kitchen. Everything was so old fashioned. Rose couldn't believe her eyes, she felt like a tourist, and pretty much looked like one too with her gaping mouth. Agnes led her into a wide open space that appeared to the exit, and entrance to the castle. Along the walls gold statues hung and high above the ceilings chandeliers shined brightly. The English flags hung around the thrones, and it was then that Rose realized she was in a castle. The room had a cathedral feeling, the windows were painted abstractly in different colors. The huge entrance doors were carved exquisitely, the detailing appearing to have men in horses fighting with bows and arrows. Leading upwards, grey knights lined up against the walls. Rose peered closely through the mask and realized they weren't real humans just the body armor.

"Wow this is amazing..." She whispered as the giant painting high above the ground caught her attention. Pillars and columns held up the arched ceilings. The room was an empty waste of space but the size was huge. An entire apartment could fit in just the room alone.

"Why is this castle so big Agnes?"

Rose turned to her and stopped walking.

"Well Lass, as you know the King and Queen have many Guards to protect them and who also inhabit this castle. Everyone, including the maids have their own bed chambers as well. The King and Queen are located on the top floor, while we are on the very bottom, unfortunately too close to the torture chambers down below. Our duty is to serve the Highness' and the Guards who protect our castle and country."

"When the hell did I ever decide to be a slave for some lazy people?" Rose said appalled. "Rose! You cannot speak like that, have some respect." Agnes was terrified of Rose's behavior. She had seen too many beatings for insolent behavior and she was not about to witness one more. "If any other Lass, or worse, Guard hears you speaking like that you'll have you bum aching with fire for a whole week." Rose bit her lip and squinted. "Sorry..."

"Quickly ladies line up!"

Agnes and Rose looked back as a dozen maids ran towards them and lined up side by side. A blonde haired woman brushed against Rose and smiled.

"Hey Rosie, I'm glad to see you finally awake." She winked and Rose flushed. She was embarrassed and could only mutter a weak thanks.

"Why are we lining up?"

"The King has arrived from his voyage. We must all greet him respectfully." Agnes whispered. Rose held her hands together. God, her heart was beating furiously. The thought that this could all be just a bad dream enticed her but she was looking forward to seeing a real King. The loud creaking of the doors interrupted her troubled thoughts. Rose zoned out the giggles and whispering from the women around her to focus on the King as he strolled in alongside two Guards. The King was tall and handsome, his brown hair hung down onto his shoulders. He wore a red over coat and around his body the sling of a sword. Rose quickly realized who she was staring at, having seen him in dozens of textbooks in her time, she couldn't forget his face. It was King Henry VIII, the King who so desperately wanted a son that he went through four wives, mistresses and affairs just to have. He was known to have died from obesity at the age of fifty five.

"They're all so handsome don't you agree?" The blonde next to Rose whispered into her ear. Rose nodded not really noticing anyone's features until her gaze stopped on someone in particular. Her heart froze to such a strong intensity that it burned throughout her whole chest. She opened her mouth to speak but couldn't as she watched Leon stride in behind the King. His face was focused with eyes set forward, walking at the same pace as everyone around him. Rose smiled, so happy to see him again.

"Leon!" She cried stepping forward, ready to run into his arms. The ladies gasped behind her in unison. Her cry startled him, and her heart melted with the vision of him running towards her. He'd swing her in the air and kiss her and tell her everything was going to be okay. She longed to feel his touch against hers and to hear him say how much he missed her when he left, yet instead, he frowned coldly at her and it was then that the vision of what could have been shattered.

Ten

His face hardened in confusion, he had no idea who the woman calling his name was. He studied her from the corner of his eye as he continued to walk forward. "Whose that Lass?"

"I have no bloody idea." Leon replied.

He looked at her again, but he was sure he had never seen her before. Had he ravished her once upon a time ago? He's had so many women that it was hard to keep track of all of their faces.

Rose stood frozen like a statue. Jaw dropped and tears streaming down her face. His cold glare was like an arrow piercing her straight through the heart. She backed away slowly, realizing the rest of the guards were watching her, all but Leon. His back faced her.

"Rose, please get in your position now!" Agnes whispered wildly behind her. *"Why doesn't he recognized me...is it because of how I look? Or is it because he doesn't remember me?"* "No, no, no this can't be happening..." Rose whispered. She wasn't listening to Agnes' pleas, only her own thoughts rung in her ears. She opened her mouth to scream his name again, louder this time, figuring that maybe he didn't recognize her voice but she was pulled backwards. Rose stumbled and caught her balance before she could make more of a scene then there already was.

"Rose, you can be beheaded for running towards the King in that manner!" Agnes said with eyes wide with horror. Rose flushed. She had forgotten that she was not alone. "I'm sorry...I..." She couldn't explain without sounding completely crazy.

"Is that you're lover?" Isabel, the blonde woman, asked.

Her blue eyes were wide with curiosity. "Yes…well no…well I don't know." Rose muttered. "Don't worry Rose he probably couldn't greet you in front of the King like that. Try to speak to him later. There, there don't cry." Her comforting words brought peace to Rose's mind, what she said was true. Her picture perfect romance scene was too crazy to become true anyways. Rose was determined to find him later, she had too.

It was a long day of following Agnes around, Rose was so anxious she could barely contain herself. She had learned how to pour tea, clean laundry which in this time required a bucket of hot water and her hands, and had learned the etiquette of serving tea and trays of food.

All the while her mind was on finding Leon again. Her eyes wandered through every hallway and open door for him, but instead she'd get seductive glances from the other men to whom she would accidentally make eye contact with. It was nearly five when Agnes turned to her to say they would be serving tea and biscuits to the Guards. Rose smiled, finally after a long day she might actually see him again and figure out why he ignored her.

Rose walked quickly behind Agnes into the kitchen where she set out a dozen tea cups, a tray and the kettle. "Now you know what to do my dear, please don't get into any more trouble." Agnes warned. There was warmth of compassion behind her voice. "I'll try not to." Rose half smiled. Her heart beat faster as she approached the dining room door. From the outside she could hear the laughter of men and that made her feel small and self-conscience. Even without makeup Rose had confidence in her looks but it was just that—that scared her. A room full of testosterone and a single woman, whose breast were high and tight against a slim fitting corset, she didn't picture it well. Rose cleared her throat and pulled the door open. A few heads turned her way as she walked in but the loudest speakers had no realization of her presence. She thanked god for not making it an awkward entrance.

Rose didn't dare look up into the faces of more than a dozen men. They filled every seat of the long rectangular table. Leon was somewhere in this room and she hoped that he would see her first. She starts pouring the tea into the cups, slowly lifting her lashes up to take quick glances around the room. She spots Leon at the very end of the table laughing. Her body grows warm, remembering how nice it felt to see him smile so happily.

"I haven't quite seen you before?"

Alarmed, Rose jumped and rattled a tea cup. She cried and grabbed it quickly, setting the tray harshly on the table. She panted as the man beside her smiled.

"I apologize I didn't mean to frighten you." Rose gasped. The man bore a striking resemblance to Andrew, except this man's blonde hair was long and curly and eyes a lighter green. They gleamed at her as he noticed her eyes set on his and a redness dusting her cheeks. She was beautiful he thought, like a porcelain doll.

"My names Thomas, what's yours?"

Rose was baffled, not expecting men of this century to hit on her. What depressed her was the fact that Leon was in the same room and not once had he looked her way. Even after their night of making love, she thought she meant something to him. She couldn't help the sad expression that fell on her face.

"M-my names Rose, nice to meet you." The words came out of her mouth lifelessly and she didn't mean to sound so barren towards him. He nodded at her with a smile, at the same time noticing the sadness in her voice. Thomas took the cup out of the tray, noting her nervous hands, wanting to be at the very least a bit useful towards her. He became instantly curious about the woman with the sad green eyes.

"Thank you my lady."

Rose forced a smile and moved on to the next person, and then to the next until finally she was in front of Leon. She was sure he had seen her, and was positive he was ignoring her. Rose forced herself to look at him deeply, so he could see the hurt in her eyes down to the pit of her soul. He arched his brow, confused as to why she had not given him his cup of tea yet.

"Is...there a problem?" Leon said finally, annoyance behind his usual warm voice. The lady in front of him was strikingly beautiful, and for a moment he regretted his harsh tone. Her eyes were wide and sorrowful, and Leon had no idea why she looked at him in that way. Rose clutched the sides of the tray firmly, trying to keep her hands from shaking.

Thomas stopped his conversation to look over at Rose, and suddenly no one else was talking. There was a lump in her throat that burned the more she held back her tears, she had promised herself she wouldn't cry in front of him, but that promise was getting harder to keep it.

"Don't you know who I am?" Rose finally said. The words came out rough and shaky. Leon smirked and looked around.

"I have never seen you before, mam. Now will you please hand me my tea."

"Leon..."

His brow rose. "How do you know my name?" He asked. His tone was sarcastic and he tried hard to hide the smile on his face. Rose could feel her heart tearing into pieces again. The heat rushed to her cheeks, and she stood shaking and embarrassed.

Suddenly, she grew angry, wanting to rip the smirk out of his face.

"It's me, Rose..." She didn't know what else to say.

"Hmm, Rose? I've met many Rose's."

Leon laughed and his friends joined him. They always found amusement in Leon's affairs. The man had a woman coming up to him at least once a day and it never got old. Rose takes a step back as tears fall from her face, she shuts her eyes and takes a deep breath.

"You asshole." She says, hurt clearly apparent in her voice. Leon's lips part in a gasp. He was appalled, this being the first time a woman had disrespected him so in front of everyone. He squeezed down on his fist, containing his anger. The room hollered with even more laughter.

"Did she just call you a donkey Leon, I've never heard a woman call you that!" A man next to him cried and laughed hysterically, the beer in his hand slipped from his fingers and the crowd laughed harder. All the while Leon grew angrier. *Who the hell is this woman? "*

"Well, maybe we have met before. My apologies, I don't seem to remember the faces of the whores I have slept with."

Flaming red, Rose drops the tray to the ground and the room gasps with shock. Thomas stands up quickly.

"That's enough Leon!"

"I get it, I came here for nothing!" The tea cups shatter into the ground like her heart and hot tea splashes onto his boots. He curses and gives her a death glare. What happened next was by impulse. Rose's swing was cut short as Leon's hand catches hers before it could reach his face. She stumbles forward and almost into his arms, but uses her free hand to balance herself from his shoulder. She looks up slowly into dark, cold eyes just inches from hers.

That familiar warmth of his hand resonated through her whole body, but instead of bringing happiness it just saddened her even more. This person wasn't the man she fell for.

Leon had too much pride to let a woman belittle him. He had controlled his grip on her palm to such an extent that it wouldn't hurt her, but warn her. Yet as angry as he was, he couldn't deny the spark that had surged through him when he had taken her hand into his. Or the familiarity of her stunning face as it grew closer towards him. He shook his thoughts away.

"You dare raise your hand at me!" Leon roared. His breath hit against her cheeks as she faced away and shut her eyes.

"I'm done with all of this. You're a fool...no I'm a fool for believing what you said. Screw you and your life. I'm done helping you, I should have never came here!" Rose cried. The words hurt her more than it could ever hurt him. His hand still held hers tightly and she began to feel the ache through her fingers.

"If you want me to remember you so badly, meet me in my bed chamber tonight, maybe if I fuck you hard enough I'll remember who you are again!" Rose pulled her hand back in disgust as Thomas took her free arm.

"I'm not one of you *whore's* and I'll never be!" Rose was shouting now. Leon could only smirk and think how amusing this all really was. He watched as his good friend Thomas slipped his arm between hers and a strange feeling swept through him.

"Please, take this crazy woman away, she has ruined my mood, and by dear god, have her out of this castle." Leon said as he grabbed a handkerchief and dusted his trousers.

Rose held onto Thomas, only because she felt as if she would faint at any moment. Her head spun in circles as she was led outside. Her lips were firm, set in a straight line of disbelief. Was it possible that she had only dreamt of the future? Was it that she was never there in the first place? A strong ache pulsated through her head and she stopped to groan.

"Are you alright!" Thomas leaned down, being almost a foot larger than her, she barely reached his shoulders. Rose looked up embarrassed, her cheeks flaming red. "Yes...I'm sorry I caused such a scene."

"I apologize for my friend, he's a bit malicious towards woman. He must have hurt you... I have seen you before this morning, was it you who called his name?" Rose nodded, hating every second that moment.

"Please Lass, forget that man, he is not worth falling for. You are too beautiful cry over any man." Something about Thomas made her heart feel warm. Rose didn't know whether it was the size of the man that made feel like he could protect her from dragons, or if it was the warmth in his eyes when he spoke. For the first time today, Rose gave a genuine smile. "Thank you...I don't know what would have happened if it wasn't for you."

He flashed her a pearly white smile, and at that moment Rose felt better, even if he seemed to remind her a bit of Andrew. It was nice to have someone look out for her in this god forsaken place.

"Can I show you the garden tomorrow night? We can talk, if it's alright with you." How could Rose reject when she was so lost and lonely in this new world. "Yes, I'd love too. Thank you." They turned their attention towards the running footsteps coming their way.

"My dear God Rose, what have you done?" Agnes scurried towards her with the same distraught expression she had held all day long. She stopped breathless. "I told you to stay out of trouble!"

Rose squeezed her knuckles. She wanted so badly to tell Agnes everything, so maybe she could understand, but this world was not like hers. They would probably burn her for being a *witch* if she told anyone where she came from.

"I'm sorry I ju-"

"Mam, it was not this lady's fault, but mines please disregard her behavior, everything will be taken care of." Rose looked at Thomas with wide eyes. Her heart began to emerge from the dark hole that consumed her chest. Finally, some faith in humanity was restored. He took her hand into his and lifted it to his lips and the flashback of Andrew came back into mind, she shuttered in that second and reminded herself that he was a completely different person.

"Until tomorrow, my lady." Thomas says. He kissed her hand and slipped his fingers around her wrist. She felt so small and fragile beside him. Awkwardly, she smiled, knowing all too well Agnes was burning a hole in her face.

"You seemed to attract many eyes today Miss Rose." Agnes was smiling, the wrinkles on her face arching upwards, making her fatigue obvious.

"I do not..." Rose could only say.

They began to walk back towards their dormitories. There was silence between the two, Rose was lost in her own agonizing thoughts and memories. Her chest still numb from the reaction Leon had given her. "That Leon man that you mentioned this morning, did you meet him?" Agnes asked cautiously, knowing the thought of him was troubling Rose. She froze, remembering the pain as if it just happened.

"Yeah...but he doesn't know who I am."

"Don't mind him then, Thomas is a gentleman, he will treat you right." Rose laughed. "I'm not interested in Thomas, I just want to be friends." Agnes raised her brow.

"A friendship between a young man and woman? I have not lived to see it once, except in the lives of children." Rose stared at her in surprise, "Are we not allowed to have friends?" Agnes laughed. "Friends is just another word for *lovers* my dear." Wow, Rose thought. This time period was really, really jacked up.

"So what the hell was that all about?" Ethan dropped his mug onto the table and pulled a chair over to sit in. "What are you talking about?" Leon asked, shifting his gaze away from the attractive woman who had been eyeing him from across the room.
"The Porcelain doll, as everyone's been calling her."
"Ethan, give me names I beg of you."
"Alright, alright, Rose, the woman who called you an asshole." Ethan snorted and held back his laugh, knowing all too well how angry Leon would get. "I came here to have a good time, please don't speak of that ridiculous woman I know nothing about." Leon was annoyed. Just the sound of her name made him lose his temper.
"You really don't know her?"
Leon took a long gulp of his Ale before setting it harshly on the wooden counter. He raked his hands through his hair which was falling in his face, obscuring his view of the big breasted females walking towards them. His overcoat was making his body hot so he flung it off.
"No Henry, that woman is crazy."
To be honest, Leon had not stopped thinking about her since the moment he set eyes on her. He tried hard to remember where they had met, but his memory had no recollection of such a time. Also, what kept him on edge

was the strange feeling in his chest that emerged when he saw her tears, it was so nostalgic, as if he'd seen them before. In his mind he knew exactly what to do, and the thought of it scared him. He had never embraced a woman shedding tears, except the times he would hold a woman after losing stealing their innocence. But even then he didn't care, he never cared about a woman, if it were not for sex.

"Hey Lad, care if I join?" It was Thomas. Leon shrugged, not caring at all, his mind set on choosing which Lass he'd take home tonight. "Those are a lot of cups, you couldn't have possibly drank them all Leon?" Thomas laughed, knowing all too well the answer to his question.

"You know me you fool, this is nothing." Leon hollered for a couple more. When the waitress came back Leon slid his arm around her waist and sat her down on his leg. The young lady giggled and trailed a heart on his face seductively. Being the gentleman that he was, Leon reached and grabbed her breast, her startled jump satisfying him.

"You look delicious." He whispered into her ear as he nipped it and trailed kisses down her neck. She laughed and grabbed his shoulders. It was then that Leon froze and a flash back of Rose's hand on his body reappeared. In that moment he could *feel* her grasp and it made him utterly uncomfortable. He hated it.

"I shall see you later, my lady." Leon shot her a smile that promised a night of pleasure and she blushed, running to another customer. When he looked over at Thomas, he was pushing away the lassies that clung around his shoulders.

"What are you doing Lad?" Leon asked, surprised at his friends unusual behavior towards woman today. Any other day he would have had four women straddled onto him, and the next day would be filled with details of what he would have each of them do to him.

"That Rose woman, there isn't anything between you two?" Thomas said suddenly. Leon was startled that he would mention her name. He groaned, rolling his eyes and gulping down his beer.

"Her again? No. there is not."

"Okay. Remember those words, I shall pursue her from now on." Thomas' eyes were serious, he couldn't doubt his friend. Leon laughed through the strange heaviness in his chest. "That lass? Are you sure about that?"

"Yes, Leon."

He crossed his arms and sat back. But Leon was curious and couldn't help but ask. "What makes you want to chase her?" Thomas gave him a sideways glance and smiled. "Her attitude and confidence, and also that sadness behind her eyes. I want to change that."

Leon cleared his throat, knowing he was the culprit towards that. Although he didn't know how or why, and it just plain out confused him. He was paying for a murder he never committed.

"Well good luck to you, she looks easy, I know you'll be able to charm her into your bedroom."

Thomas squeezed his fist. He knew Leon's spiteful and resentful personality was in his nature so he couldn't blame him. Thomas just wished he could be a bit more sympathetic towards people. Leon had a reason to hate the world, but not everyone that inhabited it. He had known Leon since they were young children, their families were neighbors who raised a farm together. They grew up as brothers. But one cursed night changed Leon's life forever, when the war broke out overnight and his home was invaded. His mother and sister were raped and his father hung. Thomas' family managed to escape, and meanwhile, Leon and Thomas had been hunting in the woods. He changed from then on until adulthood. Leon stopped caring about the world and himself.

"Please be more respectful Leon, how many times have I told you this."

Leon rolled his eyes. "The only people I should worry about respecting are the King and Queen, or they'll have my head!" He laughed, clapping hands with Ethan who also agreed. Thomas ignored his ignorance.

"One more over here!"

Thomas sipped his ale and fell back into his memories. Leon's recklessness is what the King favors. He is a very bold leader in battle, he owns no fear regarding his own life, nor anyone else's. Leon doesn't own any emotions. Thomas and Leon are the head soldiers in battle and the Kings' most trusted guards, therefore Thomas tries hard to ignore his reckless behavior. They were partners, nonetheless.

When Thomas looks back up Leon is wrapped around another female, as he would usually be every night. Thomas couldn't blame his actions, he had done the same thing just a few nights ago. "Well, you two continue to chat. I'll be taking this beauty to see the moonlight by the lake." Leon winked at Thomas and he couldn't help but laugh. "Have fun." He knew they would be doing more than just sightseeing.

Eleven

When Rose awoke she was surprised to see a strip of sunlight against her wall. The small window on the corner of the room seemed to align perfectly with the sun set and she was glad to finally see beyond the darkness.

She looked upwards towards the ceiling in a daze. She had spent last night crying her eyes out and she could feel the result of it on her lids. The hope of waking up in her time had diminished the moment she felt the uncomfortable ache from the spring mattress on her back. Rose didn't have to open her eyes to see. The stench of burning wood had crept into her room last night through the window, and she now smelt as if she'd been sitting by a fire all night. Rose craved, and needed a decent shower and she was determined to have one before her duties began.

Rose had learned that after hours, and on the weekends she was allowed to do what she pleased. That meant that tomorrow, Saturday, she would go home. Or try to find a way to. There was no point in staying here any longer. Rose walked over to her dresser and pulled it open. To her surprise, more gowns hung on the rack. A red, white, blue, and emerald colored one. She smiled and felt the fabric with her hands. It was made of the softest material, silk. Before she could wonder how they came to be, there was a knock on her door.

"May I?" Agnes said.

"Yes, come in."

Agnes smiled as she entered the room, a towel hung over her arm. "Ah, dearie you have seen my surprise."

"You put these here? Agnes they're beautiful, thank you." She smiled and rested her hand on Rose's arm.

"I figured you would need some new dresses, while you were in your coma, the Queen thought you would never wake so we were ordered to empty your dresser, unfortunately. But these should fit you just fine."

Rose had no recollection of anything beyond yesterday so she didn't feel anger or remorse. "I'll wear this emerald one tomorrow." Rose said clutching the fabric.

"How about tonight…with Thomas." Agnes gave Rose a wink and laughed. "I'm just pulling you're leg. Come, I'll show you were you can freshen up."

She found Agnes' humor to be quite uncomfortable. There wasn't anyone in this world she wanted to impress anymore.

Rose had learned all of the maid's names last night and put an extra effort in remembering who everyone was. She found it easy to categorize them by age, and who she had more in common with. Only three woman besides her were nearly the same age, the red haired fair maiden with the green eyes was called Ellen, the brunette young lady who appeared to be just over sixteen was named Alice, and the blonde, Isabel. The other women were much older than them, in fact they were old enough to be their mothers.

"Why are we not allowed to be free if we get…fired?"
Agnes huffed. "It's a bloody stinking rule that needs to be banished. We live many years of our lives serving the highnesses and what do we get in return? Not a single thing."

"That's horrible…" Rose whispered. Worry started to creep on her, and the realization that she might never find a way back home and she'd have to spend her life being a maid, or worse, pricking her fingers with sewing needles.

"Is there a way around that fate?" Rose asked. "Well, if you get married my dear, then they'll let you go. If arranged by the King and Queen of course. But no one has done so, if you haven't noticed but the other ladies, and myself included have been here since we were young." Roses' eyes shot open. "What do you mean, if arranged? Can't I choose my own husband?" Agnes whirled around, nearly crashing into Rose. "Of course not! If anyone defies the Highnesses arrangement they'll be beheaded."

"But what about love, how can you love someone you're forced to marry?" Agnes patted her back. "Awh, dear that is but a simple wish us women have. To be free and marry who we please. To have the freedom men have, they can just point and choose a lady, and they'll be theirs."

Rose couldn't believe what she was hearing. She needed to go back, there was no way in hell she could stay here and be married off to an old fart she didn't even know.

"Here it is. Please be speedy, we must carry out our duties for the day." She was handed the towel and dress. "I will."

When Rose entered the room she was surprised to find nearly all the maids bathing in tubs. It must have been the strangest thing Rose had ever seen. It was equivalent to a modern day gym room, without the walls and privacy. White porcelain tubs lined the walls, and she counted a dozen.

"Hey Rose! Good morning to yah!" Ellen, the ginger, cried from the middle of the room. She waved towards her and Rose waved back. An embarrassed flush filled her face. She walked towards an empty tub just across from Ellen and slowly began removing her clothes. *"This is not awkward, this is not awkward, god, who am I kidding, this is awkward!"*

She closed her eyes and tried to pretend she was at home, in her fancy bathroom, but all the chattering made it nearly impossible.

With one last foolish motivational speech, Rose was in the tub, bare and naked. The warm water was refreshing on her skin. She grabbed the soap and rubbed it onto her body, scraping hard against it hoping it would be enough to rid the stench of sweat from her skin. The soap smelled like lilacs blooming in the spring, and for the first time she felt relaxed. She knew she promised Agnes she'd be quick but a couple of long minutes would not hurt.

"So tell me about Lord Leon Evenwood." Isabel laughed as Rose's eyes sprung open. Rose didn't know whether to respond or be distracted by the nakedness of the woman in front of her, slipping into the tubs warm water. She had hoped Isabel would forget him.

She let out a huge sigh as she slipped into the tub. She arched her arms on the side and turned to her with a smile on her face.

"I haven't forgotten and I want to know." Her smile was large, noticing how embarrassed Rose was. She had no chance but to go with the flow of things. "We met one night, and things got emotional...then the next morning he was gone and I never saw him again."

"He left you without a simple goodbye?!" Ellen cried, eavesdropping on our conversation. Rose looked up in surprise and nodded.

"That halfwit, Rose I should have warned you about him. But you never paid any mind to him before you're accident. Why do you suddenly mention him now?" Rose had forgotten that in this time period she had a pass, she couldn't keep confusing everyone, she had to be careful with her words. They probably thought she was crazy enough already.

"I guess the impact made me remember." Isabel's' face scrunched. "He's the worst of the worst, a drunkard and a whore magnet. Don't get involved with him Rose, I don't want to see you get hurt." She smiled and Rose felt her sincerity.

"Thanks ladies. I won't anymore, I nearly slapped the guy in the face and could have if he didn't stop me!" Rose splashed the water. "What! You did not!" The two girls gaped. "Why wouldn't I? He treated me like trash, I wanted to do much worst to him."

"I'm very glad someone stood up to him Rose, but you have to be careful! Men are capable of doing anything. Especially to someone attractive such as yourself. Why do you think we are advised not to roam the halls during late hours of the night, who knows what the guards would do after a night of drinking?" Isabel held her arms and shuddered, thinking deeply of the times she barely escaped her attacks.

Rose had not thought of that, nor realized that there wasn't a phone to call the police with. God, she really wished she had studied this time period a bit more.

"I will keep that in mind. Thank you for the warning." Goosebumps had crept alongside her body now just thinking about it. "Don't worry, a tough woman like you can handle anything. You're alive now, by miracle, you are surely a legend around these walls."
"Handle anything?"

Rose didn't know why the thought of Thomas holding her down flashed in her mind. A big strong man like him, she would not be able to handle. Her cheeks were blushing. She submerged herself in the water, waiting nearly a minute until she sprang up gasping for air. Rose held her heart and the anxiety was strong. That lost, sad, heartbroken feeling had made its way back into her heart and it was aching hard. Why did it randomly happen? She wondered. She was fine until his face appeared in her mind again.

Rose met Agnes outside the bathing room, she was sitting on a stool reading a book. "Finally freshened up, feels nice eh? You can come here whenever you want." Rose smiled and thanked her. Grateful for having someone to guide her through these times.

"Today you will meet the Queen, she has summoned you to her quarters. Please wear this." In her hands was the Emerald dress. Rose had no idea one had to look nice and clean just to speak to someone, then again it wasn't just anyone. Rose didn't hesitate.

"And here, rub this berry on your lips and cheeks."

The dress fit her perfectly. She stared at her reflection from the mirror and admired the difference a nice dress and makeup could make her feel. Who was she changing into and why? What happened to the real Rose? She was becoming lost in an identity that she didn't belong to and it frightened her. Her lips were as red as blood and she realized that her cheeks flushed naturally, there was no need for blush.

The bun on her head was wrapped around tightly, secured by a lace bonnet. "There, look at you, beautiful!" Agnes fixed the loose strands of hair around her ears and guided her towards the door.

"Let's hurry now."

Rose followed Agnes to the top floor, where they were no longer under the floor boards like a bunch of mice, looked away to use when needed. The thought of it angered her. Rose was not one to be used.

"You look good enough to be a royal." Agnes whispered when she noticed how much attention Rose was getting.

Rose laughed. "I wish!" It would definitely make her life easier, she thought. The wooden panelings on the wall seemed endless as they walked the long corridors.

She could only pray that they'd get to their destination faster, she wanted to avoid running into *him*.

"Speaking of the devil..." Rose whispered.

They halted to a stop suddenly as the guards walked towards them.

"Bow!" Agnes hissed.

"Oh!"

Awkwardly, Rose bent her head down, maybe at a much steeper angle, she had no idea what she was doing. She lifted her head just as Leon appeared. His eyes stopped on hers and held her gaze. Memories of their times together flooded her mind. The nights they would laugh and spend endless hours chatting, and the time he had saved her from falling down the steps, or that night he rescued her at the bar. She fought hard not to think about the night they shared together and the last words he said before he left, *I love you*. He had said them with such honesty that he believed her. Rose tried hard, but she lost and it overcame her. She pulled away from his wide eyed stare and looked towards the floor, the hurt in her chest growing stronger. She knew it wasn't his fault that he couldn't remember her, but it didn't stop the pain from hurting. To think that a couple of days ago she was in his arms, and now they were merely strangers, pained her more than anything.

"Is that her?" She heard whispering and looked up.

The men gawked at her like fresh meat, smiling from ear to ear, all but Leon. He didn't understand why his feet were glued to the ground and why the hell he couldn't move. His eyes had fixed on the most beautiful woman he had ever seen. But the moment he realized who she was he had darted his gaze forward. In that moment he was embarrassed. Who would have thought a crazy woman like that could clean up so well. His insides turned and bloody hell, did his chest hurt so suddenly. He couldn't understand what was causing the ache but he knew it had something to do with the woman in front of him. The dream last night had been so vivid, he had woken up drenched in sweat. How had that woman invaded him even in his sleep? She had managed to darken his mood and when he awoke he simply stared into the darkness in bewilderment. He dared never to speak of his dream to anyone, hell, he was ashamed of it. He had told her he loved her and that they would be together again. Leon shivered as he heard himself say those words, something he never dared to tell a woman, much less her.

"Good morning, my lady. You look stunning today." Rose smiled at Thomas and bit her lip. "I am meeting the Queen...so I needed a change." Rose muttered. The attention of everyone was turned towards them, she could even see Leon's facial expression change. Thomas stepped from behind Leon and kissed her hand.

"I shall see you later, I hope?"
Rose nodded. Her heart thrashed wildly as she held her breath. Thomas smiled and walked on forward. "Let's go." He commanded. Leon looked at her with his brows burrowed, lost in his own array of thoughts and confusion.
"Rose?"

Startled, she looked up at Agnes a few feet away and held her hands tightly. Even though Leon didn't remember her she had come back in time. Leon was going to get murdered for something he didn't do. She had forgotten about the reason why he had asked for her help. All along she's been selfishly thinking about herself. If the one thing she could do for Leon was help him, then she would be willing to. That was the only way to really let him go, maybe then, time would be reversed again.

Rose just had to get passed the fact that he was a complete asshole who didn't deserve her help, but then again, he didn't deserve to die. Maybe she could use Thomas to help her as well. *"Suck it up Rose, you're not here for love or to be with him, you're here to save his life!'*

It was as if a dark cloud was lifted off her chest with this new realization. She ran to catch up with Agnes and turned to look back. Watching the man she loved walk away from her again.

"Meet Margaret, my daughter, as you know her." The Queen said. Rose had never been so nervous in her life, she didn't know whether to wave and smile or just say hello. She bowed. "She is as beautiful as you." Rose said and a large grin spread across Margaret's face. "I hear you suffered memory loss, it's very unfortunate." Rose shook her head, trying to choose her words carefully. "I would suffer a thousand injuries than to let you or your family get hurt, you're majesty."

"That is very noble of you Rose. I am elated to have you serve us. I have ordered you're belongings to be transferred to this floor. You will now be serving my daughter, and guards, as well as having a proper, more accommodating chamber." She was being upgraded, like getting a better position in a company, Rose didn't know whether to feel happy or angry. Angry at the fact that she would be serving the ruthless liar who gets Leon murdered, or happy that she was close enough to see him more often.

"Thank you, you're majesty. I will serve her well."

"I believe you will. Agnes will show you to your bedroom now."

Rose bowed one last time and peeped a glimpse at Margaret. She could tell what type of women she was just by looking into her eyes. She could not be trusted. As instructed Agnes led Rose to her room. When the door was opened she gasped. The room was carpeted, with golden drapes hanging on the windows and a large queen sized bed. On it were golden sheets and pillows. God, Rose missed sleeping on a pillow.

She walked in the room, noting a new dresser on the side and a room with a private toilet and tub for herself. "What is this, a master suite?" Agnes didn't understand but seeing Rose so happy made her smile. "I'm so happy for you Rose. You deserve this for saving her life, the Queen is a very righteous person." Rose should feel happy but there was a wave of sadness knowing she would not be seeing Agnes every day and she was sure she would miss her.

"I'll still see you around won't I?"

Agnes nodded and that made Rose feel better.

"Also, you are not required to wear the maid dresses anymore. You are to wear what was put into your dresser." Rose realized she was sleeping in a prison cell before this. "Now, I'll let you get settled."

Twelve

Serving Margaret was no easy task. By nearly five o'clock Rose was exhausted. She had met Agnes in the parlor and helped her prepare the dishes. She was sad to know that Leon was nowhere to be seen. Apart of her needed to see him, just so she could remember who she really was.

It was when the old grandfather clock stroke that Rose realized her shift was over and that Thomas was waiting for her outside. She hurried down the hall and through multiple corridors, hoping no one would see her running. Night had already fallen and Rose halted to a stop in front of a dark alcove deck which overlooked the village and lake below. She was so mesmerized by the size of the moon that she didn't realize there was someone else enjoying the view.

"Wow…"She whispered.

Clutching the stone railing, she tip-toed and leaned forward dangerously, to see how far the water stretched downwards.

"Be careful, or you might get a much closer view than you could ever wish for."

Startled by his sudden presence, Rose screamed. Her body moved forward and she felt the weight of gravity crushing her for a split second. In an instant she was pulled back from her death and swung into the arms of someone. It was nostalgic, his touch too familiar. But she couldn't quite concentrate with the sound of her beating heart thrashing wildly in her chest. Panting, she found it hard to differentiate the reason why it did. Was it because her chest was planted against a hard chiseled body or because she almost plummeted to her death?

The force of the spin had caused her bun to undo, and for the first time in a while she felt the comforting strands of her long hair against her skin.

"A-are you alright?"

Rose froze, moving her face away slowly from Leon's chest. She hoped he didn't recognize her. The urge to run away was overbearing, but she was paralyzed. Rose swallowed hard and squinted, battling against emotions and the urge to hold him again.

"Y-yes, thanks...I..." Her words faded as she looked up to see his hand clutching a strand of her hair. His eyes direct on it, like he's never seen it before. And that's when Rose remembered what Agnes had told her, how women were not allowed to show their hair down to any man besides their husband. Rose stepped back, her hair gliding down his palm. The look on Leon's face was priceless.

"You again?" His voice cracked. He wanted to insult her, say something to distract her from what he just did but he realized he had nothing bad to say. How could he hurt someone so innocent looking, whose eyes were shining wide from the moonlight right in front of him. He didn't know whether it was the alcohol that was making him feel this way, but he felt extremely attracted to her.

He had never seen a woman whose hair was so long that it curled around her chest and shoulders so teasingly. He knew it was wrong to keep looking, that he should tell her to put it up but he was spellbound by her beauty. Leon took a step forward towards her, Rose took a step back. He stopped, embarrassed by his actions.

"I won't hurt you."

The words flowed from his lips.

"—and if I ever did, I apologize. I have not been myself lately. But tell me, where have we met before? Please enlighten me."

Rose stared wide eyed and tried to speak. Her cheeks flushed, she couldn't tell him something so ridiculous like the *truth*. She thought fast. "I'm the one who should apologize. I...confused you for someone else." She looked down, realizing her feet were functioning and began to walk away from him when suddenly he took her hand.

"That is clearly not the truth, you knew my name, and you almost hit me. I must have caused you great pain for you to dare such a thing towards someone of my stature." His dark eyes were piercing hers, daring her to make up another lie. But they were filled with fear and he could tell how unstable his presence was making her.

"I'm sorry, I, um, he has the same name as you, and you bear a close resemblance to him...my past lover." Leon knew her reply didn't make any sense but he was not going to fight about it. The warmth of her hand still in his snapped him back to reality and he quickly let go. He found it felt more comforting to hold it and gazed at it for a second more before looking back up as she tied her hair. He wanted more time with her, to talk to her, his sudden curiosity for the porcelain doll was overbearing and he was disappointed when she turned to walk away.

"There you are. I was looking all over for you..." Thomas smile faded rapidly as he noticed Leon by her side.

"Leon? Has he hurt you?"

Rose must have looked as pale as she felt, she was shaking, contemplating if she should go for it and just tell him the truth. Things would have been easier that way. But Thomas now held her shoulders and glared at him, and she found she could not tell him even if she wanted to. Rose knew Thomas was only trying to protect her, but there was no need. She suddenly felt smaller between Thomas and Leon, and wanted ever so badly to be by his side instead.

"I've done nothing to hurt her Thomas, calm down." Leon's glare through the moon light was fierce, his eyes were filled with daggers and Rose wondered why he looked so angry.

"Come, let's go." Thomas took Rose before she could protest. She turned back to see Leon staring at her as they walked away. His hard, chiseled face held distraught and she wanted so badly to know why.

"I apologize again for whatever my friend has said to you." Thomas broke the silence after a couple of minutes. Rose tried to hide her smile, her mind kept replaying the same scene over and over again. The way his strong arms pulled her towards his body and how amazing it felt to hear his heart beat against his chest again.

"No, it's fine. He apologized to me for what he said, I apologized as well I had mistaken him for someone else..." Thomas looked down in surprise. "Really?" He questioned doubtfully. Her eyes had been miserable, even before he had seen her speak to Leon. How was it possible that she had mistaken him with someone else? "Yes, definitely."

Rose felt bad lying to Thomas, but she couldn't have him creeping into her business. Thomas led her down a corridor and finally through a large door that led towards a fountain outside. Around it large bushes and flowers surrounded the area. The sound of crickets filled the night air. A warm breeze blew, sending a chill down her spine. The moon was high above them, guiding them down the long path that led through the oversized garden. Rose gawked at the roses trailing their feet.

"Notice how the moonlight washes over the roses, making them shine more than any other flower." Thomas pointed out and she nodded, agreeing as well. Rose looked up to him and smiled, telling him how sad the life span of a rose was once they were taken from their roots. She told Thomas that was the reason why she didn't like to receive roses from men, because of the symbolism of something so beautiful dying so quickly. Like a relationship. Or a first love. Thomas enjoyed listening to her soft voice, it was the first time he had heard her talk so much. He felt lucky to have her trust him as well as tell him about her horrible accident. It was no wonder Rose was a bit strange in the beginning. "It's so nice to have a friend to talk to, I was beginning to feel so lonely." Rose admitted.

Her trust in this man was increasing and she only hoped he felt the same way. Rose knew she would need his help later on. "Am I considered a friend?" The question surprised Rose and she laughed. "Of course, what else would we be?" Thomas hesitated for a moment. He didn't want to be *friends* with this woman, he wanted much more. Friendship between a man and a woman didn't exist and he looked down at her questioning her statement, but there was not a hint of humor behind her words. He laughed anyways.

"I think it will be very hard to stay friends with a woman like you." She held her hands together, not knowing whether that was a good or bad thing. They continued to walk for what seemed like an hour. The sky had grown darker and Rose was beginning to feel nervous. The bushes they had passed by would shake, and sometimes Rose would get goose bumps, feeling as if there was someone watching them, creeping slowly behind them in the darkness.

They had finally reached the diamond lake Thomas had been talking about. The water did shine like tiny crystals, Rose was so captivated by its gleam that she paid no mind to the path she walked on. Suddenly she screamed and stumbled forward. Cursing her fate for causing her to lose her balance twice in one night.

"Are you alright!"

He had caught her waist in his hands. Her body hovered just above the ground now, just a few more inches and she was positive she would have been going back to her chambers with a bump on her head. She panted, arms tight around his neck. Rose sighed as she looked down towards the culprit of her fall, the root of a branch that had grown awkwardly in the middle of the path.

"I thought something grabbed my foot, oh god..."

It took a second for Rose to realize that Thomas wasn't paying attention, but instead gazing into her eyes. She froze, her mind beginning to panic but she couldn't move. He leaned in closer and closer until his lips were on hers. Roses' eyes were huge, the stubbles on his face scratched against hers as Thomas kissed her deeply and pulled her up against him, arching his neck down to reach her face. The attraction she felt towards him wasn't love, but lust. She knew she could drown herself in him if she wanted to but in her heart Rose felt nothing, no one else could compare to how she had felt with Leon when he kissed her. She was but an empty shell whose heart seized to exist, so Rose knew she couldn't lead him on.

He pulled her away slowly studying her face. Rose could only blink rapidly and look away. She could feel her face heating up again.

"Please excuse me..."

Thomas was embarrassed, the impulse to kiss her had been too strong to bear and he hoped it didn't scare her off."

"Oh stop it darling, you're embarrassing me."

Thomas and Rose turned towards the voice a couple of feet in front of them. A woman was laughing and dancing under the moonlight. Her dress had come undone and she was pulling it down her shoulders.

"Wow…well this is awkward." Rose whispered, curious to find out who was speaking yet not knowing whether she should look away.

"You are beautiful my lady, but not quite the most beautiful woman I have ever seen." Roses' heart stopped. She knew that voice. Leon found this Lass surprisingly annoying. He just wanted to rip her clothes off and have her, so the ecstasy of love making can distract him from his pathetic life.

"Who is the most beautiful woman you've ever seen then?" The woman said, too buzzed off alcohol to care. "She has the palest skin and darkest hair, a mysterious lady, with the lightest eyes. A combination so different and so perfect, as if the night and morning sun have come together and formed the definition of a woman." Leon stumbled against a rock and laughed as he caught his balance. The whole world was spinning in a circle around his head. He unbuttoned his collar shirt, feeling the breeze against his perspiring skin refreshing. "I daresay you are lying my lord, for such a woman does not exist."

He caught her shoulders and held her against him, kissing her neck down to her collar bone and then up again until he found her mouth. Roses stood still, breathing slowly. Her chest aching. Damn, why did she have to run into him like this?

"Let's go Rose." Thomas said, knowing all too well the hurt it caused her but she didn't move. What was happening in front of her was real and was what she needed to see to get over him. Leon wasn't hers anymore, and she was quite sure he never was to begin with.

She looked up one more time with tears in her eyes. He was staring at her, eyes wide and guilty and it seemed as if the alcohol was draining from his system. "Rose..." Leon whispered. It was the first time he had called out her name. The look in her eyes seemed like a wound in his chest and he couldn't figure out why he felt so guilty. He had done nothing wrong, Leon had never met her before so why was it that she looked at him that way? It pained him like an unwanted wave of emotions.

"Who is that?" The whore he was with turned to look at Rose. She gasped as she noticed her dark colored hair and pale complexion. Her lips as red as her name. "Her?" The woman was young, barely in her twenties. She scoffed up at Leon and pulled away from his grasp. "I'm done here!" She cried before running off and disappearing into the darkness. There was a moment of silence between Leon and Rose, they just stared at each other with wide eyed expressions.

"Out here in this spot again Lad? I say you take your business to somewhere more private." Thomas said, he looked at Rose from the corner of his eyes to see her reaction. She stiffened and swallowed. Her lips were trembling and he could see she was hurting. Rose's lie was a clear as the day now. She shook her head in disbelief, hoping it'd clear away the troubling thoughts in her mind. Rose couldn't deal with either of them, she turned on her heel and ran away, ignoring the cries that followed. She ran until she was panting and crashed onto the ground, scraping her arm against the hard pebbles beneath. "Shit!" Rose didn't move from the ground, she just cried hard and let the tears wash down her face. The pain in her chest was agonizing. She leaned her head down on the ground and wailed, she was too distressed to care about anything.

Thomas had Leon on the ground. "You're not allowed to go after her!" Thomas shouted. Leon swung his fist and knocked him over. "Don't you dare put your hands on me again Thomas." Leon growled as he staggered up and found his balance. Thomas' lip was bleeding, he could taste the bitterness in his mouth. "Damn you two, you both ruined my mood." Leon scowled and ran his fingers through his hair. "Did you not see the hurt you caused her, what is your problem Leon!"

"I did nothing to hurt her." Her watery eyes came back to mind and Leon pushed her image away.

"She is clearly in love with you, and by dear god, if you hurt her one more time I swear to you."

Leon clenched his fist, who was he to threaten him? He could do whatever he wanted, hurt whomever he pleased. "If she is so in love with me then what is she doing with another man after hours?" Leon hated to admit how much that bothered him. He felt so angry the moment he saw her with Thomas. He would prefer her to be with anyone but him, not his brother. He looked across Thomas' shoulder, in the direction that she had run through and sighed. Leon couldn't help but feel worry in his chest. A young woman should not be wandering alone at night.

"That woman is nothing to me." He muttered. But the lie was as obvious as his drunkenness. Leon grunted and drew is head back, his head beginning to ache stronger. He couldn't let Thomas know how the woman had been affecting him and making him feel, but at the same time he would not allow Thomas to tell him what to do. Leon had finally apologized to her, and thinking he was one step closer to knowing more about her she was now angry at him, and probably never wanted to see or speak to him again. The thought bothered him and he cursed under his breath.

"Are you blind?" Thomas said angrily. This time things had to change and he was not going to let the woman he wanted to be with waver. He would win her heart and take Leon's place in it. "Just stay away from her." He threatened.

"Stay away from her?" Leon laughed but then his face hardened and his eyes darkened.

"I will not take orders from you, *brother.*"

Thirteen

Leon was determined to find Rose that Saturday morning. A week had passed since the incident by the lake and he had barely seen glimpses of her. She kept her eyes low near him and seemed to ignore his presence. It got to a point where he could no longer deal with it. After last nights' dream he felt more compelled than ever to see her again. What he had kept to himself was much more than empty lies. Since his first encounter with Rose, he had not stopped dreaming about her. And what scared him the most wasn't that, it was the feeling in his chest every morning. The pain of knowing it was just a dream, after feeling how real it felt.

They were strange dreams, in a world he's never seen, people he's never met, music he's never heard and strange lights, it was all too much to understand. But she was there in them, every time. He had saved her from a fall down the steps while she held some *sort* of device, and strangely he could still remember the feeling of her body against his. In last night's dream they had made love. It was full of heated passion and he remembered it so clearly, as if it could have been a memory. He had jerked up from his bed suddenly after saying the words, *I love you.*

Leon had to figure out why this woman was affecting him so badly. He wondered as far as to question if she were a witch. He had found her room and was standing outside the door. He knocked, not knowing why he felt so uneasy. After a couple of seconds he realized what a fool he was. The maids were off today. Anger rose quickly to the thought of her with Thomas. Leon had to figure things out quickly and get her out of his mind.

Rose and the girls were shopping around the village market, entering each store and looking at everything. Rose had not felt so relaxed in such a long time. She had cleared her head of Leon for good the past week and she was confident she would not succumbed to his charming self anymore.

Rose purchased a few gowns with the salary pay she was given yesterday and was now following Isabel and Ellen as they chatted about how good looking some men were. Startled, Rose dodged some children who nearly knocked her off her feet chasing one another. This brought her back to the scratches on her arm. She had barely spoken to Thomas either, mostly because she was so embarrassed and knew she couldn't return his feelings. Yet, he still greeted her every morning and gave her a warm smile, as if reassuring her that he understood and that it was okay.

"Did you hear Rose?"

"Eh?" Rose shook herself from her daydream.

"I said we should get back before it gets dark. We shouldn't be out here at night." Rose could only imagine why.

"That's fine."

Rose was the only one who spotted Margaret a yard away. She hid behind some barrels and looked left and right. She seemed to be whispering to someone behind her. Rose instantly panicked. *"Could she be sneaking out of the castle with the man she had an affair with? Or will have one with. What should I do...should I follow her? I have to find out who she's with, if not how could I ever help Leon."* She suddenly remembered the article on Margaret's' diary. When Margaret learned she was to be wed with a Prince, she told her lover to take her virginity. Marriage in this time was only to be allowed if the two adjoining people were Catholics and if the woman was pure. By losing her virginity, it meant she was not qualified for marriage and therefore she would not be forced to wed. But because Margaret was so young and immature, when the King and Queen confronted her about her blood stained sheets, she confessed to having been raped. In order to protect her lover she lied, claiming it was Leon who had raped her.

It all made sense to Rose now, Leon was the perfect person to blame. Of course everyone would believe it was him. He was a Casanova womanizer, who didn't give a damn about the world. Margaret couldn't have chosen a better person for her lie.

"Hey if it's not too much trouble, can you ladies do me a favor and take my dresses up to my room for me, I'll meet you both a little later." Rose said handing Ellen her things.

"Sure thing."

She waited until Ellen and Isabel had walked further away then turned and ran towards the direction Margaret had gone. She could see her up ahead covered in a black cloak, hand in hand with a man. She wanted so desperately to see his face. Dodging the villagers, Rose caught up to them and quickly backed into a stone wall and out sight. She peeked at them as they walked towards a fruit stand. Margaret picked up an apple and smiled, whispering something to her lover. His face was down making it difficult to see. But whoever he was, she knew he was tall and dark haired. The villagers were looking at Rose as if she were crazy. She blushed and crept forward as Margaret continued to move.

It had gotten darker out and Rose was exhausted. She had seen them walk in and out of shops for almost two hours. It was getting harder to see them through the darkness that was beginning to fall on earth. For a second Rose decided to rest. She sat on a stool and sighed, wondering where the hell she was.

After a couple of minutes of thinking, she realized that she had not seen Margaret leave the shop.

"Oh crap!"

Rose ran forward and into the small store, it was barely ten feet wide. The shop keeper's eyes fell on her in surprise as she scanned the room quickly. They were gone.

"How could I be so stupid...?" Rose whispered.

She was angry at herself for losing them so quickly but the aching of her feet and legs distracted her anger. Sudden thirst quenched at her throat madly, she could barely speak. She would do anything for a glass of ice cold wine. Rose could see the castle up ahead, it was just a short distance away. But a crowded bar caught her attention and she immediately craved any cold drink. She walked briskly passed the eerie looking men huddled in groups and alley ways. They looked up at her as she walked by, eyeing her up and down.

Rose wasn't the only one who feared the nightlife. She didn't realize until now how quickly the streets had emptied when moments before they were filled with woman and children.

When she reached the bright lighted pub bar it was as if she escaped the entity chasing her, waiting to prey on her when she wasn't looking. But as she walked in, immediately dozens of heads turned. Rose held her breath, feeling like she walked straight into a wolves cave.

"Hey there beautiful!"

Someone whistled but she didn't dare turn to see who. The room was filled with men and the only women were those serving the drinks, half naked, some even topless.

"Oh god, what did I get myself into." She whispered.

The room's bitter scent was nauseating and Rose looked for a nearby exit to take, while analyzing how quickly she could get to the castle running at lightning speed. Maybe if she screamed while running it could scare off any potential predators. The thought was useless, figuring she'd probably trip in the process. She reached the counter where a short bald man eyed her questionably.

"Are ye here for a job lassie?" Rose glanced at the waitress then back at him.

"Hell no I'm not, I just want a cup of wine."

The man laughed. "You're the first Lass I've seen walk in here alone asking for a wine. Ye have some serious guts to dare drink in a room with drunken men, have ye no shame lass? Please scurry home now before ye get in some serious trouble." Rose knew the man was right. She was completely insane right now, then again she hasn't been sane since she got here. "I-I'll be on my way then."

She turned around towards the crowded room feeling disgusting. Off in the corner there were couples making love, in front of everyone. Right beside them a man was groping a young girl, who looked to be as young as his daughter would be, if he even had one. She scanned the room as her heart thrashed loudly in her head, drowning out the chattering and laughter of men, clinking there mugs together and shouting. On the far left a table turned and a fight broke out. The room cheered them on and Rose shrieked backwards as they headed her way. She found herself in the middle of the room walking quickly towards the exit. Anywhere else was safer than here, she thought.

"My Lord your cup of Ale."

Rose didn't know what compelled her to turn her head, and if she was surprised to see Leon. Six empty mugs already lined up in front of him, yet he reached for another.

The women took advantage of him. They wrapped their arms around his neck and sat on his lap, caressing his chest seductively. Rose was suddenly angry. Couldn't Leon act human for one damn day without having a whore wrapped around his *junk*? When Rose looked back up from the ground he was standing in front of her.

"You!" Leon cried.

Her eyes went wild.

"The one with the sharp tongue, I've been looking for you, my lady." He said stumbling forward. He caught her shoulder and found his balance. "Why...have you been looking for me?" Rose forgot how angry she was at that moment. She never thought Leon would want to talk to her, let alone look for her. He leaned his chin downwards at her and she looked into his glossy eyes.

"That sharp tongue of yours, I want to taste it."

Her eyes widened and before she could speak his mouth and hands were on her. His tongue was gliding over hers and she found the more she tried to scream the deeper and more vicious the kiss became. His hand found her backside and he cupped it, bringing it against his body and Rose could *feel* how much he wanted her. Gathering strength Rose shoved him back and slapped him. The slap was loud enough to capture everyone's attention. There was silence in the room and for a long second Rose just glared at him. She was shaking now and cursing at herself for having enjoyed it even for a second.

"I'm not one of your whore's Leon, you have no right to touch me! I'll cut your hands off the next time you try some shit like that again. You should know me, you should know I'm not that type of woman!"

Rose turned to run out of the room when suddenly he grabbed her hand and whisked her towards the exit, all the while she screamed for him to let go but his grip was hard. Finally they turned a corner and he swung her against the wall. His hands shot out beside her face, blocking her only means of escape.

"I don't want to hurt you Rose."

"If you don't want to hurt me then let me go, let me live in peace already." The words hurt to say.

"Why, why am I having dreams of you? Why do you appear in my head every single night? Why have I kissed you a thousand times and held you in my arms, how can I know the feeling of it so well if I've never even held your hand before."

Rose could hear the anguish in his voice and suddenly there was a new side of him she had never seen. He was hurting, confused, intoxicated and probably using alcohol as a way to drown out his sorrows. For the first time, Rose saw a glimpse of the sad man in front of her.

"Now please, dear, tell me who you are." He swiped his finger under her chin and sent a wave of goose bumps down her skin.

"You know me, from the future..." She replies hesitantly, not knowing what else she could possibly say. He laughs and Rose begins to lose her patience. "Enlighten me lass, what are we in the future?" His grin was sly but seductive, she held a stern gaze.

"Well I'm a twenty four year old woman, with a degree in Science, majoring in Business, and you're a ghost. Living in my house, begging me to help you." He laughs again this time holding his stomach in agony. Rose squints from the stench of alcohol protruding from his mouth.

"Am I really?"

Leon holds back another laugh, noticing there was no humor behind her serious eyes. Her lips were straight and she was frowning, rolling her eyes with impatience. " — and why would I need a woman's help?"

He arched his brow and tried to keep a straight face but the alcohol was rising and he couldn't help but smile. "Because you were an idiot, who was framed and murdered by the King so you came to me and asked me to help you by coming back to your fucked up time period. Not only did I manage to come back, but you don't remember anything! Not even about us! God Leon..."

His eyes sprung up from her chest, the humor in his voice disappeared completely.

"Murdered?"

She kept her lips firm, angry at him for all the things he had said and done to her. But worrying that this may not have been the best way to tell him, no matter how angry she was.

"Are you out of your mind?" His jaw dropped and he took a step back. "Yes! Completely out of my mind for ever agreeing to help you...and falling for you. God, you played me good. You tell me you love me and make love to me the night before you leave, then when I come back to you..." Rose had said too much. She was breathing heavily now.

"You should have just taken all of our memories with you, that way I could have forgotten all about you." She said almost a whisper. Leon looked down at her, half gaping and half crazy. He didn't understand why those words hurt him. He didn't want to believe her, but last night's dream was the answer.

He had dreamt of their love making and of many more memories. He looked her in the eyes, trying to find the answer, wanting to see the lie in them, but they were weak, barely looking into his. Leon didn't know what to say.

"I apologize for causing you pain...If I knew then what I know now I would have never approached you Rose."

His words warmed her core and at the same time hurt. Even if things turned out this way, those memories were precious to Rose, she couldn't deny that.

Fourteen

The moonlight cast shadows against the stone houses, creating a walkway of light towards the castle. Rose held Leon's arm, as he insisted. She had rejected, too proud to lean on him but deep down fireworks were exploding and gravity was lifting. It didn't matter if there were creepers staring at them through the darkness, or if bats passed by their heads quickly, Rose felt safe and in that moment she let the feelings she suppressed for so long unleash.

"So, tell me again how I am killed?"

The sound of his voice surprised her. She had been so lost in her thoughts that she didn't realize they were already climbing the steps to the castle entrance.

She looked up at his stone like face. The intensity in his eyes was fierce and she knew if she didn't confess, Leon was not going to keep still. Rose sighed and stopped walking, leaving them in the middle of the steps.

"It's like this Leon…you get framed…I'm afraid to tell you more because I'm afraid of how much the future could change. I can't just tell you everything and have it alter my existence as well."

"You not telling me *will* alter everything. For heaven's sake, I will go into this castle and threaten anyone from framing me!" Leon shouted. He marched his way up and Rose panicked.

"Wait!"

She slipped forward and gasped. Rose was tired of falling, tired of everything. She knew there was no way her and Leon could be together anyways. Once she helped him out she had to go back home, where she belonged.

"Are you alright?"

Leon's heart had stopped and a jolt of guilt ran through his blood. He kneeled down before her and reached for her hand. The look in her eyes when she looked up was enough to stop the mightiest warrior from murder.

Rose doesn't take his hand.

"The princess...she's the one who does it."

"What...?"

"There's nothing you can do Leon, and there's no way for me to prove it for you like you asked. The magazine didn't come back in time with me." Leon was as confused as she pictured him to be. Rose struggled with her words.

"You're accused of raping the princess...and in your home you are murdered. But the thing is...I don't remember what year, or date, or even time it happens. I just have to find out who the princess' lover is, the man she saved in your place, and then I'll be able to help you."

A look of disgust fell upon his face. He sat down on the top step and held his head in disdain. "I would *never* rape Princess Margaret."

Rose watched in pain as he curled his fingers through his hair and shut his eyes. He wanted to believe he was in another dream, moments away from waking up and away from this woman and her crazy stories.

"Are you sure you're not a witch..." He whispered.

Rose sat up quickly, any bit of remorse for him vanishing. "Seriously? Do I look like a witch? I'm trying to save your life and you accuse me of such ridiculousness!"

She ignored his pleas and headed inside. Running through the dark corridors, flight of stairs and finally into her room out of breath. She had never made it up there so fast with her heart pounding furiously. Why was being next to him so hard?

Leon contemplated knocking on her door. He kicked his foot back against the wall and crossed his arms, thinking of all the reasons why he should and why he shouldn't. She had obviously been hurt by something he said and all he wanted was to apologize, to explain how hard it was to believe her and admit how crazy he was to.

He found it hard to watch her go, something deep in his chest pained to see her run from him, to see the hurt in her eyes when they watered. Knowing all too well he was to blame, but not knowing why. What had their lives been like, and why couldn't he remember? He wanted nothing more than to. Tussling his hair back in an exasperated sigh, he turned towards the door knob and twisted it open.

Rose screamed. She had just pulled down her dress and was settling into her night gown the moment the door had swung open. The candle light was not bright enough to see the intruders face.

Leon ran forward and clasped her mouth shut. "Be quiet, it's just me!" He hissed. The last thing he wanted was for her to wake the whole castle up. He shut the door with his foot and suddenly there was silence.

Rose breathed heavily, stopping her nightgown from falling down her shoulders.

"What in the world Leon!" She cried stepping back until the back of her knees reached the mattress. Memories of before flashed into her mind like a déjà vu.

"I'm sorry I intruded but I just..." Leon's voice trailed off, suddenly realizing he had barged in. Rose was in her under garments, and her hair hung low against her body. *"Damn. Look away Leon."* She would be condemned if anyone found out. He was not allowed to see her this way. It was disrespectful, unworthy of him, but his eyes could not pry away from such a beautiful sight. He took a moment to admire her beauty. Her red colored cheeks against such pale skin, her eyes were wide, embarrassed and flustered. Roses' white almost see-through night gown sent a shiver down to his groin, he could not pretend he didn't notice her breast peeking through the silk fabric and the way her curls hung right beside them. Leon felt hot in his over coat and long chiffon shirt. All he wanted was to take it off. But the longing to feel her body ached more, way down to his core.

Rose crossed her arms knowing all too well what he had been staring at. She was embarrassed, but still couldn't help wondering why she should be if he had once explored her body.

"What do you want?"

Her lips shook, not because of the cold draft coming through the window, but of the lingering thoughts in her head. Leon cleared his throat, fighting back the vision of what he would do with her.

"I just wanted to apologize...and let you know that I will trust your words."

Rose could feel her body relax.

"Oh...I understand. I won't let you down." She bit her lip. His gaze suddenly fell on her face. "Will you be willing to help me then? As I have asked you before...at a time I don't remember..." His dark grey eyes were warm and Rose could see the Leon she knew.

"Yes. I'll help you in any way I can."

The room temperature was rising. Rose didn't mean for her voice to sound so seductive and she could tell he noticed. "Why...do I have such a strong urge to hold you?" Leon said. Rose held her breath, replaying his words in her head a thousand times. What could she say? Was there anything to say that would be acceptable? Her lips were shut, knowing if she spoke she would only say something stupid and drive him away.

She didn't want that.

Rose wanted him nearer. The five foot distance between them seemed like miles and she only wished he was a bit closer. Answering her wishes Leon closed the gap between them and wrapped his arms around her, not knowing what compelled him to do so. He heard her gasp beneath him and the hunger for her increased.

Her soft arms surrounded his body, returning his embrace and grasping him tighter.

"Forgive me for what I am about to do...push me away if it is what you do not want." He grabbed her face in his hands and began kissing her, deeper and deeper until they were both lost in a sensation full of lust and wonder. His hand traced her delicate skin down her face until he reached her shoulders. Taking the silk sleeve he pushed it down slowly, cautiously, waiting for her to reject, but she did not do so. Her gown fell to her feet exposing her goddess like body. Her cheeks blushed as she stared up at him, wanting him to go on. Losing herself in his very existence.

He tossed his overcoat off, his shirt following right after. He stood bare chested. His muscular body protruding more vividly that she had ever seen. His chest was broad and moving up and down to the rhythm of his fast heartbeat. Rose wanted to claw her hands against it and feel the tiny hairs on his chest over her fingertips. Her mouth watered as she imagined the taste of his neck.

She had been so focused on his upper body that she had not realized that he no longer wore any pants. He was naked. Standing like a Greek god in front of her, with his manhood clearly showing how much he wanted her, *needed* her.

Rose lunged forward and wrapped her arms around his neck, surprising him yet again. Her body against his felt so warm. He cupped her backside as she trailed kisses down his neck and chest.

"I won't stop you." She stopped to say and smiled. Leon growled hungrily and grabbed her thighs, pulling her up against him. She groped him, breathing in his masculine scent until her back fell onto the bed. He crawled forward while she edged back, teasing him with a smile. They began kissing again while Rose caressed the back of his hair, which she longed to feel for the longest time. She moaned beneath his lips making Leon shiver with the anticipation of feeling her insides. He wanted to hear her cry his name. It was more of a *need* that a want.

He dared to touch her hair, feeling the softness of it once again in his palms, Leon gripped it and kissed her crimson cheeks.

Rose held her breath as he swirled his wet tongue around her nipples. She dug her nails into his back. A warning that signaled she could no longer resist him. She spread her legs around his waist and it was then that his eyes looked into hers for approval. She leaned forward and kissed him as an answer. Rose felt a sharp pain the moment he entered her, but as his thrust got deeper it quickly subsided and all she felt was pleasure. Her face was against his breathing heavily, moaning into his ear. She was beginning to perspire and the sensation was growing closer. She could feel her body contracting, and the waves of heat and pure pleasure radiate from the explosion going through her body.

Her mouth was gaping and Rose moaned out his name, digging her nails dangerously deep into his back. Just hearing her say his name was enough to shatter every part of him. He hovered on top panting, their bodies breathing in unison.

It took Leon a moment to realize what he had done and his eyes were wide. It startled Rose.

"What's wrong?"

His eyes raked down her naked body down to her thighs. The white sheets now stained with blood. Rose sat up to look down at herself and gasped.

"Impossible...this is impossible. We made love before, how can this be. I lost myself to you once..." Rose was confused. It wasn't possible. The night they shared was the day she had lost her virginity to him. How was it possible to lose it now? *Unless it never happened.* The words made her heart stop and for a moment she questioned her own memories.

His eyes were on her, stern and sorrowful.

"I have taken the one thing you needed to be wed. Now you can never be, my lady. What have I done...?"

Rose didn't knowing whether to feel more hurt because he suddenly regretted it, or because he didn't care about her marrying someone else.

"I don't plan on marrying anyone...else." She said, half a whisper. His eyes softened and he kissed her. "You do not know the danger you are in." Rose laughed. "What danger?"

"If one day you were to be forced to wed, and you're husband realized you are not pure as said to be, you will be beaten, or banished, making cotton for days on end."

Rose swallowed. "Are you serious?" Suddenly, it wasn't humorous anymore. He could only nod. "I vow to let no harm come to you Rose, you can trust *me* on this."

She couldn't help but gaze, star struck at her gallant hero. This man who had done a complete three sixty since the last insult. She couldn't be any happier. Life was perfect at that moment, she had even forgotten their ill fate for second.

"I must go now before I am caught in your chambers." He winked and it was so seductive that Rose didn't want him to go.

"Can't you stay?" She dared to say.

He stood, adamant about leaving in the first place. Wanting nothing more than to wake up with her in his arms, feeling her hair against his face and breathing in her lilac scent. But Leon knew he couldn't. It was bad enough he had taken an innocent woman's purity without being married to her, leaving her utterly *ruined*.

"I could only wish to the god's above that I could, my lady. But as fate permits us, I cannot stay and see you punished for our affair." It pained him to even imagine it for a second. He kissed her forehead, leaving her speechless once again.

His clothes were on and his back was towards her as he walked to the door. His mind was on Thomas and his warning. But Leon paid no mind to it, he had claimed Rose his today and he would not let Thomas have her. Leon turned, wanting one last glimpse of her before leaving, and hoped that he could see her in his dreams again tonight.

Fifteen

It was the morning before Leon was to go on an expedition with the King and Guards. He had already felt uneasy about it in the first place, but after last night with Rose his chest was aching. It pained him to leave her, yet again, knowing how much it affected her last time. But he couldn't go against the King and his orders. He had to let Rose know today.

"Where did you go last night lad, I waited for you at the bar. They said you went off with some lass, is that right?" Thomas pulled the chair back and sat down. Leon didn't know if he should feel satisfied, knowing he had made love to his best friends crush. But inside he did.

"Ah, yes, she was so beautiful. But thing is I hardly remember any of it." He laughed along with him, not knowing Rose was entangled in his embrace last night.

"Are you ready for tonight?" Leon asked, in fact not caring if he were or not. He just kept looking at the clock, wondering why it was taking so long for Rose to come in and serve tea. "Ready as can be. I've packed enough for our journey. If only you could pack a few women in your bag, huh Leon?" It had become a bit awkward since their fight by the lake and Thomas had barely spoken to Leon, Leon didn't give a damn about any other woman.

He smirked, punching him in the arm. Secretly wishing he had missed and hit his face. The table chattered loudly, laughter and voices filling his head, when all he wanted to remember was the sound of her voice against his ears. He was feeling hot, and a strong desire to feel her again began to throb in his veins.

The door opened and in came Rose. Their eyes met for a second, but she looked away quickly. She didn't know why she felt so embarrassed. Maybe it was the fact that huge boundaries were crossed between them. It wasn't safe for them to show their emotions in front of others, especially in front of Thomas, whose eyes glowered with just the sight of her. She made her way around the table slowly, lifting each cup and placing it in front of each person carefully. It was when she stood beside Leon that it felt like her knees would buckle and she would fall into his lap. She imagined it for a second, tossing aside the plate, undoing his trousers and riding him in the very chair he sat. She blushed and shook her head.

"Your tea…" She whispered as she brushed against his arm to set it down on the table. Leon looked beside him, her breast catching his attention as she leaned over. His mouth watered and he had to look away, as he remembered the feeling of them on his lips and hands.

"Thank you." He muttered. Looking up as a dozen pair of eyes stared back at them. They were directed towards her body and Leon found it hard to keep his mouth shut. He had claimed Rose as his, and no one else was going to take her from him.

It was Thomas that brought him back to reality.

"Thank you, my lady. You look extraordinary today I dare say."

Rose smiled.

"You flatter me too much."

"But not enough." Thomas winked.

A guilty feeling crept up her spine. She didn't mean to sound like she was flirting, or did she even sound like that at all? She wished more than ever that she could hear Leon's thoughts. Was he angry?

His back faced her so she couldn't see the anger in his face. He clenched his fist below his chin, making believe it was Thomas' neck wrapped around his fingers.

She bowed and headed out, not wanting to look back, for she didn't know whose eyes she would lock on, Thomas' or Leon. She was relieved when she was back in the kitchen with Agnes. "You look mighty flustered, are they giving you a hard time again?"

"N-no, I'm just a bit tired." She lied.

Agnes brought her around the counter to where she had laid out bowls of different condiments and fruits. Tonight I have been told to tend to the Queens bedrooms so I won't be here with you to prepare supper for the guards. A temporary cook will also be coming, I have prepared these for you to do later."

"Thank you Agnes, I'd really be lost without you."

Rose hugged her and she laughed,

"You are like a daughter to me Rose."

It was the least she could do for her. She said goodbye and walked upstairs to where Margaret was waiting for her. Rose had to suck in her pride with her. The moment she walked into her room Margaret had sat up with her arms crossed.

"You are *late*."

"I'm sorry, princess, I was busy feeding the guards." Rose said through clenched teeth.

"That is not an excuse. But whatever, get me my towel I shall have a bath now."

Rose watched as she walked passed her and out the door with her head held high. Upon hearing the door close Rose ran for the dresser. Quickly, she searched through the drawers looking for the diary that had held the confession of her betrayal. She sighed after closing the final drawer. She had found nothing. Hands on her waist she looked around the room wondering where a young girl could keep such a thing.

Rose had taken quite some time, she grabbed the towel and ran out to meet her in the bath before Margaret could become suspicious. She was naked when she walked in. Her small slender body slipped into the tub and she let out a long sigh of pleasure.

"Oh this is amazing."

Rose took her place on the stool beside her, hating every second that she was forced to wait on her like a slave. Rose went so far as to imagine her hands on her head, forcing it under water, but she knew they'd have her head. She couldn't act foolishly.

"My hair."

Her orders were sharp.

Angrily, Rose shampooed her hair and scalp.

"Gentle!" She cried.

"Sorry."

Rose smirked. She hated taking orders from someone who was young enough to be her sister. If only they had kept her with Ellen and Isabel, she would have been happier cleaning toilets.

This wasn't a privilege but a punishment.

The day seemed to drag after the bath. Rose had to stand by her side, and off in a corner while the royal family had their dinner. It was nearly seven by the end of her shift and her feet were aching, in need of a good massage. She vowed she'd rest after preparing dinner for the guards.

Rose made her way into the kitchen to see the table Agnes had neatly prepared for her now in a cluttered mess. A short stubby man was cooking over the stove, cursing under his breath. Rose squeezed her eyes, having had enough of a bad day already. Her only medicine would be seeing Leon again, wherever he was.

The man turned to her and his gaze quickly fell from her face to her chest. He forgot what he was doing for a moment.

"Hello miss, nice to meet you." The man was odd and Rose quickly felt uncomfortable, especially with the way he had looked at her. She managed to ignore his glancing eyes and rude stares and found her heart had gleamed when she was to finally bring in the plates of food.

Delighted to feed Leon she hurried inside. His eyes stopped on hers and he smiled. The pain in her body seemed to alleviate that instant and she fought hard not to smile back. The temp followed her in to help set the plates on the table, but Rose quickly made her way towards Leon. Not wanting him to take her place. As she bent down to set his plate he leaned into her ear.

"I need to talk to you later."

Thomas stopped talking as he noticed Leon whispering to her. He frowned as they spoke to each other. What could they even be talking about? It bothered him. He had warned Leon that Rose was his. Anger was beginning to rise, and if it weren't for Rose being so close he would have lost his composure.

"I hope you enjoy your dinner." Rose said as she placed it in front of Thomas. She always enjoyed the smile he gave her but was surprised when he didn't even look up.

A sudden worry erupted and she questioned if he somehow found out about last night or if Leon had told him. That would leave her in an awkward situation. She stood in the kitchen while they ate, waiting for them to finish so she could clean and get the heck out of there and away from the creepy cook, who would try to bring up conversation that lasted merely seconds. She didn't want a conversation with him at all.

Rose carried the dozen of empty plates and placed them in the sink. She rolled up her sleeves and began to wash them, noticing how it was already past seven and the night had just fallen. She was so lost in her thoughts that it took her a moment to realize a presence behind her. Before she could turn back and look, arms wrapped around her stomach. She knew it wasn't Leon. She was already used to Leon's presence as a ghost, and no way did it feel like this.

She screamed but the cook quickly covered her mouth. He groped her breast before sliding his hand down her belly. The cook cried out as Rose dug her teeth into his hand and sprung free, running around the table, knocking down plates and pans in the process.
"Come here!" He cried.

Rose screamed again as he pinned her against the wall with his chest. It was nauseating, the way his breathing quickened at the thought of raping her. His hand slid her dress up her thighs were it stopped for a second. "Stop! Get your hands off me!" She screamed as his hand slipped from her lips. The door sprung open so hard it caused the walls to shake. The man gasped and stood frozen. A tall figure crossed the room in three strides and griped the cook by the throat, Thomas tossed him across the room and into the stone wall with a single swing.

"Let me warn you I can do worse than that, if you have any appreciation for your life I say rid yourself from this castle or I shall rid you from existence." He hissed. The man scurried up and ran out of the room in an instant. Rose was so shaken up that tears spilled from her face. She put her hands up and wept hard, disgusted by the feeling of his hands that lingered on her. She didn't even notice Leon at the door, heart racing and anger rising.

Thomas leaned down and comforted her, holding her close, and Rose felt different in unfamiliar territory that was his scent and body, so different from Leon's. But in that moment it didn't matter as she wailed. She let herself be hugged by Thomas, having no idea that Leon stood watching them. He understood the situation, and knew Rose was frightened, but he was still angry that she was in another man's arms. Angry that Thomas was in his place, and angry at Rose for not pulling away. He walked away silently before they could notice he was watching.

"Thank you Thomas...If it weren't for you..." Rose shut her eyes, not wanting to say what was on her mind.

"I would never let that happen to you."

Thomas was stern and calmer than he thought he would be. He was trying to be, for her. He didn't want to *scar* her by letting her witness a murder. He took her hands in his, the warmth of her palms warmed his body.

"I just wanted to say goodbye before I left. I thank God I came in just the right time." He sighed.

"Leaving?" Rose asked.

"Yes, didn't you hear? We are to go on an expedition with the King. We shall be back in five days' time, I fear I won't be able to remember your face."

Any other woman would have felt flattered but all Rose felt was anger. Leon had not mentioned a thing. Yet, she should have expected it. He was now notorious for disappearing after a night of making love.

"Five day's will pass by quickly, will it be dangerous on this journey?" She asked, more worried for Leon than herself at the moment.

"A bit. We have enemies all around the border, even in England. We must be cautious of who we trust, but fear not my lady. When I arrive I shall have a surprise."

It took Rose a second to catch that, after day dreaming of all the horrible things that could happen to Leon while away.

"What surprise?" She forced a smile.

"I can't say yet." He winked.

"Awe you're no fun."

Rose wiped her wet face with a nearby towel.

"How embarrassing…" She whispered.

"Need not be, my lady. It is anything but embarrassing for you. Yet shameful for the fool. I'll have his head if you let me."

The cruel and unusual punishment of this era was something Rose found repulsive so she shook her head no. The man had not managed to achieve what he was going to do, so killing him was not exactly what he deserved, even though deep down she knew he did.

"Well I have to get going, I shall miss you Rose."

He gripped her shoulder gently, then turned and walked out of the room. Moments later Leon came flying in. His face was hard and eyes set with flames.

"I have ordered that man to be executed, are you alright Rose?"

Her jaw dropped.

"Executed?"

"Well of course!" He growled. Wishing he could have the chance to do it himself.

Rose was too afraid to disagree with him.

"What were you doing with Thomas?"

His hand flew across her face, pinning her to the wall again. His eyes were cold as he glared down at her.

"He saved me Leon!"

She couldn't believe how ridiculous he was being.

"Are you going to fuck him as a reward for saving you too?" Leon was spouting nonsense and he knew it. But the jealousy was strong and he had to claim back what was his.

The slap was unexpected.

He gasped, the anger fading away into realization.

Tears fell from her face again, her eyes narrowed at him in disbelief.

"All he did was hold me Leon, he held me as I cried because I was almost raped. I wished it were you who saved me but what could I do? I'm not a whore who sleeps around with everyone. But I guess I am to you, since I slept with you now huh?"

He didn't know what to say or how to apologize.

"I didn't mean it that way Rose…" He frowned, questioning his intelligence at that moment.

"You shouldn't look angry either, you didn't even tell me you were leaving on an expedition. Where you just going to leave without telling me?!"

Rose was wild, her heart was aching and she couldn't stop herself. "Were you going to leave without even saying goodbye?" The words hit him hard knowing how desperate he was to have a chance to see her again.

"I told you we had to talk Rose…I was going to talk about that."

Rose grew silent, giving her breathing a chance to become normal again. "Oh…" She felt like a fool.

He held her cheek with his hand and kissed her quickly, knowing too well the door was open and there was too much of a risk of being seen.

"I would never do that to you, why don't you trust me Rose?"

"The same reason why you don't trust me with Thomas." She shot back.

"Fair enough…" Leon whispered.

" — don't think for a second I won't miss you."

Her anger was subsiding faster than she thought it would and she found herself smiling.

"I'll miss you too…"

"Now hurry to your room, I'll watch you from a distance until you get there safely. I'll see you again in no time."

Rose left the room, turning back at the door to smile at him. They both knew the feeling of attraction between them was getting stronger and Leon could only wish he had kissed her one more time before she left.

Sixteen

"**W**hat has occupied your mind so, that you have held the worry of a thousand years?" Isabel sat down beside Rose and put her hand on her shoulder. She couldn't stop thinking about Leon and how he was doing. Was he hurt? Or even alive? The thought of never seeing him again hurt her. He was the sole purpose of her existence in this world, without him she could not live.

"I miss someone..." Rose replied and Isabel instantly smiled.

"Oh I see, please tell me who." Her eyes were eager, like those of a child, wild and anxious. Isabel was trust worthy, she knew that much. There was no harm in liking someone in this era, at least so she hoped.

"Lord Leon...It's been nearly 4 days and I feel like my soul has vanished." It was exactly how the hollow hole in her chest felt. Even the rooms where they sat in seemed quieter than normal. Rose felt so lonely. The pen that Isabel held dropped and she gleamed.

"Rose dear you are in love! Not to worry though, tomorrow at the masquerade ball you shall see your prince again." She stood up and danced in circles and Rose couldn't help but laugh as her friend showed her the popular dances of this time. She felt a bit better.

Seeing him again was all she looked forward to, watching him walk through the open doors and feeling her heart race again. She was tired of following Margaret around and looking for clues she couldn't find. Rose had spent last night creeping around the halls, waiting to see if anyone would enter her room, but there was no one. Around midnight, she had decided the wait was too long and her small legs were getting tired so she retreated, promising tonight she'd be on watch again.

"It's so great that we are allowed to attend the ball as well. It's going to be so swell!" Rose nodded in agreement, not really knowing what she just said. She was too preoccupied in her own world to care.

The clock stroke five and Rose knew she should get back to Margaret before she lashed out on her. Margaret was watching the clock, annoyed at how late Rose always seemed to be and contemplated whether she should replace her with another maid. Being next to Rose was unbearable, knowing that she was a witness to their love making one night in the parlor. It was heaven sent that she had no recollection of the time, having been so paranoid she could barely eat in front of her parents, wondering if she had shared the news with them.

Although her conscious was free, she had felt a bit of remorse when Arthur tossed down the vase towards her, he did not know she had been secretly watching him that day. Margaret nearly lost her mind when she realized her mother was right beside her. Arthur had almost killed her, the Queen! If things had not gone the way they did Arthur would have been hung and she would have lost everyone she loved. Margaret had replayed that night countless times in her mind, anger rising each time.

As Rose walked in, head down to the ground Margaret felt a bit of guilt. She shouldn't be as harsh, at least as a favor for saving her mother.

"Hello there, you are right on time today." Margaret said with a smile.

Rose arched her brow, startled at the sudden friendliness in her voice. Her room was lit up with sunshine, and it was then that for the first time her personality seemed to shine as well.

"I will not disappoint you from now on." She muttered. Margaret smirked. Replaying the countless times that she had. But one couldn't blame a woman who had to relearn everything from scratch.

"Come fix my hair, I have a dinner to go to in a while. Also choose a dress for tomorrow, one for you as well." Roses' eyes widened.

"For me?"

Margaret nodded. Seeing this as a proper way to repay her, and hoping that this guilt in her chest would finally let her be. Rose crossed the room to where she sat and picked up her golden curls. Pulling it up and swirling it around, she pinned it against her head. Rose was utterly confused, why in the world would she give her a dress, and why was she being so nice? It was suspicious.

All Margaret could think about was seeing Arthur tonight. Her stomach was fluttering with butterflies thinking of how he ravished her on their last encounter. She could not wait to feel his lips on hers again, and if Rose wasn't in the room, she would be twirling in circles and singing merrily.

"All done, your highness."

Rose crossed the room to her dresser. She pulled the wooden handles open to where an array of different colored dresses hung perfectly together. There were more than a dozen dresses. Rose couldn't help but gape, how was she to choose a dress for such an important ball? She stared back at Margaret who was smiling at her startled expression.

She roomed her hands down the silk fabrics until she came across a golden white dress. She held it high, the dress coming down to her knees, it was rich and elegant, what she imagined a princess would wear. "I think this dress would complement you perfectly." Rose said turning to her, she was relieved when she smiled.

"You think? Well I do love the color. Good choice Rose." As much as Rose thought she couldn't stand Margaret, inside she felt they shared a bit of similarity. They were both women who enjoyed clothing and looking beautiful, even if they were ages apart and from different social classes.

"Now you choose. I shall let you keep one, as well as do your makeup. My maid has to look pretty as well." Rose stiffens, hating the fact that she felt happy and a bit closer to the woman who gets Leon killed for her own selfish needs. A part of Rose told her she shouldn't blame her, she was young and in love. Rose had done a few naughty things for love as well. But never to *that* extent. Rose choose a red and golden corset dress. She turned towards her.

"Is this one okay?"

"Oh yes, I haven't worn that one in ages." Margaret said. "Be here tomorrow, I shall lend you my supplies." Rose nodded. "Thank you." With a smile Margaret turned and skipped towards the door. "I will expect you here in the morning." She said as she opened it and quickly slipped by it. Rose stood there staring blanking around the room. Had that really happened? She hangs back the dress and closes the drawers, shutting the door shut behind her.

It was night fall when Rose ran with Ellen down the corridor, they stopped under the alcove and peered into the main entrance as a couple of guards came walking in.

"Why are they here, weren't they supposed to arrive tomorrow?" Rose asked as she scanned each man's face desperately searching for Leon's. But to no avail he did not stand amongst them.

"Didn't you know? Some guards are sent ahead first to check the path from any possible traps against the King and his Army." Her heart dropped thinking back on the trap she had read in the book, she had no clue when it would happen nor did she remember telling Leon.

"Are you looking for someone in particular?' Ellen grinned. "I know who it is." She winked and nudged her arm. Rose blushed, elbowing her and tell her to lower her voice, she didn't want anyone to know. "Yeah, well don't let anyone else know I beg of you." Rose wrapped her arm around hers and they began to stroll back to the kitchen when suddenly someone caught her eye. Someone who was staring intently at her.

The man looked familiar, but she did not know from where. As their eyes met he looked away but Rose kept her gaze questionably. His long straight black hair parted in the middle and she couldn't help but feel how horrifyingly unattractive it was, somewhere deep inside she *had* that thought before, but when? Rose was sure she had never seen that man in her life, but the way he looked at her made her feel they had met once. Rose shook her head. It could be a simple coincidence. A thirsty man staring at two beautiful woman, standing in the dark and watching him, how inviting did that look? Rose turned on her heel quickly with Ellen. "Whoa!" she cried.

"That man gives me the chills." Rose muttered. She needed to get rid of the eerie feeling that lingered in her chest. As they entered the kitchen they found Agnes and Isabel on the table chatting. They invited them in and offered tea, which Rose couldn't refuse. They ate and drank their meals, while chatting about the castle rumors and the handsome men. Rose mentioned Margaret and how she had become so friendly overnight, which they'll all agreed was fishy. It was nearly midnight, and the ladies were having so much fun conversing they didn't notice the time until the old grandfather clock besides them rang. They sat up and laughed, stunned at their lack of sleep and said their goodbyes. Rose was the last to leave, purposely waiting until she could no longer hear their footsteps to start her investigation. The castle was quiet after hours. Sometimes you could hear the wooden floors creaking, other times Rose would hear doors open and close. She would jump and hide in a dark corner until she was certain it was nothing. Rose made her way to the second floor, where Margaret's bedroom was as well as her own. She roamed the corridors, quickly creeping through the corners, past the offices and lounge rooms were the men would hang out after their duties. After half an hour of roaming mindlessly in the dimmed lit halls Rose was beginning to lose hope, when suddenly she heard a giggle coming from the library room right in front on her. She crouched down on her knees and inched forward towards the open door way. The candles in the room were not enough and Rose found it hard to find where Margaret was. She spotted movement by the window and instantly was frozen.

"Stop it Arthur, or someone will hear me." Margaret whispered, she took his hands and slid them down her waist.

"My lady, but it is you who laughs at the mere touch of my lips on your neck." Arthur says with a smile, he runs his finger down her face, it reaches and stops at her lips. He tips her head back and gives her a deep kiss. Rose holds her mouth shut, wishing it was daylight for she could barely make out the man. "Come." He motions her to follow him and Rose gasp as he steps in front of the candle light. It was the man she had just seen, the one who had left her with goose bumps on her skin. Rose found it hard to watch after

150

they began to make out in the oversized lounge chair. Still bent to the ground, Rose squeezed her hands together. What was she to do? Just barge in there and point fingers, threatening the *princess* and her lover? She was sure Margaret would find a way to get her hung before she could tell the Queen and King.

The darkness was consuming her and she could no longer stand a second more in it. Rose stood up and silently walked away, satisfied to know she had finally figured out who the mysterious lover was, a guard, maybe even one of Leon's friends. She couldn't wait to let him know, she had to before it was too late.

Seventeen

Rose struggled to line her eyes with the charcoal stick she was given, her hands trembled a bit. She didn't remember the last time she wore makeup. A tint made out of raspberries was used as lipstick and tiny bowls of colorful flours were laid out across the vanity. She could only think how easy modern day makeup was to get. All you did was go to the local drug store and pick it up, but in this era you had to make your own. She patted blush on her cheeks, which gave her a rosy color that she didn't in fact need, she had it naturally. Her jaw dropped in awe as she saw herself in the reflection of the mirror, she looked so elegant and out of place. Today she was no maid, but Rose. She could be herself for once.

The castle walls echoed with the sound of music coming from the ball room. Reminding her that she should hurry before she missed the grand entrance. Rose slipped on her masquerade mask, becoming totally unrecognizable. She wished she could let her hair down for once, Rose always felt a women's outfit wasn't complete without her hair, the most important accessory. She could imagine the ridicule she'd get if she walked in there with her hair loose, she would be beaten and just the thought of it made her shutter.

Her journey to the ball was quick, and she recognized Ellen and Isabel by the wine table whispering to each other. Would they recognize her? As Rose approached them they grew silent.

"You're Majesty?"

They bowed their heads and Rose sputtered into a laughing fit. "Oh my goodness, is that you Rose?" Isabel cried, bringing her hands up to feel her silk sleeve. Ellen shook Rose, playfully hitting her for giving them such a fright.

"My god, Rose, you look beautiful. You're beauty surpasses the princess!" Rose laughed. "Ladies, I don't think that's true." Rose would never admit it, but she knew she was more attractive than that freckled face Margaret.

"Let's dance!" Isabel took their hands and led them into the center of the room where others were circling in pairs. Rose took in the moment to remember the times she had watched princess movies and how similar the moment was.

"I don't know how to dance." Ellen whispered, laughing hysterically at Rose's awkward footsteps. Rose had no idea what she was doing, her modern time dancing consisted of grinding against each other, sex with clothes on. She would be banished from the face of the earth if such an indecent act like that was done.

"Relax and just follow them, it's very simple."

For a long moment, Rose felt bliss. Her heart was carefree, twirling and taking in the sound of laughter and music around her, engulfing in the serene environment, knowing how precious moments like these were. She was passed along from friend to friend, and they circled each other. Their dresses spinning above the gleaming floors.

Suddenly the music stopped, leaving the girls out of breath as they halted and turned towards the castle doors, they began to open. Her heart was in her throat, Rose could almost cry.

"Please make way for King Henry."

Ladies ran to form a straight line on the left, while the men stood opposite on the right, leaving a huge gap for the King and his men to walk through. Rose's fingers were shaking and she had to hold them down before anyone could notice. They bowed as King Henry walked by, a melancholy smile plastered on his face. He headed towards his throne, besides the Queen and Margaret's. They stood, smiling at him. The Queen's eyes shone, her love for him clearly apparent. They kissed and finally the King sat down. The guards began to walk by and Rose was disappointed when Leon didn't recognize her. She put her hand to her chest, telling herself it was because of the mask. Thomas marched besides him and she suddenly remembered that she wanted to speak to him. As awkward as it was between them, she needed his help to testify against Leon.

She was surprised when they stopped in the middle of the room and turned towards them. Rose froze as the dozens of men looked hungrily at the females. "W-what's going on?" Rose whispers to Ellen.

"The dance begins silly."

Rose had no idea this was part of the greeting and she suddenly hated the woman standing in front of Leon. The music began to play and her hand was taken. She didn't recognize who the man was but he smiled at her, noticing her beauty the moment he stepped into the room. His hand was cold and unfamiliar. Rose didn't like it, but she took it anyways and let herself be spun in circles. They nearly bumped into a pair and she laughed as the man pulled her forward before they crashed into each other. Before she knew it he let go, and suddenly she was in the arms of someone else. The interval lasted thirty seconds, until again she was passed around. Unknowingly, Rose was searching for Leon through the crowd, wanting so badly to fall into him, but instead she was pulled into Thomas' arms. It took him a second to realize who she was. It was when he looked into her wide green eyes that his heart skipped a beat, he recognized those eyes, he'd dreamt of them before. For a moment Rose wondered if she should pretend to be someone else, but when Thomas smiled she knew he had found out.

"Why Rose, I almost didn't recognize you."

His grin was wide and his eyes sparkled. The beauty in his arms was unbearable. Thomas wanted to hold her close, tell her stories of their adventure and tell her how much he's missed her. An ache rose up his chest, remembering that their feelings weren't mutual.

"The makeup is good isn't it?" Rose laughed.

"It suits you well."

Thirty seconds passed and she was still in his arms, his grasp was tight, he didn't want to let her go. Rose sensed this and became frightened. She was no longer happy in her serene moment. Her body was stiff now, and his hands were like acid. It burned and she wanted nothing more than to be released from his hands Nervously, she looked into his eyes, his golden curls hung loosely around his head and she hated how much he resembled Andrew in that moment.

"It's been so long since I last saw you, have you been well?"

"Yes…no one has tried to bully me as of late."

Rose forced a laughed, dodging pairs as they swung by the ballroom. Rose could hear Ellen laughing from a distance and she smiled, wondering whose foot she had stepped on now.

"There's something I must tell you, but not now. I don't want to let you go, but I have to." Thomas admitted. Rose swallowed hard and forced a smile, about to say something ridiculous when she was interrupted.

"Great, thanks." Leon said as he snatched her hand from his. Rose gasped as she tripped forward into his chest. Her hands were on him and she was panting, the beat of her heart rising from the heat of his body. She questioned him with her eyes, wondering why he had pulled her from Thomas so harshly. But the thoughts vanished as he smiled and his eyes lit up. His fingers slipped around hers and they spun in circles and suddenly Rose was where she belonged.

"We meet again, my lady." Leon whispered.

"I've been waiting so long to see you, are you okay? You weren't hurt were you?" Rose wanted to ask a million questions but knew now wasn't the time. "Yes I am alright and no, there's not a soul in this world that could hurt me, besides *one* person. Did you miss me?" he asked and Rose smiled. "Of course…every minute of every day. I can finally breathe now."

Leon felt something powerful in his chest when she said those words. He wanted to hold her tight and kiss her. So many thoughts and emotions barraged his mind. He had been worried sick thinking of her, vowing he'd murder anyone who'd try to touch or hurt her. His heart was relieved to finally see her again.

"My Angel, you are like the sun on a cloudy day. I feel as if all my aches and pains of fighting have suddenly vanished and it is as if I am standing in a peaceful meadow, soaking up the sun's rays." Leon caressed her blushing cheeks with his thumb and it sent a shiver down her spine. She wanted to nibble on the finger that sent a wave of emotions to her groin and it was then that she missed the feeling of his naked body against hers.

"I don't want you to let me go…but it'll be obvious if you don't." Rose said after a while of gazing into each other's eyes, both lost in the thoughts of what they would do to each other if they were alone. "You're right. I mustn't be so foolish. I'll meet you later by the balcony?"

Rose nodded before letting go and dancing her way into someone else. Two freezing cold hands grabbed hers and suddenly she was frozen. Her eyes widened and it was obvious how startled she was. Arthur laughed. "I'm sorry if I have frightened you?" The words were stuck in her throat and she felt like a fool. *"Get yourself together Rose!"* "I'm sorry, I thought I was about to trip and fall embarrassingly on my face. I thank you for saving me." She lied. He smiled, but his face seemed sinister. Arthur watched her face for any sign of acknowledgement, but Margaret had been right, she did not remember him or that night at all and he was prepared to *keep* it that way.

"I would not let someone so beautiful fall, I must assure you."

As disgusted as Rose was she smiled, counting down the seconds until they were to switch partners again.

It was an hour before Rose could no longer twirl without feeling nauseous, she staggered to the wine table and picked up another glass, her heart still hammering from Arthur's presence. She was taking advantage of drinking, knowing it was not every day that they were allowed to do this. She looked around the room as she sipped the bitter tasting wine, watching as Leon talked with his friends far off in the corner. They were laughing and having a good time. Arthur stood a few feet away with Thomas and a couple of other men. She looked away fast, up at the chandelier, before he could catch her staring. Suddenly Rose felt lonely. Isabel and Ellen were still dancing happily and she was just there, standing alone. The room faded and Rose could only hear her thoughts until suddenly one of the guards approached her.

"Have we met? If not do you care for a stroll?" A rather short man stood in front of her with his hand reaching for hers. "No, and no thank you, I'd rather stay here." She said quickly, rejecting him and taking a step back as he stepped forward.

"Why? You think you're too good for me?" His face got angry. Rose grew frightened, tightening her fingers around the cup she held, prepared to use it in self-defense. "N-no it's not that...it's..."

"Yes, she's too good for you Robert, let her be." Leon growled as he marched forward and stopped in front of Rose. For once she was relieved to see his back. He had seen him approach her from a distance and could no longer keep still. Robert was drunk and no way in hell would he let him touch his woman.

"Who are you to her? Mind your own business." Robert snapped, clearly too high off alcohol to realize how quickly Leon could rip the tongue out of his mouth and twist it around his throat with it. Leon laughed. That sarcastic laugh he always seemed to do when he was angered. His fist were shaking, and his ominous gaze warned Robert of what he was capable of.

"Robert, I'll have you know I can twist your head off in a second. So if you care for your life be gone now before I demonstrate on you." Robert sneered, finding humor in his empty threat.

"Fuck you, Leon."

Rose caught his arm quickly before he could punch him in the face. "Please don't Leon, ignore him he's drunk." Rose begged. Her eyes were large and filled with fear. Slowly he let his hand fall. For the first time in history, he had listened to a woman's words. Normally he would have done what he felt like, not once had he cared what anyone else said. Even he was beginning to surprise himself. He would do anything for Rose, listen to her every request and fulfill it with all his heart, this was not like him and he wasn't sure if he liked it.

He walked with her, preparing to head out the room where he could ravish her in secrecy when all of a sudden the King began to speak and the room silenced.

"My men have done a great duty of protecting this land and myself. Enjoy yourselves tonight. But quickly I will announce the engagements the Queen and I have approved, please listen up."

Rose and Leon stopped walking.

"I guess we should listen." He said but Rose didn't want to waste any second with Leon. She sighed, caring less about anyone's engagement. The couples separated on the dance floor and faced the King. Glasses of wine were brought down from their lips, it was rude to drink while someone of great power spoke. The rooms devoted attention was on him, expect Roses. She was too busy eyeing Leon from the corner of her eye.

"Nicholas, I hereby grant approval of your engagement with Lady Esmeralda De Cal."

A woman shrieked up ahead and Rose' heart sank. How horrific that must be, she thought as the lady began to sob into the arms of her friend. It was heart breaking to watch. "I hate this century." Rose hissed as the list continued. She was forced to watch the agony of some women, just a few without dignity smiled and bowed at Henry.

"I hereby grant Lord Thomas."

Rose and Leon's eyes widened in surprise of his name.

"—approval of his marriage with Lady Rose Emilia Beaumont."

Eighteen

That moment seemed eternal. She shut her eyes to keep herself from fainting. The sound of her heart shattering was like the sound of a giant mirror breaking, the pieces hit the ground like hail and bounced back to hit her, digging into her deepest wounds. The room clapped but all Rose could hear was the sound of her beating heart. She held herself together as tears fell from her face.

"No, no..." She whispered.

"I don't approve..."Rose was shaking now and grabbing her shoulders as the goose bumps ran up her arms. She was hysterical now and Leon was still. His body rigid like a solid block of ice. His eyes were wild and bewildered, his lips parted and he found he no longer had a voice. A charge of lightning was running through his body and it took all the force in the world from finding Thomas and breaking his neck in half. How could he betray him like that? Grinding his teeth together he fought the urge to strangle his best friend. His eyes caught Rose as she lunged forward, prepare to refuse Thomas' request, he caught her arm in that moment and pulled her back. Her face was distraught and tears were falling from her anguished eyes. His heart hurt to see her like that.

"Don't you dare Rose you'll be killed!" Leon cried. He was shaking and Rose could feel it on her shoulder. "Leon I can't marry him, I don't want to. I'd rather die than be with someone I don't love!" Rose was panting now, her chest heaving dangerously. Leon's face was but a blur and she needed to hang on to him.

"Please, calm down, you're going to bring attention to yourself." Leon was fighting hard to keep his composure but he was ready to explode.

"No, no, no." Rose sobbed into her hands and turned her back towards the crowd. The happiness in her chest had vanished and in that moment she wanted to disappear into the floorboard. "I'll make him pay for this. Don't worry Rose." Leon knew he was making empty promises, he didn't know if he could even trust his own words. Once something was approved by the King, it was dishonorable to refuse or take it back. There was nothing he could do. But one thing was for sure in his head, Rose was his and the thought of her with him was enough to *kill* him.

The words rang back in his head and as he watched his friend smile and be congratulated, he couldn't deny the urge surging through his veins.

"C'mon. Let's get out of here Rose."

He took her hand and they flew down the corridor, away from the party that had suddenly become so agonizing. Rose had never ran with eyes so blurry with tears. She didn't know where they were headed, and frankly she didn't care. Leon pulled her into the kitchen, shut the door, and then ran into the small dark pantry shutting that door behind them as well. They were panting, and Leon's body was against hers. His breath was on her face and she could feel his chest rise and fall. The adrenaline was rushing through his body, both from anger and his *want* for her. Viciously he picked her up and wrapped her legs around his waist. He kissed her with love, passion, anger, and hurt. Rose could feel his emotions against each harsh kiss. He pinned her against the shelves, so fast it caused things to fall on the ground but they didn't care. They were hot and sweaty now, breathing fiercely like they just ran a marathon. Their need for each other was beyond anyone's imagination. He was rough on her, grabbing her head and tilting it back, pushing her deeper against him. It hurt her, but Rose found the pain to be pleasurable. She'd rather feel anything than the pain her heart possessed. He kissed her neck down to the top of her breast, lapping his tongue around her perk nipples. She wrapped her arms around his neck and moaned against his ear. His hands were mad, roaming her legs, thighs, waist and bottom. Leon's anger was being unleashed in his every touch, and for a moment she was afraid.

"I *want* you Leon." Rose said breathlessly.

He moaned deeply against her face as he placed her on the ground and pulled down her underwear. She kicked it aside and grabbed him again, wrapping her fingers through his hair the way he liked, knowing that there will be a time when she would no longer be able to do this.

Leon was growling hungrily as he unfastened his belt. In a swift movement her legs were wrapped around his waist and he was inside her. Pounding her body against the wall as she matched his rhythm. Her body bounced on his and the feeling of it was erotic, turning him on even more. He moaned, thrusting deeper into her, and she cried out, clinging onto his shoulders and digging her nails onto his back. The pleasure of her neck being devoured was too much to bear. His warm tongue on her skin sent waves of ecstasy through her groin and she groaned, wanting him to move harder so she could lose herself completely in a world where only he existed.

Leon pulls her sleeves down and she helps him, freeing her breast from her dress. With one hand he grabs the soft mound and instantly craves to taste her silk skin in his mouth. He's beating her furiously and his breath is quickening, his muscles tightening as he holds her body steadily. Leon moans and before they know it they both shatter into an endless array of passion. Both lost in the waves of pleasure that run through every inch of their body. They hold onto each other tightly in that moment, afraid if they let go they'd be lost into an oblivion of darkness and loneliness.

"I'm sorry Rose. It should have been me. I should have asked for your hand in marriage…yet, once again I am too late." Leon pressed his back against the wall and raked his hair back in the way he always did when he was angry. Rose tried to console him, tell him it wasn't his fault, but it didn't change the torment in his heart.

"I will make Thomas cancel this engagement." Leon scorned. Rose didn't know what to say, but it was suddenly apparent how Leon felt about her. Did he love her? He must have. The hurt in his eyes was beyond anything Rose had ever seen. Their feelings were mutual and there was no need for them to admit it. They could *feel* it. Like an aura flowing from their bodies. Rose was meant for him. Leon was meant for her. But then the horrid realization came again, Rose was not from this time and she did not know how long she was going to stay here anyways.

Leon knew that too, but he was too in love to care and somewhere deep in his heart he didn't want to believe that someday, soon, Rose would be gone from his life entirely. He frowned, she could not be forced to wed at a time like this. Marrying Thomas would mean leaving the castle and going off to live with him. If that happened Rose would not be able to help him. Things were much more complicated, even worse than they already were.

Rose had to talk to Thomas. Now. Before she went any crazier. She stroked his cheek softly and his stone expression changed.

"Leon…"

He looked up, his dark eyes softening.

"I…"

Those three words were hard to say at a time like this. She didn't want to pull him in any deeper if it would hurt him in the end. The small room seemed much darker in that moment and. Arthurs face came back to mind.

"I found out who Margaret's lover is."

His eyes widened instantly. He had expected her to say something else. Leon couldn't help but feel a bit of disappointment.

"Tell me who it is." She sighed, nervously twirling her fingers around her hand reluctant to say much more.

"It's Arthur."

"What? Arthur?!" Leon averts his gaze and turns to storm out of the room and directly where Rose had imagined but she grabbed his arm quickly and stopped him.

"Why do you stop me Rose?" He frowned, his eyes so intense it sends a chill down her spine.

"Because you can't just run in there and kill him. The princess will have you killed for killing the man she loves. It doesn't matter how ignorant Margaret is, it's her word against yours and if you aren't believed, even I know, they'll kill you for lying. I don't want you to die Leon, please, just listen to me and wait. We can figure out a way to save you some other way." Her eyes are pleading, begging him to understand.

Leon calmed down as her reasoning began to make sense. His temper fluctuated, and thankfully she had stopped him from making a huge mistake. His jaw tightens, before meeting her gaze and softening again.

"You are a smart woman."

Rose stares into his eyes, knowing in his mind he was battling his own demons and the bittersweet ache of pain and pleasure seep into her heart.

"I try to be."

Taking her hand, he wraps it around his arm and pulls her forward. They exit the pantry that now held one more of their memories.

"We should get back, or they'll be suspicious." Leon said, his voice was shaking, the realization of what's to come hitting him again where it hurt the most.

"I have to talk to Thomas." Her words surprised him. "You couldn't possibly?" He shot her a look, his face hardening with the thought of the two of them together. "I'm going to tell him I won't marry him and please don't stop me." Rose said letting go of his hand as they neared the music filled room.

"Okay. I'll be over there watching you." Leon could only agree and watch her as she made her way into the open room. Rose searched for Thomas, but the amount of people made it difficult. Before she could set out in her search Isabel and Ellen shouted her name.

"Rose! Oh dear god, are you alright? Did you hear?" They grabbed her arm and dragged her to a corner where no one else could eavesdrop. "It's so awful, I am heartbroken for you." Ellen cried and hugged her, bringing back the sadness Rose had bottled back up in her chest.

"Yes, I heard. But I am not getting married to him." Their eyes were large, stunned by her brave remark. "Rose, you cannot go against the Kings wishes!"

"But it is not the Kings wish it is Thomas." Rose mutters angrily. It wasn't fair how women had no say in their own marriage or lives.

"We know you're in love with Leon, but Rose, Thomas is not bad. He is a gentleman who cares for you. Not to mention very good looking as well." Her eyes gaze between theirs, amazed at how they both agreed with her statement. Rose saw no gentleman in Thomas. He was sick, and when she got her hands on him there was no stopping what she would do.

"Please Isabel, don't say anymore." Rose said, her voice was wretched in sadness.

"I'm sorry...I'm just worried about you. We don't want anything to happen to you Rose."

She knew their feelings were genuine and she thanked and hugged them tight before turning on her heel to find Thomas, who she spotted at the wine table gulping down glass after glass. Rose approached him slowly, seeing in his burrowed brows and vexed face how angry he was. He didn't notice her presence right behind him.

"Thomas, we need to talk."

His eyes pierced hers and she found it hard to look away. The anger in his eyes intensified and he suddenly found the sight of her repulsive. Rose stood like a deer in head lights, wondering if the rage in his eyes was caused by her and Leon.

"There you are. Where did you run off to with Leon?"

"You were watching me?" Rose cried in disgust.

He didn't answer but instead took another glass of wine, the alcohol did well in drowning out the pain, and he realized that after the fifth glass his heart was beginning to go numb.

"I will not marry you Thomas."

Her voice was loud and clear, loud enough to capture a few people's attention. Thomas noticed the sudden attention and grabbed her arm. "Let's go." She staggered behind him as he pulled her forward and out of the room, taking a left they walked into the dark balcony. Her heart was beating fast now, and Rose didn't know if it was the chill of the night air that caused her skin to crawl, or if it was the way Thomas was staring at her.

"You will marry me Rose." His voice intensified. He leaned over the ledge to stare down at the lake below, he tried to calm himself but the alcohol was taking affect and the room was spinning.

"I will *not* Thomas what is wrong with you?!" She cried and ran to his side. "Please, you can't, I can't. Let's find people we love and marry them!" Rose was begging now and he could hear it in her voice. He turned to her, finding it hard to hold back the hurt.

"Rose, I love you. I can care for you, you can also love me in time." She shook her head.

"I-I don't want to! I can't Thomas for reason's I can't say right now but I just can't."

His chiseled face tightened and his lips straightened.

"Is it because of Leon? Do you love him?"

She froze, her mouth open with the answer on the tip of her tongue. "That doesn't matter." She said. Denying her love for him was hard, and even if she lied he would be able to see it in her eyes. Rose looked up at the moon, praying god would help her.

"I'm not a fool Rose, I've known you loved him since I first laid eyes on you. Leon and I have always been close, I know him more than anyone. He has been fascinated by women since he was a toddler, possibly. He is not a man to settle down with, and I know you don't deserve a man like that. I claimed you as mines before you even knew it, but in your eyes, he was all you could ever see..."

Rose was shaking now, she grabbed the stone ledge with all her might, holding herself from falling off into her unconsciousness. Her face was hot and flustered and she looked into his startled eyes with so much hate, that he could feel the sting of it down to his core. "If you knew this than why the *hell* would you tell the King you want to marry me?" She screamed the words through trembling lips, letting the confession be finally known, no longer able to hold back. Rose was crying, not knowing whether to be angry at herself or the man in front of her.

"Because I'll have you regardless Rose. I *will* win your heart." He was stern and his ignorance set her on edge. She squinted. "No...no you never will because I'm in love with Leon and I always will be! Even if you lock me up from the world I will never love anyone more him, understand?"

Thomas' eyes flashed and he moved towards her, pinning her back against the ledge. "Regardless, you will marry me Rose." He threatened her, his grip on her arm harder than expected. She stared into his menacing eyes in horror. His body loomed over hers and she felt small and weak, he could crush her if he wanted too.
"Get your hands off her!" Leon shouted.

He crossed the room and lunged Thomas back, he stumbled onto the ground and groaned with rage. Rose's confession still rung in his head and he wished he could hear her say those words again and again. Thomas stood back up, a sly grin of amusement on his lips. He spit and was prepared to tackle him when suddenly Rose stepped in between them, her arms spread wide to her side, foolishly protection Leon.

"Step out of the way Rose." Thomas growled. His voice was eminent with anger. Not once had he imagined things would be so difficult. He imagined Rose succumbing to his desire and Leon fading from her life. He wanted to do things the nice way, but after this, he wasn't confident he look at her the same way. Leon gently squeezed her hand and dragged her behind him.

"Why are you doing this Thomas?" Leon asked, wanting to know what foul substance had corrupted in his friends head. Thomas had never been so wicked, among their group of friends he was always the most honorable, respectful man.

"Because I feel like it Leon, you don't have to question me, no one questions you when you feel like *fucking* random whores in the night. You don't deserve Rose when you don't give a damn about anything. A person like you belongs in a dirty bar, not with someone so innocent."

Leon didn't even reply, instead he grunted and swung his fist into his jaw. He could no longer withstand the offensive insults coming from his mouth. Blood splat out instantly as Thomas was knocked down to the ground again. Rose was screaming for them to stop, holding back Leon, afraid he'd get in trouble if he continued. She knew he was capable of flipping Thomas off the balcony and into the river beds below. It would instantly solve everything but what good would it be for Leon? He would be gone as well.

"Please, shut up Rose." Thomas cried, growing tired of her useless cries. "Don't speak to her like that." Leon shot back, mentally planning how to make his death seem like an accident. Rose held his arms back but she was beginning to lose her grip. He was strong and she could no longer ignore the ache on her fingers.

"She is my fiancée I will do as I *please* with her." There was a hint of sexualness behind his words and that was enough to set Leon off. He lunged forward and crushed Thomas into the wall. He beat his face into the stone until Leon was pushed back. He fell back, but rolled away quickly before Thomas could jump on him. They fought for several seconds until Leon suddenly realized Rose screaming for him to stop, he pushed Thomas off and staggered to his feet. His vision blurred for a second and he ran to her, apologizing and wiping her tears away.

"You will be hung for adultery." Thomas said as he staggered up, he caught the railing for support and panted.

"I don't care." Leon said.

With that being said, Thomas wiped his bloody lip and disappeared into the darkness.

Nineteen

Rose could feel her swollen lids before even opening them. She had spent the whole night crying and drowning in her misery. The alcohol from last night was still in her system and she was starting to feel the side effects. The sunlight was making her headache stronger so she dug her face deeper into the plush pillow.

It was another Saturday and she thanked god it was because she was not in the mood to walk around with a fake smile plastered on her face. Last night had been tough, she had come to a conclusion, and it killed her inside, but she *had* to do it. It was the only way Thomas would help her. The King would be more willing to believe something coming from his fellow guard than an unknown maid.

But before going into town to clear her mind, she had to let Leon know of her plans. Dreadfully, she pulled the covers off her body and slipped down to the ground. Rose dressed quickly, in a white satin gown. She powdered her face and applied makeup before settling her hair back in the usual bun.

The door closed behind her loudly and she jumped, her nerves were getting the best of her and she had to calm down.

Rose made her way into the kitchen, where she managed to force a bit of bread and water down her throat. Her body was not allowing her to function the way it should. It was filled with too much anxiety.

It was when she saw Thomas enter the room that she crashed into a chair and dropped her plate. It shattered on the ground like her dignity, and she didn't dare move.

"Are you alright?" Thomas made his way around the table and took her elbow in his hand. Rose fought the urge to push him away and tell him not to touch her. But there was a reason why fate had led him into the same room she was in and she sighed.

"Thomas...I need to tell you something."

He sighed.

"Rose, first, I apologize for my actions last night...I was drunk. But I meant what I said, I will not back out of this marriage." Her eyes widened. "Even if my life was at stake?" His green eyes narrowed into hers.

"You would rather die, than be my wife?"

"No...but I can promise you that for the rest of your life *we* will be unhappy. Never will I smile with you, nor enjoy our *nights* in bed together, our children will mean nothing to me. You might as well sell me off. I will be as hollow as an empty porcelain doll, as you men call me. Not a day in your life will have peace." He grunted, clearly trying to hold back what was on his mind. Thomas didn't want that. He had always pictured himself having a happy family surrounded by smiling children. The rage in his heart quickened and he looked towards the ground.

"But...there's one condition. There's something that if you do for me...I promise I will marry you, and I will treat you well..."Her lips shook as she spoke and Rose trembled now beneath his startled gaze. She was selling herself off and it was not fair, she wanted to spend the remaining time in this era with Leon, not with *him*. The only satisfaction Rose got was knowing that she wouldn't be married to Thomas forever. One day she will suddenly disappear. It was bittersweet.

"What is it, I will do anything."

"First, I need you to trust and believe me, can you do that?" Rose looked around the room before continuing, noting the couple of people far off in the corner eating their breakfast. No one was paying attention to them, and she didn't even think they noticed they were in the room as well.

"Okay?"

She sat down, tired of looking up at him and feeling like her knees were about to break. He took the seat next to her and caressed her hand. She kept still, like a statue, the traces of his fingertips burning against her skin.

"Speak, what is it that bothers you?" Rose hesitated before looking back into his eyes.

"Leon's life is in danger and I need you to trust me that I am not crazy nor that I am witch." She thought back to Leon's accusation and rolled her eyes. Her lie was about to begin, she cleared her throat.

"As you know I was in a coma, for a while, after saving the Queens' life. After I awoke...I set out to town to try and remember my past but I just couldn't. While there I bumped into this old woman, the instant she touched my hand she shut her eyes and told me that someone near to me would be murdered. It was Leon. I was told about Princess Margaret and her affair with a fellow guard...In order to protect her lover, after suspicions begin to arise around her she accuses Leon of raping her. The King, of course believes her and has him executed."

Thomas was smirking while scratching the stubbles of hair on his chin, he stared back at his wide eyed fiancée and wondered how much she had drunk last night. "I'm not lying Thomas, I'm asking you to believe me!" There was seriousness behind her voice and Thomas was in fact beginning to believe her.

"So your telling me, Leon was, well is going to be accused of rape? When and where? Just tell me and I shall deal with it."

Rose sighed.

"That's the thing, I wasn't told when these things would happen. Now the deal is that I need you to testify with me. I need you to help prove Leon's innocence." He pursed his lips together and gripped his knuckles with his free hand.

"You love him that much, that you're willing to throw your happiness away just to save his life?" Thomas was astonished, he had never met anyone like Rose and it killed him to know her feelings. He only wished she felt that way about it.

"Yes." She replied boldly.

"Okay, we have a deal then..."

There was a moment of silence between them. They were both lost in their own anguished thoughts, hurting for different reasons. "I fear that the time is close though, your friend Arthur is Margaret's lover. I saw them in the library one night..."

Rose was hoping she had made the right choice in telling Thomas. A part of her was glad that he had agreed and believed her ridiculous story, yet the other part was crumbling into pieces thinking about Leon's reaction when he finds out about her plan.

"Arthur? Are you positive Rose?"

"Yes, absolutely. Even though Margaret is the one who blames Leon, it must be Arthur who chooses to use his name.

Thomas put his hands under his chin and frowned. "That would make sense. Of course he would choose Leon, he's a manwhore everybody knows that."

Rose shoots him a look of silence.

"Anyways, I just need to gather proof of their relationship before this happens. I need you to be there for me if he is accused before I find a way to prove his innocence. The King will believe you more than he would ever believe me."

"That is indeed correct...Leon and I have not always gotten along, but no one deserves to die like that. I will help you Rose, and I shall keep my word." She let out a huge breath and smiled, the tension in her voice had finally disappeared. The weight of the world seemed to be lifted off her shoulders, with Thomas' help she was confident Leon could be saved. That's all she cared about, and that's all that made her smile.

"I have to get going now, I have to visit my family and tell them about our engagement." Rose cringed as he took her hand. She looked down to it, knowing very well she should pull away, but Rose couldn't. The deal was set and that meant she had to keep her end of the bargain. "I'll be out doing some shopping in the village." Rose said hoping to change the subject. "How splendid, care if I join you later?"
She bit her lip and squinted.
"I kind off wanted to be alone, you know, to process all this."
He squeezed her hand reassuringly.
"I understand. I'll walk you out."
As they walked down the corridor Rose's heart felt heavy, she was miserable. Thomas was a nice guy, but he was not for her. They were not meant to be together.
"What is fate doing with my life? Is there anything that could possibly make this moment any worse?" Rose shut her eyes tightly and when she opened them again they were at the gate and Leon was standing right in front of them. His eyes were wild, fire blazing around the iris. His lips formed into a tight line and fist tightened, prepared to rip Thomas in half. In that moment, even Rose was terrified.

Thomas didn't let go, but instead stopped right in front of him. Roses' jaw dropped as she looked between their fierce gazes. Their eyes were fighting a war only they could see. Leon ordered him to let go of her hand but Thomas refused. Before Leon could cause a scene Rose interrupted.

"Stop it Leon, I'm the one who took his hand." The look of hurt on his face nearly blew Rose off her feet. Her eyes were watering and she had to look up at the sky for a second.

"Please, Leon, let us be." She couldn't hold it in anymore. The tears flew down her cheeks and she cursed herself for being so damn weak. Her lips trembled and she reached for her face to wipe the tears. Thomas let go and it surprised the both of them.

"I'll go first."

He understood what was going on between them, and swore it would be the last time he would let Rose and Leon be alone. Just this one time he would let her properly say goodbye.

Rose stood embarrassed in front of him, cheeks heating a hundred shades of red. "What's going on Rose, why are you with him?" His lips parted, and he blinked several times, hoping the image he saw before him was just a dream. He fought hard to control his tone but the anger in him was beginning to seize his emotions.

"Because I want to be..." Rose muttered, she avoided his gaze and looked towards the empty space besides him.

"You're lying." He sneered.

She squinted through the pain and tried not to look into his eyes, for she knew she'd crumble like sand and run into his arms.

"I decided to give in Leon, there's no way to stop him anyways. Besides, one day I will go back to my time, I just have to put up with this marriage until then."

"Rose, you couldn't possibly mean that. I know you, you're stronger than that. You wouldn't let a man dictate you like this!"

"It's the only way Leon..."

Rose began to run passed him when he suddenly took her hand. "Tell me the truth Rose, that's all I need and then I will let you go, if it is what you desire." She shook her head, she was breaking. Rose knew the moment he touched her she would fall apart.

"I-I told him I would marry him if he helped me prove your innocence. Thomas agreed, after threatening him and saying how our marriage will be unhappy and dreadful, how I will never smile, or talk to him or love him." The words came out less intelligent than she hoped but she was not in the right state of mind. Leon's mouth dropped. "Are you out of your mind Rose?!"

"Please, just understand that I don't want anything to happen to you. I don't care about my happiness as long as you're okay." She said through sobs. The hurt in his heart was like a hammer pounding on his chest. It was hard to look at her and he suddenly grew angry.

"Did you ever stop to think about my feelings?"

Leon stood still, his face was hard, his eyes cold.

"I did Leon...but you can live without me. I'd rather you *live*. I came here for that reason and I will keep my promise to you."

"Live? Rose have you forgotten your impurity? You cannot go on with this marriage, if you do you know what will happen to you! God, how could you do this? He held his head in distraught. He was done, no longer could he put up with this love triangle. If Rose really wanted to do things her way, then he would let her.

"Because...I just have to. I don't care."

He laughed sarcastically and shook his head.

"You're ignorant Rose. Go on and marry him, have his children, and enjoy your life. Don't you ever appear in front of me again, better yet, don't even bother helping me. I thought I finally found someone worth living for, but now that I won't have you, there's no point now is there? I might as well be condemned a traitor if that so happens to be my fate." He swung her hand away and stormed off, pushing aside the strangers that crossed his path.

Rose found her balance and leaned against the fence. Leon's confession hit her harder than she could ever imagine and for a long moment she stared into the sky and sighed. It was better this way, she thought. If she stayed out of his way, it would be easier on the both of them. From now on her only duty was to stay strong, for him as well as herself. *This sacrifice will be worth it,* was all she had to say to keep from breaking.

Twenty

The sky was a bright blue with barely any clouds to shield the villagers from the sun. Its rays warmed her face and made her body temperature rise. It was hard to choose between going back inside the lonely castle to hide from the heat, or walk amongst it like everyone else. The decision was simple, being back in the hell hole was suffocating her and Rose knew she'd end up crying again in her bedroom. There was laughter all around her and it made her feel miserable. She wished she was with Leon right now, talking and laughing like they usually did.

The scent of freshly baked bread rose in the air and Rose followed the scent. Her stomach growled, threatening to eat itself if she were to postpone dinner any longer. For a dime she bought a loaf and continued her walk down the street market and towards the river ahead. She noticed a young boy to her left with his hands out stretched in front of him. The boy was dirty and his clothes were tattered. Rose stopped eating and looked down at her food, it was enough to feed a family and suddenly she was embarrassed. Kneeling down towards him she gave the young boy a smile in which he returned.

"Here, take it." Rose handed him the loaf and his eyes widened, as if it were the first time anyone had ever done such a thing. Rose quickly added a few coins into his palm before standing up and dusting her gown.

"Feed your family."

Her smile was warm and inviting and the boy couldn't help but thank her repeatedly before turning on his heel and running away.

"That felt good."

Generosity was not common in this era, seeing how people barely had enough to feed themselves. Rose looked up to a dozen pair of eyes on her. Did they notice? Of course. Women turned and whispered into each other's ears, a few of them smiled her way and a mother of three bowed her head down. Biting her lip she nodded back, startled by the reaction from the public. In her time, no one gave a damn whether a homeless man was helped. They had no sympathy for people, and never stopped to think that not all of the homeless were lazy to get jobs, some really had a reason they couldn't. Depression, disabilities, there were so many reasons people didn't seem to think of.

Rose continued her walk down what seemed to be the food market, and stopped to buy an apple. She ate it as she took in the site of the hay scattered sheds and stone houses. Horses were tied to poles by them and it reminded her of garages. Horses were as valuable as cars were in her time.

"Wait!"

A small boy cried from behind her. She looked back to see the homeless boy running with a grin on his face and a red rose in his hand. An older woman walked behind him, her eyes wide and tired from shouting after him to walk. Rose kneeled down as he wrapped his arms around her, startled by such innocent affection she hugged him back. "I wanted to give you this..." He blushed and handed her the rose.

"It's beautiful, thank you so much."

It was the sweetest moment she had ever had and she wanted to thank him because for that one second the worries in her heart disappeared. The smiling young boy would grow up to be a ladies man for sure, and Rose hoped it would be in a good way.

"No, thank you." The old lady finally caught up, out of breath and holding her aching back. Quickly rising to her feet, Rose held her steady.

"Are you alright?"

The old woman had not looked at the young lady that had so graciously given them a meal until now. Her eyes widened and she nearly fell.

"Oh, my, Rose! Are you alright?"

Rose frowned, darting her eyes between the young boy and his grandmother. It didn't cross her mind that the stranger knew her name.

"I'm sorry…I don't seem to know who you are…"

Her pupils dilated, making her iris appear larger. She resisted the urge to hold her and tell her how much she missed her. The days had been dreary and lonely without her presence and she had desperately waited for the day in which she could see her again. Yet as the old woman looked into Rose's frightened eyes, her happiness diminished, and suddenly she was worried.

"It's not possible, you were supposed to remember everything when you returned…"

Rose was as confused as she could ever be. When she tried to think back to a time she could have seen this woman, her head began to hurt, warning her that she could not go any farther into her memories. They had been blocked, or as Agnes had said, *lost*.

"I lost my memories after an accident, I don't remember anything past that. I was in a coma for…" Rose couldn't even remember how long. She was in her time during all the years before coming here. The old woman's eyes were horrified. They questioned her every move, trying to see any evidence of deceitfulness but Rose had the same blank, confused stare. *Had the potion gone wrong?* Rose was supposed to remember everything. She had to let her know the truth.

"Rose, I have to tell you something but not here, we need to sit you down for this." The old lady took Roses' hand and began to lead her towards her home around the corner.

"What do you mean, please I can handle it just tell me now." Rose pleaded impatiently, something inside her was stirring, it was a déjà vu moment and she was beginning to feel as though she *had* met this woman before. Sighing, the old lady turned to her and grasped her hands together.

"You are about to get very confused but trust me."

Her eyes were wide and she wanted to admit that it wasn't possible to feel any more lost than she already did. The moment stilled and a flock of birds flew dangerously low above their heads. Screams and curses were muttered towards them. With her eyes she followed a pair of children who began to chase them. A little girl with long blonde pig tails held her brothers hand. The sound of the world had muted and for that one moment she enjoyed the serene playing between siblings, he chased her and she chased him. Her eyes flew to a man right behind them whose stand of melons had broken. The wooden legs splintered in half and down came the fruit rolling through the dirt road. He chased them quickly, staggering at which to go to first and then scooping the few close by into his arms.

A shriek silenced the area and for a moment everyone stood still. Rose blinked several times, waking herself from the illusion and finding herself in the middle of a stampede of people. She gasped, startled by the sudden sound of horses galloping.

"Quickly we must get inside!" The old lady cried, snatching her grandsons arm and pulling him forward through the crowd. Rose followed behind, body after body shoving past her shoulder and nearly knocking her off her feet.

"What's going on?" She cried.

"It's an invasion, hurry!"

Her voice faded as another scream pierced the air up ahead. Rose stopped dead in her tracks as dozens of French men in horses galloped towards her. They jumped off their horses and swung their swords at the innocent people.

"Capture the woman and children!"

A man was cornered into the wall and Rose witnessed his murder as he was stabbed to death. The bile rose and she fell on her knees, slamming her mouth shut. She couldn't peel her eyes away from the bloody stone. The men wore tight red pants and long blue coats with buttons that ran across the chest and a collar that snugged against their necks, a gold trim lined up and down the sleeves in a strange design. On their heads a red and blue capped hat shielded their eyes from the sun, a strap under their chins held it in place. The swords were pulled out from the sheath wrapped around their backs and Rose watched as more men with leather boots came forward. They jumped off their horses and targeted the unlucky ones nearby.

People were crying for help and it was in that moment that Rose realized she was in the middle of a battle field. She struggled to stand up on her wobbly knees, noting that the crowd of people had separated her from the old woman. There was nowhere to run or hide. She looked around, but it seemed like the invaders were coming from every corner, Rose was surrounded and knew if she ran it would only bring attention to herself instead. She went back down on her knees and searched around, heart beating fast, she hid behind barrels a couple of feet away.

"My goodness what is this!" She cried, placing both palms over her ears, trying to block the blood curling screams of the victims. The pain in the air was real, this was no movie. The sound of screaming brought chills to every part of her body and she just wished it could end.

All of a sudden there was a sound of clashing swords, Rose looked up quickly to see the guards running towards them. Another group of red coats from the castle made their way forward. Her eyes were darting from face to face, searching for Leon but he was not amongst them.

Her mind was contemplating whether it was a good chance to run now, but her legs were frozen. Woman and children were being loaded into a jail cell type carriage. They dragged them inside, ignoring their pleas and cries for help. She didn't want to be in that situation, she couldn't be. Rose was a coward and swore she would not budge from her hiding spot, but it all changed when she spotted the little boy from before.

"Oh my god." She stood up, quite unsure why her body was reacting to her heart instead of her mind. She searched for the old lady and when she saw her on the ground she stumbled forward into tears. The young boy was reaching for her screaming, while his other arm was being pulled away.

Rose knew if she ran away without helping the poor boy she would regret it for the rest of her life. Gathering some strength and courage Rose picked up an axe that had been abandoned in the stampede and ran forward. The invaders jumped, startled by her presence. They lifted their swords towards her, daring her to come near, but she continued to walk. The axe shook in her hands, she didn't even know how to use it. The two guards looked at each other and laughed. They spoke something in French then looked back at her.

"You let go of that boy and that woman!" She cried.

"I say drop that weapon and surrender yourself."

A golden haired man stepped forward, slightly lowering his weapon.

"I will not, now let them go!"

Rose was panting now and her vision began to blur. The dirt ground had risen into the air creating a dark cloudy haze. The gravel beneath her feet was shaking, or was it her body? Suddenly he lunged towards her and she shrieked, dropping the axe onto the ground. The man held her against his body, she lifted her head up more as one arm wrapped around her throat, the other around her belly. She struggled to breathe and it took all her will power to keep from fainting.

"I'd keep still if I were you." He hissed against her ear and it sent a shiver down her spine. He grabbed her breast in one hand and she screamed again, struggling against him, kicking and shaking, trying to free herself from his grasp but he held on even tighter.

"You're a pretty one, you'd go for a fair price. Maybe I will have a taste of you before selling you off." His sick twisted laughter was disturbing. The man dragged her forward towards the other women that were now chained to the carriage. *"No, no way, I can't go in there!"* Rose banged her head against his face and he let go. Cursing and holding on to his bleeding nose. He leaned down and moaned and Rose took the chance to run forward but he darted after her, his eyes full of vengeance and anger.

"Don't you dare!"

Startled, Rose looked back as a sword struck out in front of her, halting the French man in his pursuit. She tripped on her feet and fell down hard on her bottom. Dirt now stained her body completely. Her hands and knees were bloody from her falls and she could feel the bruises.

Leon stepped in front of Rose. His eyes hungry for murder, he swung his blade upwards, nearly catching his face but he stepped back, bringing his sword up to shield himself. The man was good, he blocked every swing Leon made and it angered him. He had seen Rose from a distance and seen the way he touched her. Just the thought of it fired up his adrenaline even more and he swung his blade with more force, slash after slash until finally the man's sword flew from his hands. His eyes widened and with no remorse Leon ran and dug his blade through his heart. The man's face fell was over his shoulder and he could hear the deaf defying gasp and groan. Leon grabbed the handle with both hands and swiftly pulled it back out. The man staggered backwards and fell. Taking the blade, Leon wiped the blood off the sides of it with the dead man's coat.

"Take your filthy blood with you." He spat on the ground besides him and turned his attention to the stunned invader by the cargo of woman. He growled and ran forward.

"Everyone look away, now!" He screamed, and quickly they did as they were told. Leon drew his blade and swung it across his neck, blood squirted out in different directions and he gagged for a second before falling to his death. He ran back to Rose, whose eyes were wide and horrified.

"I told you to look away!" He shouted. But she was frozen in that direction. Rose slapped herself back into reality and shut her eyes. Leon slid his sword back into his sheath and reached for her hands. When she opened her eyes they were filled with tears. Rose stood up and wrapped her arms around his neck, she was sobbing uncontrollably because for that one second, it seemed like she would never get to see him again.

"I'm so glad you came." She whimpered. He held her close, holding back his own tears, fearing that if he had not made it in time Rose would not be in his arms right now. For a long moment they were silent, holding onto each other. The screams of death faded and suddenly, they were in their own world.

Leon knew he had to snap out of it. He had told her to stay away from him and the look in her eyes when he said that had haunted him from that very moment. To let her go meant to be apart from her, but here he was holding her close, loosing every bit of self-control he had made for himself and the hardest part was realizing that he'd rather hurt than not hold her at all.

"I have to get you out of here safely, it's too dangerous."

There was murder all around. The dirt roads were now stained with the blood of the victims of the attack as well as the perpetrators, even some allies. It was a sight that would cause any sane person to lose their minds. The surrounding was getting quieter and the remaining invaders were running towards their horses to retreat. Leon held her close and covered her eyes as his fellow guard came forward and slaughtered another man to his death. The howl of his cry caused her skin to crawl and she dug her face deeper into his chest.

"It's almost over." He whispered.

Leon was leaving the castle when he had heard of the attack, it caught him and the others off guard. They had been ordered into the court room for a meeting in which King Henry stated they would be at war with France. He had no idea what laid just outside his castle walls. The King had pulled Leon aside and told him of a traitor, who was believed to be lurking amongst them. Leon's duty was to find him and just the task alone set a heavy pressure on his chest. He could only imagine how the King was feeling after seeing the invasion and the corpses of his men all over the village. It had left hundreds of wives without husbands as well as many children without fathers. Today would be a day of grief. Wives wailed and sobbed, dropping their knees to the ground and holding their loved ones. The village was sorrowful and as she looked around it struck her down to her soul. The happy image she had enjoyed a moment ago, children laughing and singing were now replaced and she was forced to watch them cry and scream. Her eyes filled with tears as she began to wonder what had happened to the pig tailed little girl.

Her eyes dropped back to the old woman and her grandson and she gasped.

"I'll be right back."

She ran from his arms and towards the boy. Her heart quickening and praying that she was still alive, *please* god, let her be alive. Rose drops down beside her and places her hands above her chest. For a moment they tremble and she looks into the teary boys eyes. She begins to push down on her chest repeatedly. A small group gathers around them, wondering what Rose is doing, never having seen it before in their lives. Rose parts the old woman's lips and blows into her mouth, she pushes down on her chest and pauses for a moment, trying to look for movement but there is none. Leon steps besides her with narrowed eyes, never having seen a woman doing something so obscene in public.

"Rose, why are you kissing her?"

"I'm not kissing her! I'm trying to save her by filling her lungs with air, maybe it could get her heart beating again." Her voice shook.

Others around them gasped, understanding the concept they had all taken so wrongly. After several more repetitions Rose slowly pulled her hands back.

"She's gone..."

Faces turned away with sorrow and the young boy begins to sob into his dead grandmother's arms. There was a moment in which Rose felt a sudden pang of sadness and it hit her hard. Tears were falling from her eyes as she looked down at the old lady, the nostalgic beginning to rise yet again between them. In that moment, it felt as if she had known her, long ago.

"I'm so sorry."

Leon pulled her up and away from the old lady and the boy. It wasn't right to get so personal with strangers, people here minded their own business, and he didn't understand what had compelled Rose to do such a thing towards a stranger. He wanted to yell at her and tell her it wasn't okay, but she was crying again and he couldn't bear to hurt her anymore.

Roses' eye skimmed down to his stomach and she stiffened. Her lips parted but she found it hard to speak. "Oh my god Leon, you're bleeding!"

He had been strong for the longest but he couldn't neglect his wound much longer. A blue coat had impaled him as he was running to save Rose and for a moment he had even forgotten about it.

"And so is your dress, my lady." He winced and pressed his hand against it, the pain of the wound beginning to ache. Rose looked down startled. The sight of blood on her dress caused her head to spin. He caught her fast before she could faint.

"You're okay, don't worry."

She held onto his arm.

"Quickly we have to get you to a doctor!"

Leon turned towards the abandoned horse and took ahold of the saddle. He pressed his foot into the stirrup and swung his leg over to the other side. He groaned as the wound stung from the sudden movement. He reached his hand towards Rose and she took it. The eight foot creature in front of her was huge and Rose found it hard to believe anyone shorter than Leon could make it up. As if reading her thoughts he smiled.

"Come, I have you."

He held back the pain as he pulled her body up and behind his back, she wrapped her arms around him, knowing well to keep the wound covered to prevent any more blood loss. Leon squeezed his calves into the horse's body and grabbed the rein. The horse galloped forward quickly, startled, Rose screamed and grabbed onto him tighter. She loosened her grip when she felt his body cringe.

"Sorry!"

Leon forced a laugh.

"The pain is nothing compared to other wounds I have suffered." Her heart saddened, knowing well he did not lie.

Twenty-One

"This is not a hospital, why have you taken me back home?!" Rose was angry now as they halted in front of her mansion. He looked back at her and raised his brow.

"Home? This is my home. And if you haven't forgotten there are no hospitals in this time Rose."

She blushed, she had forgotten all about that the moment she looked up at her house. Leon jumped off first, then turned and helped her down. Rose put his arm on her shoulder and helped him up the stairs. He was trying to be strong but it hurt like hell. Leon fought hard not to grunt as he found it embarrassing to look so weak in front of a woman.

The front door opened and Rose gasped as she looked around. The kitchen was just a counter and a stove and the dining room to the left bore only a small sofa and table. It barely resembled her house, the twenty first century updated home that is.

"Will you call a doctor, please Leon? You'll die if this get infected!" Leon shrugs her words away. "I don't care." He smirks, quickly regretting his words as she shoots him a look.

"That's not funny at all." She rolls her eyes at his childish response.

"Let's get you on a bed." Rose leads him up the stairs and into the room while Leon stays silent, amazed at her remarkable knowledge of his home.

"How did you know this is my bed room?" His eyes sparkled with amusement.

"I told you Leon, in the future this is my house and also my bedroom."

She helps him settle on the bed and releases her grasp.

"So at a time we shared a bedroom." There was a seductive tone in his voice and Rose couldn't help but laugh, even while bleeding to death he could still crack a joke.

She looks around the room and finds it to be empty, besides a table off in the corner, sheets of paper on the top with some sort of cursive written on it. The room was so masculine, but it was nice and in this era quite modern with the silk red bed sheets.

"I'll get you a towel and anything I can find to clean the wound, stay there."

Leon smiled. "I won't be going anywhere."

Climbing down the steps in twos', Rose darts into the kitchen and finds a bottle of whisky, perfect for killing the bacteria. Finding a bucket by the floor, she runs to the bath tub and fills it with water. He watches her as she drops the items by his feet.

"Are we having drinks now?"

"Not me, but I suggest you have some before I get started on you."

Rose opens his closet and pulls a white long sleeved shirt from the wooden hanger, deciding it was the closest thing to a band aid.

"Do you have a needle and some thread?" His eyes widened.

"Whatever for!"

" — you couldn't possibly..."

"Leon, please, just in case the cut is too deep it might need stiches."

"No, I'm sure the blade just about scratched it."

Rose rolled her eyes, finding his nervousness attractive.

He gives in and points to his desk drawer where Rose gathers the items and places them besides him. She pulls back the covers before ordering him to lay down.

His eyes watched her movements intently, admiring the way her eyes would squint when she frowned and how her pink tongue would repeatedly swipe under her lips. A warm feeling would flush down to his core. He winced as Rose pulled his shirt over his head. She grabbed it and dipped it in the water.

"Now this will hurt a little."

She dabbed the wound with the tip of his shirt and cleaned it off. The bleeding was subsiding and that was a good sign, it meant that it was not as deep as she thought it was and did not require stiches, which she was glad about since Rose had no experience in stitching whatsoever.

She brought the liquor up to his lips, startled, he took a long gulp.

"I must warn you Rose, I'm a stupid drunk."

She laughed.

"Well that's too bad but you better not try anything with this cut on your body. You have to rest."

He laid his head back down and smirked. "Here is the hard part." Rose spilled the whisky onto the cloth and pressed it against the open wound. He groaned and clenched his teeth.

"Dear god what the hell Rose!"

The veins in his face were protruding and Rose stopped to give him a moment to breathe again.

"Sorry, but the alcohol kills the germs..."

She was afraid to tell him about the salt she had to sprinkle on it too. "I can handle it, continue."

Leon shouted obscene words as the pain shot through him. Rose noticed it was working, there was barely any blood left. She grabbed a handful of sheets and ordered him to open his mouth.

"What?" It was apparent in Leon's' face how terrified he was of Rose and her strange medical techniques that he had never once heard of. He wasn't sure it would work but trusting her was all he could do. It left him without a choice.

"Bite down on this."

He screamed into the cloth as she poured the salt over his wound. The sound was muffled but still loud enough to echo through the hollow house. Pulling her arms away she jumped a couple of feet back.

"Sorry!"

Her hands flew to his chest and the warmth of her palms on it made his heart beat faster. The feeling was bittersweet and he found it odd that he would take the pain a hundred times more just to feel her hand on him.

"I'm done, I promise. Sit up please."

Rose decided to tear up a piece of his thin white bed sheet instead and with a pair of scissors she worked fast. Running to him, she twirled it around his chest multiple times before finally reaching the end of the cloth and tying it together. It was snug and guaranteed not to fall off.

"Wow, you're amazing Rose."

She blushed, thanking the internet for her skills and knowledge.

"Not really..."

He grabbed her face in his hands and for a moment just looked into her eyes. She sat still, mesmerized by the way his eyes gleamed against the sunsets orange rays. "Now, about you...Rose darling, you look like you've murdered somebody." Her eyes went wild as she looked down at her blood stained gown. "I need a bath." Her cheeks blush crimson and he notices.

"No *we* need a bath."

He winks in a sexy way and Rose gets weak in the knees. "But your wound...I just did all that." She crosses her arms and sighs. Leon stands and laughs. He takes her hand in his and for a moment Rose hesitates, remembering her engagement with Thomas and her point of coming back to this era. Being near Leon meant becoming even more attached to him, even if she didn't think that possible, but it was. It made her love him even more and not ever want to leave his side. A part of her wished she could finally choose between fighting and giving in.

Leon slide his finger under her chin and pulled it up.

"I know I was awfully rude to you this morning and I apologize...It's just that everything is becoming so unexpected and challenging and the hardest part is knowing that you're not mine." He takes a deep breath and sighs, letting the anguish flow through his lungs and out. Rose takes his hand.

"Can I be yours just for today?"

The words were hard to say and her bluntness even startled her a bit. He bent down and swallowed her mouth in a passionate kiss. Her hands slid up his masculine chest and up to his neck where she held on to him, fighting hard to keep her balance and melting in his arms. His breath smelled harshly of alcohol and Rose found it surprising that she could taste it in his mouth. He pulled away, half gasping and placed his hands on her shoulders.

"I feel I am not properly bathed to kiss you, my lady, let us cleanse our bodies together."

Before she could object and admit how embarrassed she would be, he pulled her forward and into the bathroom. The shut behind him and Leon began to slip off his boots and trousers. Rose blushed and looked to the ceiling quickly. The temperature in the room was rising and she had a feeling it was coming from her own body. Slowly, she pulled down her dress from her shoulders and paused as Leon stood like a Greek god, staring, making her feel more awkward then she already did. The dress fell to the ground, leaving every part of her exposed in broad daylight. Biting her lip,

Rose reached up to her messy bun and unleashed it. Her hair fell around her face and back.

Leon cleared his throat, not knowing if he should look away or keep staring at the goddess in front of him. Her every curve was perfect, so slim and petite. He cursed in his head, damming the man who had slashed him, and prevented him from a long night of love making.

Her slender body moved forward and slipped into the warm bath tub. He followed her in and sat opposite of her so he could face the beauty in front of him. It was like a magnetic pull between them and Rose wanted to jump on him, but she knew it'd hurt him to even move, so she sat still, holding her breath.

She found the bar of soap and ran it across her arms and then under her neck. He watched her hungrily, intent on her body and the way her breast moved just above the water. He could feel his attraction towards her hardening, and knew that the rose peddles floating above were blocking her sight of it.

In her mind she was fighting the urge to stay away from him but she could no longer resist. She slipped forward and wrapped her arms around his neck. He let out a low moan as her bottom swiped across his manhood and stopped against it. Leon could only imagine grabbing her tight in his hands and pounding her against him. Rose was blushing now, feeling his erection against her.

"Let me clean you up." She smiled seductively and ran her soapy hands along his face, neck and arms. She enjoyed the way his muscles clenched beneath her fingers and the way his lips would part as she applied pressure on a certain area. Her sex ached, and her teasing was beginning to consume her as well.

"The hell with this." Leon muttered into her ear. His hands caught her waist and he slammed her down onto him. Rose cried out and fell against his chest. "Your wound Leon!" She said, startled by the foreign feeling in her groin. He pushed her down again and she moaned, Rose could feel him reach the very top and her body wanted more, deeper.

"It's okay." He groaned against her and slammed her into him once again. Her breast brushed against his chest and he could feel her nipples hardening, turning him on even more. Rose held on to his shoulders and moved to his rhythm. Water was splashing onto the ground but neither of them cared. The waves they had created were now a typhoon as they moved endlessly against each other, moaning and gasping, clinging onto each other.

His strong hands were tight against her waist and even the pain of it was beginning to be pleasurable. Rose kissed him, sweeping her tongue into his just to feel the wetness of it in her mouth. She craved much more, she wanted to taste him as well. Rose pulls herself out, leaving him gasping, eyes wide with question. "Stand." She ordered. There was delight in his eyes for a moment.

"Darling, if you say so."

Drops of water slide down his massive body and Rose sits on her knees, staring horrified at what had been inside her just a moment ago. She looks up into his sultry eyes and he knows what she is about to do. Something inside him tells him he should stop her, that she shouldn't ruin herself any more than he had done, but his lips are frozen shut, until he feels the tip of her warm tongue circle him. He moans and grabs her head, hoping his action was gentle, too focused on the feeling of her mouth around him. Her wet lips surround his head, hitting every nerve and he pushes himself into her, the pleasure of her warm insides riding up to his core. He shivers, his hands beginning to shake as she moves into him and out. Leon's panting now as she quickens her pace and his body quivers. His defenses are down and it's the first time he finds himself trusting another human being with his body. Rose strokes him with her hand and she could hear him moaning now. His hands are roaming through her hair, following her pace and she feels his veins throb in her mouth, he shakes, and suddenly an explosion of warm liquid seeps down her throat. She grabs onto his waist and shut her eyes as he finishes and releases his grasp on her hair. Rose backs away and coughs, suddenly embarrassed she can't help but laugh. His quickly down, holding her and asking if she's alright. Rose turns back and smiles.

"That was unexpected." Leon says, a wide grin spread across his lips. He stands and reaches for her hand. "Let's get out of here before we prune to death, my love."

Twenty-Two

Rose sits on the couch watching Leon prepare tea. Her gown had been washed and she now wore it like new, no signs of violence on it anymore. Her mind travels back to yesterday and the old lady. The woman was clearly trying to tell her *something* important. The look in her eyes still clung in Roses' mind and she couldn't help but shiver. Rose could not figure out what it could have possibly been and it bothered her. Going back to that dreaded town and castle was the last thing she wanted to do. If only time stood still, and she could spend her days with Leon, sleeping by his side and holding his hand. He would kiss her softly and tuck her fallen hair behind her ear. Rose shook herself out of her ridiculous day dream and turned her attention towards Leon.

He set down their tea and biscuits on the table and settled into the chair in front of her. There was a dreaded sadness behind his eyes but he still smiled at her and motioned for her to eat.

"Leon...can't we just run away together?"

Her question surprised him and his cup shook in his hand. He couldn't deny that he had questioned that as well. But his duty to his King was something he could not run away from. Henry would set out to find and kill him if he were to do something that dangerous. Her life would be in danger as well, she was safer at the castle and with Thomas.

He squeezed his fist under the table. Just the thought of him sent his blood boiling. The only satisfaction was knowing that Rose would not be his wife forever and the feeling was bittersweet. She would be gone from his life as well. When he looked back into her eyes they were tearing. He grabbed her hand and caressed her palm with his thumb.

"Fate has been cruel to us Rose, but I am afraid that is not an option. I would never risk your life."

Rose sighed. "My life without you..."She hesitates and looks up, blinking back the tears.

"I don't know if I can carry on."

His face softens and he squeezes her hand. "Please, don't say things like that. You can and you will. You are a strong woman Rose, and I am lucky to have come across someone like you. So willing to help a man like me without caring for your own happiness." The words pained him to say and he found himself breathless, the ache of his wound and heart combining into a sharp stab.

"So you will let me help you? You can't push me away Leon. Not again."

It takes him a moment to reply, but he nods, knowing he'd disappoint her with his true response. He wanted Rose to do nothing more for him honestly. If there was someone after his life, it put hers in danger as well. What he could possibly lose had been lost already, Leon had no one else to live for and he knew Thomas, although it pained him, could take care of Rose in the meantime.

"Since we already know Margaret's lover is Arthur, I just have to get some kind of evidence. That way Thomas can approach the King and let him know."

Leon had finally understood why such a deal between Thomas and her had been made. In fact, it was better off for Thomas to approach King Henry with such accusations than a maid. His heart sank, knowing the sacrifice between them was too much to bear. Thomas and he were the Kings most trustworthy men, that's why Henry had assigned him such a task.

"Okay. I will also look for evidence, in the meantime I have to let you know something you cannot tell anyone. There is a traitor among our castle walls and I have been instructed to capture this man or woman. Please be very careful."

Roses' eyes frowned in confusion.

"I don't remember reading about a traitor…"

" —ugh how stupid could I have been."

She knew the answer to all their questions was in the magazine article she never got the chance to finish. If she had, all this would have been a lot easier.

"My dear, you are anything but stupid."

He stood up and approached her.

"Leon…"

Bending down, he arches her face and gives her a deep kiss, knowing it would be a while before he had a chance to do it again. Flushed, Rose stands and hug him tightly and it is dangerous, as their hearts connect and for a moment they refuse to let go.

"We should get going. You didn't go back last night and I'm sure Thomas must be worried about you."

Rose shrugged.

"He will realize I spent the night with you once he sees us together."

Leon laughed, his eyes brightening with mischievous humor.

" —and I will be very satisfied."

It's nearly noon when they reach the castle. The village had been busy, people spent their day cleaning up and fixing their stands. The roads had been cleaned, and now hundreds of crosses were hammered into the trees that ran all along the river, symbolizing the ones who had lost their lives in the attack. It was hard for Rose to look at and she found herself shutting her eyes as they passed each one.

"Does your wound feel better?" Rose asked as they stopped just outside the doors, they had agreed to part in separate ways. "Much better thanks to you." He placed his hand on her smiling face.

"Can't we just go back?" Rose moaned, she batted her lashes flirtatiously and caught Leon's flush.

The birds ahead were chirping in sync and for a moment the world felt so serene. A soft wind blew and she watched his hair move through the breeze. He was so perfect and she didn't want to be apart from him. The happiness in her heart would die and she could feel it subsiding as the seconds passed.

"I wish, but that would be far too suspicious. If anyone ask, I was wounded in battle and you nursed me. That is what we shall say, understood?"

Rose nodded.

"Okay. I'll see you later."

He kissed her forehead quickly and strolled inside. Rose waited a couple of minutes before walking in, not wanting it to look any worse than it already did.

She made her way across the room and surprisingly no one seemed to notice her presence. Climbing the steps she walked towards the bridge that separated the left side of the castle with the right. The stone bridge was unique in which statues of men were built feet apart on the ledge. Rose would always stare at them as she made her way across, wondering how people in this time could have the tools necessary to build such a thing. The castle was pretty much made up of statues on every corner, possibly ancestors of the King. With the amount of gold plaques that hung on the walls, it was obvious how rich Henry was.

"You're majesty, I have returned." Leon kneels down before the King and bows. Henry smiles, motioning him to his feet. "I knew I would not lose my strongest warrior in battle, but what ails you?"

Leon's staggered walk had been obvious when he entered the room. Thomas noticed immediately.

"I have just a mere cut on my stomach, but it is nothing I assure you I am alright." Leon straightens his back, not wanting the others to witness his weakness. "All is well. In two days we shall go on our expedition to Scotland to gain our alliance. The King and I have arranged a marriage between their Prince Edward to my daughter Margaret. We are to pay our respects to their country, their alliance is what we need to take over France."

Leon stood frozen for a moment, realizing that he would be away from Rose for more than a month. He looked back up to the King and nodded, bowing he turned and took his leave. His blood was hot, *dammit*. He was not prepared to leave her so soon. Leon feared the look in her eyes when he told her and it hurt him deeper than the wound. He needed to see her and quick.

"Leon."

He halted, the voice that had become poison to his blood came nearer. "Are you alright lad? I didn't see you yesterday, I thought the worst." Leon smirked, failing to hide his annoyance.

"I was protecting Rose. She was nearly killed, if I had not come in time she would not be alive right now." His eyes widened, alarmed, but feeling relieved to know that she was still alive. He had searched all night for her, fearing she had been captured along with the other missing women.

"Where is she? I need to see her."

Thomas could feel Leon's anger rise. His eyes were dark and menacing. He no longer held the carefree smile he had once worn, Leon changed. Even his friends had noticed his absence from the bars and for a moment Thomas wondered if Rose had been the one to change him. Rose had changed Thomas as well, in a way he didn't like. Ever since she appeared in their lives, their friendship had begun to fade.

"Let her be. She is tired from last night." Leon hid the satisfied smile of the night they spent but Thomas could see it from within him. He smirks and each word he spits out hurts more than the last.

"Don't worry, I took *really* good care of her."

"You spent the night with my wife?" Thomas growled in a low voice only he could hear. Leon smirked.

"She's not your wife yet."

Thomas clenched his teeth.

"She will be by tomorrow."

His reply caught Leon off guard.

"What?"

Thomas ignored his question, trying to contain the emotions in his heart. "You know damn well to take a woman's virtue before marriage." He was angry now, flames of fury burning inside him as they walked towards a more secluded area to talk.

"What do you mean she'll be your wife tomorrow?" Leon grabs a handful of shirt in his hand and pushes him against the wall. Neither of them on the same topic, each going mad within their own misfortunes.

"We are to be wed tomorrow. The King had granted my permission yesterday before the attack. Besides, Rose and I made a deal. Only I can help you Leon so if you know what's good for you, you'll let us be."

Leon's mind went as blank as an empty canvas, his hands dropped down to his side and he stepped back. There was too much going on at once and processing it was like digging another wound onto his body. He had not expected such a quick marriage. Leon had neglected his confidence. Being wed so soon meant that Rose would no longer live in the castle, she would be sent to Thomas' home, where he'd impregnate her and have her raise their children until his final battle where he would then be allowed to go home.

Leon blinked several times through the colorful spots in his eyes and groaned, holding onto his stomach he used the wall as support. Thomas stood silent in the shadow, watching him. Never before had he seen his friend so distraught,

"She was mine before she was ever yours." Leon growled. He didn't know what he was saying, all he tried to do was contain himself.

"No, Leon. You lost your chance with her the moment you broke her heart."

Leon swallowed the lump in his throat, remembering back to the time she had witnessed his affair by the lake and ran. The moment he had first laid eyes on her and called her a whore. He had indeed hurt her too many times to count and but had done greater damage on his own heart.

"I am in *love* with Rose."

Thomas stiffened, having been the first time he's ever heard his friend say those words.

"But for her safety, I won't get in the way. Just promise me that you will never hurt her the way I did. Take care of her. Love her uncontrollably. Do not banish her, for her virtue has been taken by me. It is your choice whether you chose to continue this marriage because of that."

Thomas stood still, face expressionless, not knowing whether he should be surprised or not.

"It does not bother me but it is fine. I will make her love me one day."

Leon squeezed his eyes and grimaced, the words like nails scratching against an easel.

He patted Thomas on the back and forced a smile.

"Good catch, my friend."

It was then that Leon realized the extent of his love for Rose. His love so strong that he was willing to set her free, when all he really wanted to do was run to her and take her offer. They'd run away to the farthest country, but then they'd have nothing. No place to live or food. No shelter during the harsh winter months. Leon couldn't let Rose live that way. She deserved better than that and that reasoning was enough to let her go.

Rose had heard the news of her marriage before Leon had could tell her, but she did not know he was going to travel to another country for more than a month. It proved that just when she thought things couldn't get any worse, they did. For a long moment she wailed in his arms and he caressed her hair, telling her things were going to be okay, but they were just lies and Rose knew that. They were in the garden were they had agreed to meet and the day was surprisingly cold, just like her heart. In his arms is where she wanted to be and when he told her he had to go her heart broke into pieces. Sadly, she said goodbye and watched him disappear through the trees. Leon was not strong enough to withstand his tears much longer. He had left her side before she could see how he truly felt.

As Rose made her way back into the castle, head down to the ground wiping her tears, she bumps into Thomas. Rose looked up at him with murderous eyes.

"How dare you!" She swung her hand towards his face but he caught her wrist. "I agreed to marry you, but not so quickly!" Rose was yelling now and he was dragging her back into the garden.

"Let me go!" She pulled her hands away from his grasp and panted. "Listen, I did not think anything of it. We are to be married sooner or later, why not sooner?"

"You just want me gone from this castle and away from Leon, that's why!" Rose began pounding her fist on his chest, her measly hands doing nothing against his broadness. He sighed.

"You're right. That is my reason why. I cannot have you fooling around with a man while we are to be wed. I will not accept that."

"Well I don't accept this marriage! I can't leave until I help him and if I am forced to leave then I can't, and our contract means nothing. I will *not* marry you."

Her breathing is heavier now and the light headed feeling begins to rise. He catches her arms as her body leans to the left and in that moment she finds her balance again.

"You are not well, you must sit." He urges for her to take a seat on the bench but she doesn't budge from her stance.

"Rose, please, I don't want to fight with you." He takes her by the shoulder.

"Get your hands off me. Only Leon is allowed to touch me, his hands are much warmer, gentler. His touch is much softer than yours." She mocks, knowing all too well it angered him to hear.

"Oh yeah?"

Rose gasped as he grabs her face and begins to kiss her. She shakes her head but he keeps a still grip, causing her to tuck her lips in between her mouth. He groans and pushes her body against his, his large hands feeling down the small of her back and down to her bottom, he presses her against him harder. Rose struggles beneath him, hands flying and scratching him everywhere until he lets go with a sharp gasp.

"You're disgusting!" She cries and steps back, stumbling down the stone step and falling to the ground. She winces in pain as he looms over her, his eyes lost in the realization of what he had just done.

"I'd rather die than have you force me into everything!" Thomas takes a step back and looks down at her terrorized face. She was staring at him as if he were a monster, and for that moment he believed he was. He had never treated a woman like he had just now and it pained him to know how much he had changed; what anger and jealousy had done to his heart.

"...I'll see you tomorrow." He turns on his heel and leaves, drowning out the sound of her crying with his own thoughts.

Twenty-Three

"**M**other, I will not marry him!" Margaret is heard from the halls screaming. "You are a *Princess*, do not be so stubborn, he is a good match. It is for the good of our country." Rose stills for a moment.

"Please, I cannot!" Margaret is crying and for a moment Rose can sympathize for her, knowing they were both in the same situation.
"The marriage is finalized, we will have no further discussion on this matter."

Rose could hear Margaret's running footsteps cross the room and disappear down the direction of her bed chamber. The time was getting closer, she could feel it.

The wheel of fate had just begun to turn and now that Margaret knew of her arranged marriage Rose knew what she was going to do next. It was her job to stop that from happening at all cost. She ran forward and after Margaret, stopping out of breath at her door. It was after hours and she would wonder what Rose was doing but maybe just talking with her, woman to woman could somehow alter fate itself.

Rose knocked and held her breath, but there was no answer. Her eyes widened as she turned the knob and realized she was not in the room. Margaret must have run off to find Arthur and let him know. It was an opportunity Rose could not refuse. She shut the door behind her and grabbed the candle beside the table. The light was enough to see a couple of feet ahead. The adrenaline was pulsing through her veins as she feared what would happen if she were caught but she moved quickly, looking through the drawers for her diary, but again she found nothing. The dresser held nothing but her clothing, even the underside of her bed was clean. After a couple of minutes of endless searching Rose stopped. *"Okay Rose, If you had a diary where would you hide it? Somewhere no one could ever find it?"*

She took a deep, calming breath and thought hard for a long moment. Suddenly, her eyes lit up as she thought of the one spot she had not looked, a spot where Margaret always warned her to stay away from. Rose set down the candle and plunged her hand between the mattresses. Her heart stopped when she felt the hard cover on her fingers tips, within an instant it was in her hands and she had fled the room. Running through dim corridors she made her way towards Leon's room.

She stopped out of breath, realizing she had made the five minute walk to his room into a minute. She knocked and a couple of seconds passed until he opened the door. She smiled and pushed passed his confused look.

"Rose, what in the world are you doing here this late?" He whispered.

"Leon, that's not important. What's important is what I have here in my hands."

His eyes trailed down to the leather covered book.

"What is that?"

"Her diary, I finally found it. My proof must be in here somewhere I just know it." He watched nervously as she sat on his bed and motioned for him to follow.

"Rose, I'm terrified right now. Woman are not allowed in a man's bed chambers, you know that."

Rose rolled her eyes.

"Who will find out?"

Rose takes his hand and pulls him to her. She was so happy, she couldn't help but grin. "We must be quiet then." She winked and Leon could feel his temperature rising. He didn't know how a woman could be so irresistible.

Rose began to turn the pages, each with a date on the top. She skimmed through the passages until her eyes stopped on Arthur's name. Each page was filled with details of their secret encounters and love for each other. It wasn't until Rose turned to the last page that her heart sunk. It was the page she had read about in the future. Her last journal entry was done today, early this morning. It spoke of their plan to lose her virtue, that way she would be unable to wed Prince Edward. Leon read besides her, freezing as his name appeared.
It stated how they would use *him* as a rapist.

Rose grabbed his hand and tucked it tightly in hers, she could feel his surprise as well.

"I never doubted you Rose, but it scares me to know how much of what you said was true..." His eyes were lost in disbelief. He brought her hand up to his lips and kissed it.
"I won't let her get away with this, Leon."

Rose dared not to read the rest but she couldn't resist, the temptation was much too great. She dropped the book from her shaking hands and it slammed shut on the ground.
"What's the matter?"

He held her as she wailed in his chest. "Leon, their planning on doing all this tomorrow night! I know how this ends if we don't stop them history will not change and you will die..."

"Darling, please calm down, nothing is going to happen to me." Her eyes were clouded with tears but she still looked up at him. How could someone be so calm knowing their life was in danger? Rose didn't understand and she held onto him tighter.

"If I don't stop this you'll be blamed Leon! When the King comes back from his expedition with you and the others, he will find out. It's all a trap as well Leon, my god, did I even tell you?"

Rose was losing her mind, it was all beginning to make sense now. Before, she was not sure which expedition was a trap but now that she knew about Margaret's plan she was certain it was the upcoming one.

"One thing at a time, my love. Take a deep breath and explain." Rose tells him through tears about the trap.

"During the expedition the traitor will lead a detour towards Woodham, not far from the castle but not that close either, that is where the French attack you guys off guard. When the King and what survive of his men return to castle he hears of his daughter's rape and in rage has you executed."

"But I am his best commander in battle. It's not possible."

"Leon, after being betrayed, having half his men killed and daughter raped, knowing she can no longer marry the Prince of Scotland and he could longer have the alliance he needed to conquer France, he goes a little crazy..."

Leon's face falls.

"How can we put an end to this? Do you know who the traitor is?"

She shakes her head no, telling him how much she wished she did. You must give the diary to Thomas. Margaret will question you first for it, she will never assume one of us has it."

Rose looks up to him and he is staring into space. "Tomorrow you will be wed as well." Silence fell among them for a second. "Yeah...there was a wedding gown in my room this morning. That is how I found out, Isabel and Ellen told me Thomas had announced it yesterday before the attack."

She sighed and he embraced her. It pained him to see her so distraught, the lively person she used to be was beginning to vanish and he feared he would never see her laugh again. He kissed her up and down her cheek until she gave him the smile he longed to see. She turned his face and kissed him, jumping back as he pushed her down onto the mattress. He hovered above her for a moment to admire her beauty and the way her eye lit up when she smiled. Rose tried not to cry, vowing she would not shed another tear. Leon leaned down and kissed her gently, brushing his lips against hers teasingly. The moment heated and before they knew it, they were on each other. Using the lust and passion as an excuse to forget the harsh reality they were forced to face.

They stopped out of breath, laughing in each other's arms. "I don't want to go." Rose pleaded. He sat up on one elbow and caressed her flushed cheeks.

"You must. I will walk you to your room."

"No Leon, it's far too dangerous. What if someone sees us?"

He smiles wickedly.

"Let them think what they want."

Rose shoves him away playfully and stands up, dragging her gown back over her body. "I'll be fine on my own, please drop this off to Thomas for me. I don't want to speak to him."

He takes the diary from her and begins to feel the sadness over whelm him. When would it ever be appropriate to see her again? Even he did not know and the thought had eaten away at him all day. He would be forced to walk passed her like a stranger, tucking away the memories they shared as if they never existed. Life was not worth living that way. The only thing that kept him going was wanting to spend the remaining time she had in this century, with her. Yet now, that wasn't even possible. Leon always feared that their last encounter would truly be their last, and now was one of those moments.

Rose hugged him goodbye before turning towards the door, taking with her the scent of him that lingered on her skin. The sky had darkened and the dim candles against the wall barely lit the corridors. Getting back to her room would require much greater attention to her surroundings, she feared she'd awaken the castle if she were to trip over some obstacle in the way. She traced the walls with her finger tips as she crept against it silently, her footsteps muted by the soft cotton slippers on her feet. All Rose could think about was taking a warm bath and changing into her night gown. Her dress held the horrors of the day before and it frightened Rose to see her own reflection, for the moment she did the memories would flood her mind like a raging river. The hairs on her back stood to an end as the darkness began to trap her, making her feel much smaller and defenseless. The sensation of someone or *something* following her through the corners was deep in her pores, and although she knew it was just her mind creating images of dark figures, she couldn't help but regret not taking Leon's offer.

The night was eerie and the wind blew fiercely against the windows, making them rattle furiously in response. Her heart quickens and Rose picks up her pace. She's halfway to her room when suddenly, she hears a quiet whisper. Rose stiffens and plants her back against the cold stone. Without even looking, Rose could hear the voices of two men whispering back and forth to each other. They were on the balcony, where Leon and Thomas had last fought and she cursed at herself, trying to think of another route to reach her room.

"The plan is all set at Woodham, the troops will be assigned on each end, the north and the west, that way when the King arrives there is no means of escape.

Have you contacted the King of Frances' head commander? Has he agreed to our plan?"

Rose brings her hand up and covers her mouth, her eyes are wide realizing it is Arthur is talking. She drops down to her knees and becomes paralyzed. Her mind shouts at her to run to Leon again but she can't, Rose doesn't budge.

"Yes. He has agreed. No suspicions have arisen am I correct? Are you positive that Rose woman does not remember what you said?" Roses' heart begins to pound in her chest, she swallows, noting the way her body was beginning to shake.
"Yes."

Arthur laughs and he quickly softens his voice. "I thought I had taken care of her for good when I dropped that vase on her, but the damn thing didn't kill her. Lucky her, the impact caused her memory to be gone for good. Too bad it missed the Queen as well, my aim had been a bit off, but she's just a whore, there's no need to worry about someone like her."
"What…"

Rose is horrified now. "What is he talking about, remember what? He did this to me on purpose? For what reason! What could I have possibly seen or heard that he had the audacity to try and kill me? This didn't make sense…why can't I remember! I have to find Leon, I need to let him know. Get up Rose! Stand up now!"

Her mind was talking but her legs had lost the will to move. Her heart beat so loud she was afraid they would be able to hear it.
"Whore? The damn witch had me tossed out of the castle by that Thomas fellow, damn that woman. Good thing I managed to escape before they cut my fucking head off!"

Rose had been biting her lip so hard that she now noticed the taste of blood in her mouth. Tightening her fist she staggers upwards and finds her balance against the wall. Her head is spinning with the realization that Arthur and the cook were the traitors. That made so much sense. Of course Arthur would want to ruin the Princess, it was all a plan for France to capture England. They didn't want the union between Scotland and England, because only then would they surely lose any battle against them. No wonder her body had reacted so strangely at the ball when she had taken Arthurs hand. Although her mind couldn't remember what she had seen or heard, her subconscious sure did. Rose was holding her breath, realizing that she was the only woman on earth who could save England and its downfall.

"So when will Leon *rape* the Princess?" The cook says with a sly grin on his face.

Arthur smirks, his plan was working and the satisfaction of it was massive.

"Tomorrow night. The poor fool, he has no idea what is going to happen. But I am looking forward to taking young Margaret's virginity, her annoyance has been hard to deal with but I will finally get my reward soon." They laugh and a dreadful chill runs down Roses' spine. Her feet move backwards, no longer able to bare any more of their talking.

Her mind is so lost in a chaotic rollercoaster of emotions that it takes her a second to notice the burning candle on the ground besides her and the creaking holder that now swung loudly back and forth. Her heart stops as she stares petrified at the ground and up at Arthur and the man's startled face. She knows it is too dark for them to recognize her and figures if she runs for it maybe they will never know it was her who had been eavesdropping. Her plan quickly diminishes as they lunge towards her. Rose screams and starts running, their footsteps are far behind her, but beginning to close down on her. With all her might, her feet move faster and she barely escapes Arthurs grasp. Turning the corner she knocks down a statue behind her, hoping the noise was enough to awaken someone who can save her but it doesn't faze a soul.

The men jumped over the fallen statue, cursing at each other and shouting for her to stop, but only a fool would do such a thing. Rose nears the steps when suddenly her foot twists, she cries and falls forward, her chin hitting hard against the floor. The men seize the opportunity and rush forward just as she scrambles up wards. Arthur catches her arm before she could take the first step down and pulls her up against him.

"Well, look who we have here." He says out of breath.

"The hell? If it isn't the ole' witch, what a coincidence. Arthur I thought you said she didn't know?"

He glares down into her big eyes.

"She didn't, until now. You're coming with me."

"Let go of me!" Her mouth is slammed shut by his big palm and she screams into it, struggling against his strong grip on her arm.

"Keep still!" He cries while trying to silence her but Rose is uncontrollable, kicking and scratching at his face with her free hand. He growls and turns her back to him, pinning her into a choke hold. She finds it difficult to breathe and brings her hands forward to his arm, clawing at him until he has no choice but to loosen his grip, she is stronger than he thought.

"You bastard!" Rose is gasping for air now.

"Enough, I will not tolerate your existence any longer!" Arthur pushes her forward down the flight of stairs. The moment seems slow and for a long second Rose is flying in the air, her chest hits the top step harshly and she rolls down to the bottom, her body knocking against every hard edge. The cuts and scrapes mark her skin and it is when she reaches the last step and strikes her head hard on the stairwell that her vision blurs, the pain was so strong that it ran down every part of her and suddenly she's still. Rose could feel the bruises on her body, her breathing is slow and the blood begins to creep down her scalp, she could feel it along with the loud throbbing in her skull. I'm dying, she thinks as images begin to cloud her mind. Her eyes roll back in her head and suddenly the world is nothing but silence.

Twenty-Four

"Your cup of tea, my lord?"

Arthur drops his book and takes the cup from Rose's hand. Her smile allures him and for a moment he imagines his hands working up the curves of her body. His daydream vanishes as she turns and takes her leave, outside the room her mind suddenly remembers the letter in her pocket entrusted by a man she had met outside the castle. It was directed for Arthur. Rose reaches for the door handle when suddenly there is an unfamiliar voice speaking. She frowns, absolutely certain there had been no one else besides the two of them. The door is open just a crack and she edges closer, listening to the harsh distressed whispering of another person.

"Has there been any progress Arthur?"

"Relax! I will take care of this issue." He snaps back.

"If anyone finds out I am helping you destroy England, my life will be on the line. Hurry and get on with your plan so we can leave this castle already."

Arthur sighs, remembering all the troops he had to gather for the attack. "It is not that simple. We cannot take England in a day, I need more time."

Rose holds her chest, completely baffled. She barges into the room, eyes wild, completely degrading the man she thought she had fallen for. After realizing that Leon was never going to want her, she finally convinced herself to fall for someone else, but who knew that *someone* else would have been a traitor.

Her hands shakes as she points to him, his face widens in alarm and he looks to his ally then back at her. He stands up slowly, his angry gaze darting to the man who had spoken much louder than he should have.

"Rose. You don't understand." He starts towards her but Rose backs away.

"You, don't come near me. Stay away!"

Tears in her eyes, she turns on her heel and runs away.

"Aren't you going after her?" The man says.

"Leave her be. No one will believe a maid."

Rose runs until she's certain she's far enough from him and stops outside the garden. Her panting is heavy and she holds herself steady against the apple tree. Her chest is heavy, contradicting whether she heard correctly or not. But she knew it was clear as the day, the man had hid, waiting for her to leave to say what he needed to say. Rose was not crazy enough to imagine that and she rubbed her forehead, loosening the tension that was tight on her face.

"Are you alright?"

That familiar voice was as soft as cotton. Rose's eyes were wide as she looked up at Leon, the man she had so long admired from afar was standing in front of her, acknowledging her existence.

Her lips parted, Rose wanted to speak but there was a lump of nervousness in her throat and she blushed. His gaze was sensual, making her knees buckle beneath her weight and she now depended on gravity to hold her upright.

"Y-yes...your concern is much too kind, thank you."

He bows his head slightly and a bright white smile spreads across his lips.

"Whatever bothers you so, I hope I can rid for even a moment."

He leans down and Rose is paralyzed. The scent of alcohol reaches her nose before his lips are on hers. Swooping her into his arms Leon ravishes her body, feeling her skin through the slim fabric of her dress. His kiss deepens and she's falling into him, her hands cup around his chest for support and she finds it harder to keep her balance. His kiss is rough and she can taste the beer in his mouth. Her heart quickens as he steps forward and pins her between the tree and himself. He fondles with her corset for a moment and suddenly his hands are on her breast and his lips are on her neck. She gasp as a sharp pull of pleasure hits her core. Rose gulps, her dreams of being in his arms beginning to tarnish as she realizes Leon is drunk and just taking advantage of her emotions. Angry her hands swing his away from her body and she pulls her corset back into place. His face is puzzled, having been denied for the first time in his life.

"I will not give in to you like this."

His eyes roll around and he staggers forward, his hand lands just above her head and onto the tree trunk. He leans down into her ear and for a long moment Rose holds her breath, the proximity between them making her body heat.

"Fine."

His body sways as he turns and leaves her standing breathless, not knowing what to be more distraught about.

Colorful lights were appearing in her eyes. The floor where she lay was cold and the room was dark. Her lids grew heavy and she succumbed, shutting them and wincing from the pain that ran through her bones. Rose was now in front of Gretel's home, she needed someone to talk to. A woman who could give her advice.

"My dear, come in!" She reached for Roses' hands and took them, her distraught face made the struggles in her mind apparent, Gretel had seen it in her eyes the moment she opened the door.

"Tell me what ails you?"

Rose is led to a chair and she sits, turning towards Gretel with glossy eyes.

"I don't know what to do…"

Gretel is attentive now, not knowing whether Rose was going to speak of her unrequited love for Leon or something else.

"Arthur, he's a traitor and he's trying to destroy England...and worse, I think he might be from France. Oh Gretel what should I do?"

The conflicting argument in her mind was causing Rose to feel weak. Gretel gasped, shaking her head in disappointment. She found it a bit hard to believe but she knew Rose would never falsely accuse another being. Rose was gentle and kind hearted, and suddenly she felt guilty for urging her to forget Leon and look towards Arthur.

"I don't think I'm safe with this knowledge..."

"You are not Rose, you mustn't tell a soul about this."

Rose looked up in surprise. Her mother had always told her a woman must always be truthful and honest, one with a tattered heart would live a horrible life. How could she keep quiet about something so terrible?

"But the fate of England..."

"No, listen Rose. You cannot go up to the King and accuse his men of betrayal without *proof*. You would be mocking him, making him into a fool, you mustn't do anything until I tell you to do you understand? I will help you."

Her pupils dilate and Rose is pulled into her serious eyes, she knew she could trust Gretel. Her witch craft had helped her before after catching the measles when she was child. Gretel was her savior, so righteously taking her in after her parents and sister died in the attack, she was the only person Rose had left to hold on to. If there was one person in the world she could trust, it would be her.

"Okay..."

She sighs and forces a smile that seems to relax Rose a bit.

"Now go on and be calm, I will see you later?"

Rose tightly embraces her and tells her of the bittersweet encounter with Leon. She's angry and hurt that his motive was not reflected on love but alcohol and it bothered Rose that although his sudden affection had nothing to do with her, deep in her heart she couldn't deny the warmth she felt in his arms and the way her heart beat against him.

The feeling was pleasant but tinged with sadness. It caused an ache in her chest that made it almost impossible to bear. From that moment on she vows to forget such a drunkard, she was better than that and she deserved much more.

Rose groans, she starts frowning, what is she seeing? Why was the old lady from before in her mind and why was she holding her so close? A feeling in her chest rises and before she knows it tears are streaming down the sides of her blood stained face. The memories were flooding back into her mind and now her heart lay opened, bleeding and aching from the realization that the only other person she had ever loved had died in her arms a couple of days ago and she didn't even remember who she was.

Her head began to spin as the bile worked its way up her esophagus. She held it back, having no strength to move, and suddenly there was darkness once again as she faded back into her subconscious.

Rose lay on the soft cushioned bed. The room was barely lit and she didn't remember how she got there. A bandage was wrapped around her forehead and just looking up at it made her wince in pain.

"You're awake, my dear Rose."

Gretel took her hand and placed it against her cheeks, she was crying and the wetness was now on her palms.

Rose frowned, suddenly frightened.

"W-who are you...?"

Gretel's eyes widened in horror, her lips parted in a gasp.

"You don't know who I am?" The words were cluttered and Gretel had hoped the medic had been wrong, but indeed Roses' memory was gone and she was now a stranger in her eyes. Rose crawled backwards until she could no longer, the wall was edged against her back.

"Where am I? Where are my parents and sister are they alright?" Her mind was back ten years ago, after the attack left her village engulfed in flames and suddenly tears fill her eyes and Gretel's heart begins to ache.

"Don't be startled, I am just...a medic bringing you your medicine. You took quite a fall." Gretel had thought fast and when she noticed Rose relax she knew her lie was working. She had brewed the potion together with honey, hoping it'd rid the bitter taste. As much as it pained her to do, Gretel was going to do whatever it took to get revenge. Arthur had something to do with Roses' accident, she felt it and she vowed not to let him get away with it. The only way she could save Rose was to put her in a coma temporarily, where her soul would be transported into the future, the fate she had already seen in her vision. There she would meet Leon who'd bring her back into the past, Gretel had seen it all clearly. If only Rose knew her love for Leon held a purpose, their lives were intertwined and she didn't even know it. Gretel smiled as Rose took the drink and gulped it down. Arthur had no reason to hurt a woman who was unconscious, and that was enough for Gretel to feel secure about her safety.

"I'm sorry dear, but you must be strong. You *will* be okay. I love you." Gretel's words faded as Rose passed out onto the sheets.

Twenty-Five

Leon had paced in his room back and forth, contemplating whether he should go to the wedding or not. Part of him wanted to take the chance to see her in a wedding gown and pretend for a second, it was him she would marry.

Yet, the thought of it was foolish beyond belief. He couldn't possibly watch the woman he loved walk down the aisle with another man. The diary was tight against his finger and one thing was for sure, he had to let Thomas know about the attack tomorrow. For the sake of his people, Leon could not let Rose cloud his vision.

He found Thomas at the library, congratulatory handshakes were shared between others and himself. He watched for a moment as he spoke and laughed and a bitter feeling sank into him, he wanted to wipe the smile right off his face.

"Thomas, we need to talk."

He turned towards Leon and sighed, growing tired of their endless pleading to stop their marriage.

"What is it Leon, I'm on my way to the wedding."

Leon hands him the diary and there is an open mouthed expression on his face.

"What is this, a bible?"

Thomas smirks and looks up questionably, he thinks it's a joke until he sees Leon's stoned features. He's not smiling. "In there is the proof of my innocence. You mustn't tell anyone about this, not a soul, until I am accused, understood?" Thomas nods, his eyes scanning the pages then back up at him.

"Arthur?"

Leon nods.

"Rose had told me but it is still so hard to believe…"

Thomas had been friends with Arthur for a while. He was a secluded, quiet guy but never had he thought more of him. It was shocking to hear that he was the one to have Leon framed. If he hadn't promise him to keep shut, he would have been beating his face into the ground by now. Thomas quickly read through the end and gasped.

"This plan is happening today?"

"Yes, that is why I cannot let him out of my sight."

Leon crosses his arms and sits down on the sofa.

"Will he be at the wedding?"

Thomas clears his throat, noting the way Leon was trying hard to act casual.

"Yes."

"I will be on my way then."

"Wait, are you not going to congratulate me?" Thomas grabs his shoulder and Leon shakes him off. With dark sinister eyes he glares up at him, a murderous glow shines around the rim of his pupils.

"Does a deer congratulate his hunter for killing him?"

Thomas' lips straightened, his smile faded and he couldn't deny the guilt that had been creeping up his skin, indeed he felt like a murderer and he was not proud of it. It was not like Thomas to feel this way but the reason was evident.

The church was loud with the chatter from the crowd. Thomas looked around nervously, Rose had not come forward. His eyes fell on Leon who was watching Arthur from across the room. He had seen the way he smiled and there was something behind it that made

Leon wonder if he had anything to do with Roses'
delay.

"The poor lad, his wife has run away." Andrew
whispered to Leon.

But Leon knew that was not the truth. If Rose had run
away she would have taken him with her, they would
have left together. Something felt wrong and the heavy
feeling in his chest grew stronger as he watched Arthur
slip from the crowd and out through the side door.
Leon ran after him, pushing past the spectators that
stood in his way. Once outside he looked around,
noting from a distance a man running forward towards
the castle. He sped up behind him fast, yet he
disappeared into the castle. When Leon opens the door
to the parlor there is nothing but silence, the room is
empty and he could no longer hear running footsteps.
Confused, he scans around the room, hoping that
maybe Arthur would be foolish enough to be lurking
behind a table but he is nowhere to be seen.

"Dammit!" He scowls himself.

Instantly he remembers Rose and runs fast to her
room. Out of breath, he turns the knob and her door
opens into darkness. The bed is neatly made as if it
were never slept on. On the side of it is her wedding
dress, untouched from yesterday. Leon searches for her
shoes, but as he thought they were nowhere in sight.
His head is spinning now and he staggers towards the
bed. His hands clasp the wooden post before he could
fall, the realization that Rose did not return last night
hit him hard.

"Arthur." He growls.

It was not necessary to gather proof, his name
screamed in his head and that was enough to suspect
him. He finds his balance and like a fierce hurricane
ready to attack he exits the room, prepared to strangle

him to death. Leon's hands are shaking as he imagines what he would do to the man in his presence.

He's gliding down the halls now, darting between faces in search of Arthur. He's like a ticking time bomb, ready to set off at any moment. The struggle to keep calm was growing stronger. Where are you? I need to find you!

Leon barges into an old office Arthur once used. His eyes settle on the desk, he marches towards it and swings his arm across the table, sending the contents on the top flying to the ground. He's angry now. Crossing the room he stands in front of an old book case to calm himself and bangs the wall next to it. It takes him a second to realize the hollow affect his punch makes. Confused, he does it again. Both hands spring up and feel the wall. There was a secret passage behind it, and a gut feeling was telling him that he needed to see what was behind this wall. The latch to the opening is behind the bookcase so he pushes it to the side a bit further. It takes a good hard pull but the wall gives in and a small door is opened. Leon's jaw is dropped, he had heard rumors of walls like this but never had he found one.

He slips through and shuts the door behind him. Darkness surrounds him, but in the far end of the tunnel there is a small candle burning and he wonders how recently that candle had been lit. He's cautious as he nears it and slows his pace.

Suddenly there is a loud groan. The back of his hairs rise as two people begin talking, it is hard to tell what they are saying. Leon listens in, recognizing Arthur's voice.

"All is set for tomorrow. Now all we do is watch and wait for the Kings' downfall."

He stiffens, listening in more closely.

"—After that, we'll dispose of this woman, throw her into the river. She knows too much already."

"Yes sir, let's go to the pub. I could really use a beer."
The voice is unfamiliar and Leon curses under his
breath. His hand is on the handle of the blade and he
slides it out of the sheath slowly. Leon's heart quickens
knowing that Rose was the one they were talking about.
Their footsteps echo down the empty corridor as they
begin to walk away. Leon emerges into the room and
gasp. It was an underground prison cell, he had heard
of it before. Centuries ago, criminals would be tortured
in these very walls. His eyes search the empty cells but
there is no one. A groan halts him and he looks down at
the cell besides him. Rose lay on the ground, she is still
and even through the darkness he can see the blood on
her body.

"Rose!" He cries. His hands grab the rusty handles of
the cell door and he pulls backwards with all his might.
It doesn't budge. He looks around the room for
anything that resembled a key but there was nothing.
Taking his sword he swings it against the metal clasp. It
springs free and falls to the ground. Leon takes a deep
breath and runs to her side, dropping down on his
knees.

His hands are trembling as they touch her shoulder.
Her body is cold, her lips are blue. Tears run down his
face. He pounds his fist against the stone ground, a
monstrous energy building inside him.

"Those bastards..." He growls.

Squeezing his eyes shut he wipes his face.

"Leon..." A small hoarse whisper escapes her lips. Leon
drops the sword in his hands and grabs her face.

"Yes, I'm here. Speak to me Rose."

Her eyes are sore and it takes some effort to open
them. For a moment his face is nothing but a blur, she
blinks several times until he finally comes into focus.

"It hurts so much..." She mutters.

The adrenaline in his body is surging now and the only person in his mind is Arthur. He was going to murder him. The purpose of his existence in this moment was to kill him.

"My love, you shouldn't move, please. I'll get you back to safety, hold on to me." He gathers her limp body in his arms and begins to turn around when a laugh stops him in his tracks.

"Well, well look who we have here."

Arthur's eyes are menacing, and a glint of humor lies behind his dark gaze.

"You…" Leon scolds.

Rose could feel his body shaking and knew it wasn't caused by fear. He wanted to rip the man into pieces and if Leon had not been holding her in that moment, Arthur would have been on the ground, throat slit in half.

The cell door slams shut and within an instant they are both locked in. Leon runs forward and kicks it harshly, the sound causing Arthur to jump back and laugh.

"Well you made my job easier of capturing you. Thank you. You walked straight into my trap. Now my little chickens' behave while I have your country kneel to France. I could be back for you two later? But I'd rather you both rot and starve to death. Bye."

"You come back here you coward!" Leon screams. His legs swing repeatedly at the door until his efforts are effortless and he realizes that his hits have made no impact on their escape. Rose is nearly falling from his arms.

"Leon, put me down." There is fear in her voice but Leon fails to notice. He staggers backwards against the wall and slides down to the ground. His hands are at his raging temples and his chest is heaving furiously up and down.

"We *are* going to be alright…"

Rose gathers some strength and slips out of his grasp. He's too distressed to notice. His eyes are shut and he's muttering something inaudible and for a moment Rose is afraid of him. He stands up quickly and grabs his sword, in that moment Rose screams as he swings it repeatedly against the cell bars. The sound of the impact echoes through the empty dungeon loudly. It rings against her ears and she brings her hands up and covers them, leaning forward between her legs.

"Please stop!"

Leon is screaming now, kicking and punching the door. His knuckles are bleeding but the pain doesn't faze him. He's out of breath by the time he falls backwards against the wall and drops his sword again. With wide eyes she looks at Leon, Rose had never seen this murderous side of him. His eyes meet hers and for a second he's pulled into them.

"Dammit…I'm sorry Rose."

He hadn't realized he frightened her so much. Leon crawls to her and begins to examine her body, his eyes intent at every wound and scratch, swearing he'd repay double the hurt onto Arthur.

"I have to get you to a medic." His voice is cracking and it pains her to see him so weak.

Before she could reply he embraces her, holding her tight against him and even though it hurts her, her lips are pressed against each other and she doesn't say a thing.

"We'll get out of this."

Her voice is frail and she's not confident she can make it through another night. He takes her hand in his and snuggles her face against his chest. His heart is beating loudly and beneath his gaze she smiles. Rose remembered the way her chest would warm when she was in his arms, even as a ghost.

"I don't know how, but I have to warn the King of the attack. They'll be leaving tomorrow morning at six, if we don't make it out of here by then..." Leon holds his head and takes a deep breath.

"We will."

The words flew from her lips, she wasn't even sure about that but there was no use in having two negative people in this situation.

It was nearly six am when Rose awoke. She knew it was because Rose always awoke at that time. Long ago when her village was attacked, it had been six am when her sister reached for her and forced her out of bed. Ever since that day Rose had always awakened at that time. She looks up at Leon's sleeping face. Rose had been too distracted to remember her memories. Gretel had saved her life by transporting her to the future. She wasn't sure if all the memories from her life there were real or not, but it lead her to Leon and back to her time. It was a perfect potion and Rose only wish she could have remembered this all sooner before Gretel passed away. Tears filled her eyes as she remembered the times and days she shared with her. She had become her mother. Cooking and living for a child who was not even your own was something not anyone would choose upon, but Gretel did and for that she thanked her from the bottom of her heart. Rose sighed, the heavy burden in her heart was much too strong to bear. The bittersweet feeling of knowing she was never going to go back to the future was torture. Marrying Thomas would be a lifelong commitment now and she'd be apart from Leon. Life was not worth living that way, if they even made it out alive. She could only imagine what Arthur was doing to Margaret right now. Did the princess even notice her diary missing? Would that action somehow alter fate? Rose could only hope. She felt so useless trapped inside this cage like an animal.

The candle light was close to an end, there was a bit of wax left and that meant they would be in total darkness soon.

"Leon, wake up."

His eyes shot open, startled she jumps back.

"What time is it? Dear god I fell asleep."

He starts to stand when Rose suddenly grabs his arm.

"I must tell you something..."

"What?" His eyes open wide, imagining the worst.

"Leon..." Her eyes fills with tears again.

"—I'm not going anywhere."

His face is puzzled but he crouches down to meet her face.

"Why would you want to stay here?"

"No, that's not what I meant. I mean...I'm not from the future. It was a potion I drank that brought my spirit to the future...It's complicated, I can't really explain it well right now but I'm not going anywhere."

He smiles.

"That's great, wait..."

His smile fades quickly.

"Fuck!" He curses.

"So you mean to tell me, you'll be married to that asshole?"

His hands are tangled in his hair now.

"I didn't marry him...yet. And there's no guarantee that well even make it out of here..."

Rose didn't know what she preferred, dying with Leon, or living and going their separate ways. The two feelings opposed each other and it was painful to think about.

His hand rest on her shoulder and he squeezes it reassuringly.

"We shall live. I'll be satisfied just knowing you walk the same earth as me. I will always protect you from a distance."

He kisses her and Rose finds comfort in the warmth of his lips.

Leon stands up again and grabs the lock on the door.

"If only there was something sharp I could pick this with."

Time was ticking and he knew the King must have set out by now. He patted his pockets, only to find just a couple of coins laying inside. Turning towards Rose he eyes her down, she as well didn't seem to have anything.

"Wait!"

Her hands reached up to her hair and she pulls apart the pins that kept it up in place. They smiled at each other in delight as Rose runs up to him.

"Try this."

He kisses her forehead and rakes his hand down her long locks.

"You my lady, are amazing."

Rose watches as his attempts fail the first two times, growing uneasy by the second she holds onto him.

"Finally." He mutters.

The gate swings open and they look up at each other. Leon leans down and hugs her tightly. She laughs, although knowing they shouldn't be so happy just yet.

"Quickly, we must hurry!" He slips his hand into hers and pulls her forward through the darkness.

Twenty-six

"Will you be alright on your own?" Leon ask as they close back the secret door. Rose halts and turns towards him, eyes wide and famished.

"What do you mean? I'm going with you."

Leon shakes his head and walks forward. "No, no way. I can't take a woman into battle. Go to your room and lock yourself inside. I'll come back for you." Thinking it's the end of the discussion he turns from her, not wanting to see the way her face dropped when he said that.

"No. Either I go or you don't."

"—please Leon, you can't just leave me here alone. There's more traitors in this castle besides Arthur. If they see me, you know what they'll do to me." Rose was right. In fact he had felt uneasy to leave her in the castle by herself, but taking her into a battlefield was much worse. He didn't have much time to think, his head was aching with the task of reaching the King before they met at Woodham. He bites his lips and says okay. They run to the Queen's chamber and grant permission to speak to her. There, Rose stands by his side while he tells her of the scheme and names of the traitors within the castle. Her face is petrified of course, but she sends more troops to the meeting spot. She thanks them and leaves Leon with the task of warning the King.

"You are aware you'll be safe by the Queen's side." He says hoping she'd change her mind but her lips were tight and her eyes were stern. Rose doesn't reply and gives him a look that says the discussion was over. He grabs her hand and they quicken their pace as they race out into the stables. In an instant they are on a black stallion horse and are speeding past the castle trail. Her hands are around his stomach. They were going so fast that her hair was flying from the force.

"Don't let go and keep low." He shouts as they gallop into the forest. The footprints of feet were still engraved in the muddy ground and it was not long since the men had departed.

Rose clung on tighter as branches swept over their heads, they ducked just in time. They had crossed a couple of more miles when Rose realized what the hell she was doing. She should have listened to Leon, Rose was not cut out for war. The thought of never seeing him again had caused tears to fall and her heart to ache, so after finding her she vowed not to let him out of her sight.

They were reaching the top of a grassy hill overlooking the ocean when suddenly Leon begins to shout. Rose looks over his shoulder to the crowd of horses up ahead. In the middle was the Kings carriage. They were pretty far and Rose doubted they could hear his cries.

"Dammit, Woodham is just a couple of miles away."
Leon kicks into the horse and they go flying across the land. He shouts for Rose to hold on as they cross the distance between them.

Thomas was the first to notice a distinct voice from behind them. He halts his horse and turns around. Others notice his reaction and stop, watching Leon speed towards them.

"Why have we stopped?" The King ask as he sticks his head out of the window.

"Sir, there is someone charging towards us, we think it might be one of our men."

Thomas squinted. "Could it be Leon?" He had thought for sure Leon had run away with Rose last night. Thomas spent the day searching for her, demanding to know why she had stood him up. Rose had taken back her word, and so would he.

"It's Leon sir!"

"What?" King Henry steps out of the carriage as Leon pulls the reign back to stop the horse. Rose cries as the animal goes back on its two legs and then harshly back down.

"What is the meaning of this?" The King says angrily.

"You're Highness, I apologize for my sudden disappearance. I have been captured by a traitor, one of your men known as Arthur. Going to Woodham is a trap sir, we must turn around *now*." The look of distraught fell upon the Kings face.

"Are you positive about this?"

He nods and turns to look back at Rose.

"I have brought a witness, she too was captured after finding out Arthur's scheme." Rose blushes, pretty sure her look was as disastrous as the news.

"You heard the man, we shall turn back!"

The King motions for everyone to turn around and gets back into his carriage. Rose smiles and looks up at Leon. "We did it, you did it...I'm so proud of you."

Before Leon could reply the ground began to shake. Rose froze. "What's going on?"

"Quickly get the King out of here now!" The Kings horses begin to gallop away, a dozen men ordered to protect him by his side.

"Their coming Rose. Arthur must have noticed our disappearance. I'm going to get off, do you know how to ride? Rose is shaking now, gripping Leon's sleeve with all her might.

"A little...but I can't leave you."

"This I will *not* argue with you about."

He's on the ground now. Rose looks up to more than a dozen horses charging their way. He turns the horse around while Rose screams for him to get back on.

Thomas rides up beside them, a look of horror etched on his face.

"Do you know what they'll do to you if you're captured? Rose get out of here now!" Thomas shouts. He shifts his horse and stands guard. Blocking the blue coats view of Rose, knowing all too well they'd go after her directly.

"I'm sorry. I love you, please understand." Leon gazes at her. With tears in her eyes Rose holds on tight as the horse begins to charge after the King's. She looks back as the French rush forward and strike, knocking each other off their horses. Thomas is on the ground and Leon is up against someone. His sword held firmly against the blue coats. His face is tense and the veins begin to appear, even from this distance Rose could see his struggle. Pushing him forward with his head, the man is knocked off his feet and Leon swings his sword. The moment seems to slow down as the blood flies in the air, staining his face with it. Rose gasp, she's halfway across the hill when she loses control of the reign. Desperately, she grabs onto the horses' hair, but it startles the animal and it goes back on its two feet again and throws her off. She screams, startling Leon from the distance. He looks back in horror as the horse continues to run without a rider. He could see Rose on the ground.

Rose's arm is in pain. She grimaces, finding it hard to move her stunned body. The body that's been tortured enough and barely had the will to work. Her fingers reach down to her stomach, were her unborn child lay inside and she was glad her abdomen had not been struck. Rose shakes, desperately regretting that she had not told Leon she was pregnant, honestly, she was frightened of his reaction, and what he would do if she told him. It was the reason why she was not going to marry Thomas, she couldn't even if she wanted to keep her word. She had lied to him and to everyone around her. The symptoms of her pregnancy began months ago after her first night with Leon. The night he had barged into her room. The nausea she had felt all along was not caused by a simple cold and she was sure of it. There was a baby inside of her, and even through her fall nights ago Rose knew her baby was still alive inside of her. She prayed to god that whole night that she would not miscarry it, and she didn't. She had to tell Leon, even if it meant breaking the news in the middle of a battlefield.

Rose looks up and screams, a pair of blue coats on horses were heading her way. Wiping the fallen hair from her view, she stands up and starts running towards the ocean. Thomas sees her before Leon.

"Leon! Rose is in danger!" He screams while fighting off another man. Leon is struggling against an enemy and he knows he can't take much longer.

"Die!"

Leon swerves to the right and rolls onto the ground as another one charges towards him. His sword flies a few feet away. He swings his legs up, kicking the man off his feet and staggers up. As another blue coat runs towards him he swings his fist and knocks him backwards. The adrenaline was rushing through his veins. Leon was prepared to unleash the anger he had bottled up over the years. He stomps on the face of a man and screams. Sweeping his sword up from the ground he twirls and slices a head off. Thomas' eyes are wide, never having seen Leon so fierce before. Leon is surrounded now and from a distance he can see Rose running towards the bay.

"Shit!"

He looks over at Thomas who seems to read his mind. Thomas nods at him and hops onto his horse. Their differences were put aside, and for once Leon didn't mind Thomas running to Rose.

"Are you bastards ready to die?" Leon sneers.

His eyes are wild and crazy and for a moment the invaders look at each other. Leon held the handle of his sword tightly, he swung it upwards and watched as the blood dripped down the shining blade and onto his fingers. His eyes shot back to the men around him. They ran forward but Leon was quick, he took out the man on the left first, swinging his blade downwards onto his leg. He clenches his teeth as his grasp moves upwards, the face of the man in front now spit in half. It takes a second for the body to fall and when it does the remaining men halt, fear wide in their eyes. Leon was covered in blood, the look of a demon in his smile. He finishes the men instantly in one swing.

Thomas swings his sword into the blue coats horse. The animal cries and falls to the ground, taking with him the invader.

Rose screams and falls into the sand, she lifts her head up and is relieved to see Thomas. He climbs off his horse and pulls her up. Rose is surprised that he had saved her. She figured he'd be too angry to even look at her but he held her tight in his arm, his sword pointing to the man running towards them.

"Shut your eyes."

Rose listens to the order and shuts them just as the man groans and falls to his death. She peeks through her squinted lids and looks up at him. His eyes were on her, full with concern. Rose needed to tell him as well about her secret and now was the perfect time.

"Thomas, I never meant to hurt you the way I did..." He cut her off, silencing her with his finger. "I know it is not your fault, you were captured Rose, of course you couldn't make it to the wedding." She took his hand and gazed into his eyes. They softened. "I'm carrying

Leon's child..." His eyes widened instantly, surprised by her words. The shock ran down to his body and he found that he couldn't speak. His breath hitched, and for a moment he studied her to see if it was some kind of cruel joke, but her eyes held no humor. Her lips were set in a straight line and her hands traveled down to her stomach.

"Are...you certain?" Thomas shut his eyes and took in a deep breath. When he opened them again they softened and he put his hand on her shoulder. "Then I will make sure to get you out of here safely." His reply startled Rose. She had prepared to hear him yell at her and storm off but instead he looked at her with sympathetic eyes. From the start Thomas knew he could never have that happy family he had always dreamt of with her. Now this proved it, like a sign from above. There were many women in this world, he would have to find one for himself, and in the meantime he would wish his friend the best. "Does Leon know about this...?" Rose shook her head no, her gaze dropping to her feet and he could see the sadness appear in his eyes. "Don't worry, he will be thrilled." Thomas reassured her.

They look back to the battlefield and their lips part in a gasp. The ground is covered in bodies and just a dozen French soldiers were left. Their attempt of an attack was pathetic and it was futile to win against the English. Their plan had not succeeded but they still fought till the death, an order from the French King, stating that if they didn't win, they might as well not return at all.

"Oh my god..." She whispers.

Leon is surrounded again, and this time he is fighting against a *beast* of a man. The monster swings and Leon blocks it, but the force is so strong his feet slide back and his knee drops. He groans, pushing forward with all his might but he can't hold it much longer.

"I need to save him, stay here!" Thomas runs towards Leon at full speed, he doesn't notice Rose staggering behind him, ignoring his order once again but Rose could only think about Leon's safety. Her worst fear was not being able to tell him about the baby.

Thomas is out of breath when he reaches him and plants his back against his. "Let's do this Leon, just like old times." He could feel his nod and Leon smiles. "You know, you're not such an asshole after all." Thomas laughs, "I'm sorry, I shouldn't have let a woman come between us nor should I have requested to wed her knowing how much you loved her." Leon was surprised by his confession. "It's okay, it doesn't matter, what matters most is kicking this troll's ass."

The adrenaline was pulsating through his veins, and the need to kill was growing stronger. He screams and runs forward, taking the beast with him and stumbling backwards. The man cries and Leon finishes him off, jumping between his body and plunging the blade through his heart.

Rose is on the ground again, kneeling and covering her face. The blood and sounds of death was too much to bear. She's shaking and her heart is pounding furiously but she had to be strong, for her baby as well as herself. Rose tried to ignore the need to be held and told that everything was going to be okay.

"Rose, don't cry I'm coming!" Leon yells from overhead. She looks up in time to see a smile spread across his face and instantly she feels better. Rose knew he was only trying to make her feel better and that was what she loved the most about him. The way he lowered himself at times just to see a smile on her face. He lived for moments like these. He waves, and time seems to slow down again. Suddenly Roses' eye widen in horror.

"Leon!"

Time freezes for a moment as Roses' high pitched scream silences the field. She's running now towards them, catching herself with her hands as she falls. Leon feels Thomas' arms over his back and hears his groan, he falls to the ground besides him. Leon is still, sword shaking in his grasp. Furious, he turns and swings his blade across the murderer's neck, cutting his head off completely.

"Thomas!" She runs towards him as his body falls and there is a look of distraught on his face. He's wincing and shaking from the pain, and looking into Roses' eyes made it harder. Leon's eyes widen, realizing Thomas had saved his life. He drops his sword and looks down at Thomas, his eyes were squinted, his lips barely parted. Rose is on her knees besides him, holding his wound with her palms, tears flying from her face.

"R-rose..."

"Don't speak." She says through muffled sobs. Rose cursed at herself for ever wishing anything horrible upon him before. If she knew then what a nice guy he really was, she would have never had such foul thoughts.

"Why did you do that!" Leon yells. His hands are on his head and he paces back and forth. His eyes are squeezed shut and it was preventing the tears from forming. Thomas forces a smile.

"I thought about it for a second, I thought about letting him kill you. But then I saw the way Rose smiled at you and I never want her to stop smiling. Besides, she needs you to help her raise that little baby inside of her." Thomas winces and shuts his eyes.

"Be a good father Leon."

Leon bends down to meet his eyes. He had no idea what Thomas was saying.

"Take care of her, and I'm sorry." His voice fades away and his eyes roll back into his head. Rose takes her shaking hands away from him and wraps her arms around Leon, sobbing into his chest uncontrollably. Surprisingly, she didn't mind that her secret was told by someone else, especially by Thomas. Leon was still, paralyzed by the news and his friends death. Rose had to stand him back up.

"Let's go…"

The tears began to swell in his eyes and he looked down at Thomas one more time. *"Thank you,* brother." He whispers.

Twenty-Seven

"So you mean to tell me...that there is a baby inside of you?" Leon said cautiously, trying to steady his voice. His mind was racing, thinking back to their passionate love making and having never thought of the possibility of a child. Rose nodded, afraid he'd get angry, but suddenly his arms are around her and he's kissing her forehead. "That's wonderful." Leon had never thought about kids, but he had once pictured settling down and Rose was the only woman he wanted to share his life with.

Rose smiled, the anxiety in her chest finally alleviating. "So you're not mad? You won't run away from me?" Her questions were ridiculous and she knew that as well as Leon. "Why in the world would I run from you, Rose, I love you." There was warmth in his eyes when he said those words and her heart fluttered. There wasn't any other person in this world she could ever want to be with. His hand trailed down her gown and to her stomach, he got down on his knees and smiled.

"Hello there little one... I'm your father." His eyes lit up as they met Rose's. "I can't wait to meet you, I know you'll be as beautiful as your mother *or* as strong and handsome as your Father." He winked and Rose laughed, hitting him against the shoulder. Leon stood back up and kissed her until she was breathless.

As they walked into the castle doors behind the guards they are startled to find everyone clapping and cheering. Rose walked behind Leon cautiously, embarrassed to be the only female among such a large group of men. They stopped in front of the King, who was sitting beside Margaret and his Queen.

A smile spreads across his face and he points towards Leon and Rose.

"Would you two please step forward?" Leon takes her hand and grips it, feeling her nervousness fade into the oblivion. They kneel down and look up at Henry.

"I would like to thank you both, because of your courage and bravery, you have saved England from its mortal enemies." The room began to clap and Rose looks around. Ellen, Isabel, and Agnes were waving and she couldn't stop herself from smiling.

"We have lost many men in battle, but let's remember this day as a lesson. England will rise and we will prosper. Let it be the last time France tries to ambush us. As for Arthur, he has been beheaded, for trying to ruin my daughter and my country.

Margaret blushes, her eyes were red from crying and she sniffs, remembering the way Arthur tried to force her after she had refused to have sex with him. Her diary had gone missing and Margaret did not want to take any chances, but he didn't care. She thanked god a nearby guard was on patrol when he heard her scream.

"But you two have endured so much. I shall grant each of you one desire." Rose and Leon look at each other, their gazes locked but they made no effort in pulling away.

"I desire to marry this woman and spend the rest of my life with her."

The room silences to just the mere whispering of awe. The King parts his lips, ready to question him and baffled by Leon's choice. Any other man would request money, power or land. But Leon didn't need any of that, to him Rose was worth much more than life itself.

"I as well desire to marry this man and to spend the rest of my life with him." Rose is smiling now as Leon's lips curve into a grin. The love of his life was right in front of him, it was hard not to smile when he looked into her beautiful green eyes.

"Very well then. You shall be wed, and no longer have duty to our castle and country. Now we shall let the festivities begin."

The King waves to the orchestra and music begins to play. Pairs soar through the dance floor and suddenly the room is filled with joy. The sorrows of the lost men are vanished and a private group goes out to fetch the dead bodies, the King ordering to give them the proper burial they deserved. They tried not to think back on Thomas, having had so much hate for the poor guy before, they found themselves feeling guilty when they spoke of him.

Rose reaches up to Leon's blood stained face and laughs. They were beyond dirty and repulsive looking, but that didn't stop Leon from holding her close.

"Did this really just happen?"

He takes her arm and plants a soft kiss on her lips.

"Yes, my love."

Rose blushes. "I think it'd be wise to clean ourselves up and enjoy that dinner buffet they are setting up." Her stomach churns with that thought and they move through the crowd and towards the bathing room.

"Are you sincerely suggesting that or is it because you want to bathe together?" Rose stops suddenly, and a bright smile shines on his face.

"You know me too well."

Leon tilts her head upwards and onto his lips. She falls into his arms and into his kiss, the sound of the music fading to just the sound of his heart beating against her chest, the way she always loved. The world is still and in that moment they are the only ones alive, losing themselves in each other's touch and into the bittersweet taste of their lips.